"That is not Grace Urich."

❖❖❖

Dr. Ralles blinked.

"Hana—" Elsie began.

"It is not Grace Urich!"

"Won't you look at her again?" the doctor urged. "And bear in mind the altered state of her appearance."

Hana did look again. It was not altering or change she saw. It was a face folding in on itself. The rot of fallen leaves in February.

"What killed her?"

"A knife. Good sharp thrust. Now then, *is* this Grace Urich?"

Was it, after all, Grace? How in God's name could she tell for sure?

"Fingerprints," she said too loudly, her voice bouncing off the sterile walls. "Grace's fingerprints are on file at my office. We'll see what the fingerprints say."

A HANA SHANER MYSTERY

...NOW YOU DON'T

ROMA GRETH

PAGEANT BOOKS

Publisher's Note: This is a work of fiction. The characters, incidents, and dialogues are products of the author's imagination and are not to be construed as real. Any resemblance to actual events or persons, living or dead, is entirely coincidental.

PAGEANT BOOKS
225 Park Avenue South
New York, New York 10003

Cover artwork by Robert Crawford

Printed in the U.S.A.

First Pageant Books printing: August, 1988

10 9 8 7 6 5 4 3 2 1

...NOW YOU DON'T

Chapter One

IT WASN'T UNTIL she realized someone was following her that Hana Shaner thought her idea might be dangerous.

She paused, listening.

There it was again. Soft, furtive footsteps echoing against the restored buildings of center city. Clutching the handle of her suitcase more tightly, Hana turned to stare into the misty autumn evening.

Only a few hours before, the restaurants and shops had been full of tourists. Now their dim, mock-Colonial lights reflected emptiness. About fifty yards beyond a streetlight, where a cobbled lane led to the CarPark, she saw movement, hardly more than the stir of a shadow. Then it was gone. Hana hesitated. She had nearly reached the narrow brick alleyway that led between two eighteenth-century buildings to the door of Grace Urich's apartment.

In that apartment was a phone. But although there were dozens of people she could call for help, Hana felt suddenly and desperately alone. It was an unpleasant, unfamiliar sensation.

Forcing herself to walk slowly, she moved toward the alleyway. She thought she heard the footsteps again, but this time she couldn't be sure. Perhaps there were no footsteps. After all, the last two months had been enough to give anybody the jitters. Maybe her imagination was enlarging the strange quiet that settled over the historic city at dusk. Two hundred years before, this had been a wagon road filled with noise and activity. The city was proud of its restorations, but Hana wondered if it was really possible to restore anything. The long-ago people who had lived here had gone.

As Grace Urich had gone.

But not very long ago. Two months.

After turning into the alley, Hana began to run. Lantern-shaped lamps on black posts made unreal shadows that moved as she did. The alley dead-ended at the apartment door. Sweating now despite the cool, damp air, Hana rummaged for the key.

Oh, God—!

Then she remembered. She had put it in her jacket pocket.

It was in the quiet moment before she inserted the key in the lock that she heard the footfalls again, this time on the cobbles of the old wagon road, unmistakably coming closer.

The key balked. Panic dulled every sound as she pulled it out, shoved it in again, turning it first one way, then the other. Abruptly it clicked. She stumbled inside and slammed the door behind her. Suitcase bumping against balustrades, she dashed up the stairs, then stopped to fumble again with another key and another lock. Finally she was inside Grace's apartment. She dropped her bag to grope for the bolts on the door.

It was a good lock. Strong bolts. She was safe. Breathing hard, she moved to the window, tripping over a low coffee table on the way.

Drapes, left open since Grace had vanished, gave her a clear view of the little alley. She didn't want to see anything. She wanted to believe, even against her own reason, that it had been someone walking a dog. And, of course, there were other apartments in the neighborhood. Maybe . . .

At the entrance of the alley, silhouetted, someone stood. Someone in dark clothing, made darker by the night. From the tilt of the head beneath a broad-brimmed hat, she felt sure that someone was looking up at the apartment.

She shouldn't have come alone. Not the first time anyway. Maybe they were right—lawyer, servants, friends, employees—everybody who had told her she was crazy to move into Grace's apartment. Then the fear ebbed, followed by a kind of exultation. This proved it! Grace had not disappeared voluntarily. Hana was right and they were all wrong, even the police.

She wished now she had acted aggressively, tried to intercept whoever. Maybe it wasn't too late—she could get the keys and go down the stairs. Outside. She hesitated, and the dark figure backed slowly around the corner, out of her sight.

Hana did not pick up the keys; nor did she go outside. Instead, she turned on a lamp and faced the empty apartment. Three rooms, bath, original plank floors, the trim sanded to reveal the grains of old wood. Two months isn't really a long time, yet a film of dust had settled over Grace's things. The air of disuse had settled even more thickly than the dust. It was almost as if Grace had been gone as long as the people who had walked the cobblestone road beyond the alley.

Police had been here. Also the private investigators she had hired. They'd found nothing. No clue. No reason. Zilch.

The consensus was that Grace Urich had, for reasons of her own, decided one morning to walk away from her job, her bank account, her apartment, her clothing. Her life.

Since nobody else seemed to give a damn, Hana had decided she herself would find Grace. Or, if it came to that, Grace's body. Melvyn Rosen, her attorney, told her that disappearances had become epidemic. Children, young adults, old people, all were falling through the strange cracks the civilization was developing. Often they were never found. The 1980s had become a lonely, frightening time.

Restlessly, Hana began opening drawers. In the small antique oak desk. In the chest of drawers in the bedroom. Everything looked so . . . normal.

She had insisted the apartment remain as Grace had left it. And so it had, because this building—with its quaint gift shop below and the apartment on the second floor—was among the many Hana owned in downtown Conover, Pennsylvania. For generations the Shaners (originally Schoener) had prospered here, influenced local affairs, served on committees, added to the family fortune, and at last departed with much regret, leaving behind few progeny, and these as sexually conservative as themselves. Finally only Hana remained to inherit the family honors and wealth. She had maintained a low profile while her father and the aunt who raised her were alive. It was only after their deaths, when she was thirty-three, that she discovered her real talent for selling carpets.

Hana loved media, used media, and if "60 Minutes" hadn't gotten to her yet, rumors around town suggested it was only a matter of time. Beneath the glitz of TV promotions, Hana handled her inheritance well. The mill that still manufactured the famous Shaner carpets had expanded under her directorship. The large ancestral mansion, destined to become an American Stately Home, was being maintained like the shrine it was. A jewel of Colonial architecture called Blue Spring Hill, it was located beyond the edge of town and so secure behind its famous azalea garden, woodland, and fields, that not even the suburbs of the city had dared approach it.

Wondering what she was looking for, Hana slammed shut a drawer filled with tidy piles of Grace's underwear. So far she had found nothing. There had to be something others had overlooked. After all, they hadn't known Grace.

Returning to the living room, she paused again at the desk, her attention caught by a framed group picture taken at the company picnic in July. Shaner Carpets had held a company picnic every year since 1887. She was touched that Grace had framed her copy. Hana herself stood front and center, looking almost like a kid in her jeans and T-shirt. Even though her deep green eyes were too far apart for real beauty, she had often been described as a "fine-looking woman."

At forty her skin was smooth, youthful, a light tan contrasting with her short white hair. She had turned white at age twenty-five, following the tradition of the women of her family.

She felt she still followed family tradition in what she was doing now. Her father had always quoted his grandfather as saying, "Be loyal to your employees and expect the same from them." An old-fashioned philosophy, but in many ways Shaner Carpets remained an old-fashioned company.

It was eighteen months ago that Grace Urich had come to work in the office. Hana, who had developed the family habit of noticing those working with her, found Grace to be unusually efficient. Even Jimmy Klopp, her notoriously hard-to-please plant manager, appreciated her skills. Grace had really good carpet instincts. Nor was she afraid to give that little bit of extra to her job. Despite some reservations, Hana made Grace her executive assistant when the woman who had been with her for ten years left to have a baby. The reservations had less to do with Grace's performance than with her odd reticence. Grace never talked about herself unless pressured. She had come from the Midwest, she'd said. From an ordinary family who were all dead. Hana suspected an accident, decided Grace's secret—if indeed there was a secret—did not affect her work in any way, and probed no further.

On the company picnic picture Grace was laughing, her head thrown back as though she loved the sunshine of that summer day. Twenty-eight, fun-loving, witty, she had not only become an indispensable part of the Shaner business family, she had also joined their social circle. Everybody liked her. Well, she was . . . likable.

Hana heard again the sounds of the picnic. The swat of the softball being hit over on the ball diamond. Kids shrieking as they scrambled for peanuts. And that strange story Grace had told.

It was suddenly very vivid. Grace chewing on a hot dog, drinking wine from a plastic glass, and asking, "Anybody want to hear about this crazy dream I had?"

Jimmy Klopp groaning, saying, "Tell it to your therapist, Gracie, and leave us alone, will you, huh?"

Melvyn Rosen—her father had always insisted on including an attorney just in case—saying, "I like to hear about other people's dreams. Great way to study human nature."

Grace turning, instantly dramatic. "Well, there was this guy trying to sell me a set of encyclopedias—"

Jimmy groaning again.

"—only I had to buy a casket with them to get a good deal, so in my dream I told him . . ."

Hana quickly returned the picture to its place on the desk.

Why had Grace dreamed about somebody trying to sell her a casket? Did she know something nobody else did? As picnic sounds faded from her mind, the silence of the apartment became almost audible. At home there were always people around, even after Dad and Aunt Sissy died.

This was not a very good beginning, she decided. Maybe she should have left it to the professionals.

No.

She'd get over it. After all, she was Hana Shaner, one of the leading women industrialists in the country. At a time when imports were taking over America, her stocks were high, her carpets selling. Mostly, of course, because of Dutch Blue, whose chemistry was still a closely guarded secret. Once it had been called Deutsch Blue, but her father had changed the spelling during World War II. It was a bright, vivid shade, developed a century ago by her great-grandfather. Her father had strictly impressed her that the universe revolved around, not the sun, but Shaner Carpets and Dutch Blue. Grace had been pushing to expand into women's clothing with this unique color.

Nervously Hana went to the window to close the drapes.

A figure was coming up the alley.

She drew back, noticing that her hands were shaking. Angrily she clasped them together, then grabbed her keys, unbolted the door, and ran down the stairs. No Shaner had ever hidden during a crisis. She recalled the time somebody had broken into Blue Spring Hill. "Kick 'em in the nuts" had been Mr. Fred's instructions.

Easy to say, but could she? And in time?

She was at the door. One twist of the knob would bring her face-to-face with whoever waited out there. Pictures from countless TV films flashed across her mind—an opened door, a gun roaring with death. Or a knife. That was the worst. She hated knives.

Drawing a deep breath, Hana jerked open the door and pulled back for a kick.

Elsie Hardinger, large eyes blinking in the sudden burst of light from the building, screamed. Hana stopped the forward motion of her kick just in time, grabbed Elsie's arm, and pulled her inside.

"Good Lord," Elsie said.

"Were you following me?"

"Why should I follow you?" Elsie sputtered.

"What're you doing here?"

Looking offended, Elsie pulled her rather long neck farther into her all-weather coat. "Mr. Fred called me."

"Why?"

"He's worried about you being here alone. He wanted one of your friends to drop in. You were —actually—going to kick me in the crotch, weren't you?"

"Come on up," Hana invited, ignoring the question and wishing that Mr. Fred would occasionally act like the employee he was.

Along with Blue Spring Hill and carpets, she had, in a sense, inherited Mr. Fred. After all, one couldn't lay off a man who had looked after her father for so many years. They'd been great friends as well as master and servant. He'd called her father "Mr. Henry," and her father had responded by always referring to him as "Mr. Fred." Mr. Fred was an excellent housekeeper. In some ways.

"So this is where she lived," Elsie said. "Compact, isn't it?"

"Plenty big enough for one person," Hana said shortly.

"Yes, of course. And she was a loner."

"Why do you say that?"

"Don't tell me you thought she was outgoing!" Elsie shrugged awkwardly out of her coat. "Umm . . . I wish I hadn't stopped smoking. Lighting a cigarette always gave one an opportunity to collect one's thoughts."

"What thoughts do you have to collect, Elsie?"

She dropped the coat on the small rose-colored sofa, then sat beside it. "He's really worried about you. Mr. Fred is. Well, we all are. Nobody can believe that you're actually going to live in this apartment and try to—whatever it is you're trying to do."

"You *know* what I'm trying to do."

Elsie Hardinger, tour guide specializing in excursions into Amish and Mennonite farmlands, turned on her charm—a charm that had been known to extract enormous tips, especially from Manhattanites out to view their country cousins. Her soulful eyes on Hana, she managed to give the impression that a refusal would shatter her world.

"Hana. Darling, listen to me. She's gone. Two months gone. Plus a couple of days. It's terrible. It's so sad. We all know that, but we also know you must return home. And forget it. Please forget it and go home!" She gestured forlornly. "You have to face it. A drug addict, or motorcycle gang . . . that's how things are today. We're coming apart, unglued. As a people, I mean. And Grace Urich is one of the victims. Sad they never found the body. Perhaps in some field someday—on an Amish farm—the mules pulling the plow will uncover—"

"Stop, damn it! You don't even know she's dead."

"Of course she's dead. Otherwise she'd be here," Elsie observed practically.

Hana turned away. Elsie rose, patted her shoulder, then began to prowl the apartment, picking up knickknacks as if Grace might be hiding there after all.

"How marvelous that all her things are still around! Look at this—her very own desk, her own felt-tip pen." Elsie's half-lidded eyes snapped into focus. "Did you know I conducted eight hundred and seven Jack the Ripper Walking Tours when I worked in London? Even the Dickens Tour and the East End Ghettos couldn't compete with that record. What I mean, my dear, is that people get it off on Jack the Ripper. And here this apartment is—a shrine to a missing woman. I wonder if there are other places like this in Conover? After all, this town saves everything, you know. 'Homes of Murderers' . . . Have there been any really *good* murders here? I've only been in the area for a couple of years, so I don't—but there must have been! Yes, there was that Amish woman slaughtered by that boy. And surely there are others. What a marvelous idea!"

Hana wished she hadn't controlled the kick. Maybe it was what Elsie Hardinger needed. She knew exactly why Mr. Fred had called her for help. Elsie was constantly catering to Mr. Fred. Hana was sure she had bribed him a number of times to allow special—and very wealthy—tourists to glimpse not only the famous azalea garden but the inside of the Shaner mansion. Hana wondered just what the bribe had been. Mr. Fred wouldn't have done it for money. At Mr. Fred's age, one hardly imagined that . . .

But one never knew these days.

Hana smiled warmly—she hoped. "Before you go, Elsie, did you see anyone out there?"

"I'm not going, Hana. I'd never forgive myself if anything happened."

"What could happen? Anyway, Bill's coming over."

The large eyes narrowed. Bill Longenecker owned and managed the tour company for which Elsie worked.

"Mr. Fred didn't tell me you were having company."

"It's just possible Mr. Fred doesn't know everything about me."

A slightly nasty gleam came into Elsie's eyes. "Don't bet on it."

Trying to change the drift of the conversation, Hana said, "You didn't answer my question."

"Question?"

"Did you see anybody hanging about out there?"

Elsie frowned. "No. Why?"

"Just checking." Hana picked up the all-weather coat and handed it to her. "Where are you parked?"

"CarPark," Elsie grunted, moving reluctantly to the door.

Feeling guilty, Hana followed her downstairs. If she saw or heard anything—anything at all—she'd bring Elsie back inside. She hoped she wouldn't have to do that, because now she had to call Bill Longenecker and ask him to take her to dinner. Wouldn't he be surprised.

Confidently, Elsie swept out into the night. A woman who had walked in the footsteps of Jack the Ripper eight hundred and seven times apparently was not afraid of an alley in Conover. Even so, Hana went with her to the cobblestone street, then watched until she disappeared into the thickening fog. Everything was quiet now, except for the distinctive click of Elsie's orthopedic heels.

(Only on shoes designed with the professional tour guide in mind.) Elsie boasted one pair had lasted through one thousand cathedral crawls and an entire season of Madrid's ever-popular Medieval Torture Trot.

Hana hurried back inside, looked up Bill's number, and dialed, wondering why she felt so anxious as it continued to ring. Then she realized she desperately wanted him to answer.

Two summers ago, she and Bill had dated regularly for three months. He was nearly ten years her junior, a fact that now at forty she found inexplicably attractive. They had enjoyed summer shows at the theater and concerts in the park. What soured the relationship was his insistance that his Amish/Mennonite tours benefited the Plain People. Hana argued they were exploitative. It was altogether different from taking a tour of the Grand Canyon. Here the focus was not on place but on people who considered photography to be biblically forbidden.

"Tourists don't respect their wishes," she had told him angrily. "They take pictures—and your buses have even run their buggies off the road."

Bill, almost as wide-eyed and charming as Elsie Hardinger, had replied with equal heat, "I suppose you're going to tell me the little old lady who lets us into her basement to buy her quilts at three hundred per doesn't appreciate my tourists?"

Bill answered his phone.

If he was surprised at the request, he didn't show it. What he displayed instead was disturbing enthusiasm.

He chose an Italian tavern out of the restored district because he remembered her preference for Italian cuisine. It was a small place with candles, brick walls, and cooking odors that any other time would have driven her into crazy anticipation.

Tonight even homemade pasta couldn't bring her up.

He was smiling as if she had agreed to sign on for a tour of Australia and New Zealand with a stopoff at the Fiji Islands. "Hana, my dear, you take too much of the responsibility for the welfare of your employees on your shoulders."

"Grace was also my best friend."

The sauce was definitely a shade too garlicky. Nor was it very attractive on Bill's green and white sport shirt. It reminded her that Christmas was coming and she would have to be back home to control some of Mr. Fred's wilder urges in seasonal decorating.

Bill continued, "Sure, she was your friend. But how can you prove anything by moving into that dumpy apartment?"

He smiled again, reached across the table to lightly touch her hand, then dropped the subject. And Hana remembered why she had liked Bill. Except when it came to his business, he never pressed. He respected another person's private places.

They lingered over their wine. Hana found herself saying flattering things she didn't mean. He looked pleased, reminding her of a parrot that had been at the animal shelter for a year before they found a good home for it. She wondered if it was the wine, then decided she was making a fool of herself because she dreaded returning to the apartment.

To prove herself and everybody wrong she announced that she was very anxious to get back, but put up no more than token resistance when he insisted on coming with her.

Even holding on to Bill's arm as they walked from the CarPark, Hana felt a childish fear of unseen terrors. The boogeyman . . . she hadn't thought of him in ages. Probably kids today didn't even know about the boogeyman. But in her childhood, youngsters were told Germanic tales originating in the dark forests of the old country, and the boogeyman had been very real. Only heartfelt prayers at bedtime kept him at bay.

Bill chatted comfortably, apparently unaware of the possibility of lurking classic monsters.

No footsteps followed them.

When they reached the apartment, he looked about appreciatively. "I didn't know it was this nice. Any wine around?"

"I don't know—"

"The kitchen! In a place like this, it's usually under the sink."

Whistling (in the dark to scare away the boogeyman?) he went into the kitchen. Hana dropped her jacket on the recliner in front of the TV. As Bill, still whistling, slammed cupboard doors, she wandered to the window. Fog nearly obscured the streetlights now. She hoped he could get home okay. In fact, she wished Bill were at home right now.

He brought wine in two crystal goblets.

Waterford? My. She hadn't realized Grace had such grand taste. Really, there was a lot about Grace she didn't know.

Handing her a goblet, he grinned. "Here's to crime."

"What an awful toast."

"I thought it was appropriate since you're playing detective."

She let it pass. They drank their wine. They talked, sitting comfortably together on the sofa. He went on about a lot of little things, letting her rest while her mind wandered. Although Hana had never married, she hadn't reached forty without what her aunt had once described as "an odd assortment of suitors." Funny, old-fashioned word that somehow seemed appropriate because none of them had suited her for long. Bill was as odd as any. Strange that he was also so easy to be around.

She noticed that he had stopped talking, which was all right too. For a while they sat in companionable silence. Hana closed her eyes. Bill put his hand on hers, then drew her closer. She thought of their summer as he kissed her, expertly, passionately. If they renewed their relationship, he could visit here often or even move in for a while, although she had never done that. Blue Spring Hill was too full of the vibes of her staid ancestors. More than that, Hana, once she had escaped from her aunt and her father, had prized her freedom.

Then, too, there was something about Bill and had been even that summer. . . . Perhaps it was his oddly curling hair. Not that she objected to curls. But his reminded her of feathers.

She opened her eyes as he stroked her back. He had been so good at massage. . . . The sauce on his shirt was a turnoff, but in fairness it was one of the hazards of Italian food. As he pecked at her neck, she saw Grace's desk above the fluffy, distracting curls. Something was wrong. It looked emptier.

She frowned, trying to think. Something was missing.

Hana pushed Bill away, rolled off the sofa, and hurried to the desk.

The picture of the company picnic . . . where—

Then she saw it, now facedown. She knew she herself had carefully replaced it. She'd watched Elsie and was certain she hadn't touched the picture. Bill hadn't even been inside the apartment before dinner.

"What's the matter?" he asked, his voice strained.

"Somebody was here! Somebody was inside this apartment while I was out."

He sat up, smoothing his hair with his hand. "So maybe Gracie had some real good friends you don't know about. What does it matter?"

Bill had just lost.

She didn't need a relationship right now. She had one. With a crime that had forced itself into her world.

"It matters to me."

She moved slowly about the room, trying to recall where objects had been when she first entered the apartment. Bill discovered the sauce on his shirt and scraped at it with a fingernail.

"You could help me look for things out of place."

Gloomily he shook his head. "I think I'm what's out of place here. You just needed a warm body tonight, didn't you? Any warm body."

She paid particular attention to bookshelves, avoiding his eyes.

"I'm sorry, Bill—"

"Yeah, I know." He finished a bit of wine, then

picked up his coat. "If somebody was in here and if they weren't friends of Grace's, you're in trouble. You know that, don't you? Hey, if you had to live here, it would make some sense. Know what's wrong with you?"

And to think that for a moment she had considered renewing their relationship. This was what had happened at the end of that summer. He'd told her what was wrong with her, and most of it had to do with the fact that she had never been poor.

"Everything was handed to you," he went on. "You were never forced to do things on a shoestring."

"Bill, what on earth does that have to do with—"

"You're spoiled! You think you can do anything. Including something better left to the police."

"The police aren't going to do anything in this case."

"You're not either, Hana. Except get yourself into a lot of trouble."

She turned to look at him. The worry in his eyes took some of the sting from his words.

"Bill—"

"Oh, forget it. I know when it's time to leave."

As she bolted the door behind him she wondered why he was so unsympathetic about Grace. He'd known her. Everybody in their social circle had known Grace.

She shrugged it off, concentrating on the apartment again. Where would a working woman keep important things?

Mr. Fred would know. She'd have to bring him here. He probably wouldn't want to come, but she could handle Mr. Fred. Probably better than she handled her lovers, she thought, remembering Bill's eyes.

Exhausted, but pleased with the Mr. Fred inspiration, Hana carried her suitcase into the bedroom. She paused, staring at the bed, which was rumpled as if someone had just crawled out of it. Well, of course. It hadn't been changed since . . . Certainly she needed clean sheets after two months.

She hadn't realized it would be that way. She was accustomed to the meticulous ways of Mr. Fred and Sal.

Oh, shit.

Maybe Bill was right. Even though she tried not to be, Hana knew she was spoiled.

She threw her suitcase on a chair, dug out robe and pajamas, and left everything else where it was. She'd live out of her suitcase for a while, even putting her traveling toothbrush back in its case. Because somehow it was important that everything here remain the same. Hana dropped into the bed and pulled the covers to her chin. They smelled faintly of dust and cedar.

She waited for sleep.

The bed felt strange, much softer than she was accustomed to. Then there were the noises—soft, strange sounds drifting like darkness through the old house. She felt tense, wakeful.

A floorboard creaked loudly.

Hana sat up in bed.

All noises stopped.

Well, old places did settle. Anyone who had spent her life at Blue Spring Hill knew that. The apartment was quite dark. Even though she had left the drapes open, the fog outside closed around the windows like gray shutters. She could scarcely see the dark bars meant to keep out intruders. She was glad they were there. The silence was now deafening.

Carefully she lay down again. But she didn't close her eyes. Nor did she relax. She could hear her own breathing.

As if they had been waiting—whatever they were—the sounds began again. There was one like the faint dripping of water. An intermittent tapping. A creaking as if light feet were passing slowly through the rooms.

Hana knew she was breathing more quickly than usual. She hoped she wouldn't begin to hyperventilate. Okay. Think logically. What would cause the sounds? Fog dripping from the eaves of the house. A tree branch scraping somewhere. The normal expansion and contraction of old wooden floors.

Had Grace lain here and heard this? Had the noises frightened her when she first moved in, then perhaps after a while she learned to sleep through them? Had she ever talked about that? Hana couldn't recall.

Something snapped in the living room.

Hana vaulted out of bed. She stood on the chilly floor in her bare feet, but all she could hear was her own heart. She considered turning on the light. If somebody was really in the apartment she could see them. But then, they could also see her.

Why hadn't she brought a flashlight?

Feeling inept and amateurish, she moved softly toward the bedroom door. She didn't know why she had even closed it. Maybe because it had felt safer. Slowly she turned the knob and opened the door.

The room beyond was just as dark as the bedroom. She tried to listen, even tried to sense another living presence. Her feet felt cold.

Hana moved forward, trying to recall the location of furniture. She bumped into a chair. After that she went faster, intent only on getting to the light switch.

Groping along the wall, she found it.

The room became alive, warm with colors.

But empty.

She ran about the apartment, turning on all the lights. She looked in closets and under the bed. She checked the locks and the bolts on the door. She inspected all window locks. She sat in the living room and carefully looked about to make sure everything was the way it had been when she went to bed.

Except for herself the apartment was unoccupied and undisturbed.

Imagination.

What else could it be? She refused to consider the possibility of less solid intruders. If Blue Spring Hill wasn't haunted—*and it was not!*—then neither was this or any other old house.

So what was the good of sitting here staring into the corners of the room? Hana went to the bathroom again, then turned out all the lights and got back into bed. She considered leaving the lamp on. But again, to lie there in a pool of light seemed more frightening than the darkness. She was aware of her cold feet, of the taut muscles in her neck beginning to hurt.

Aware of the dripping sound again. Of the scraping. Of the creaks. Now there was a new one. A shuffling. It grew louder. As if furniture was being moved.

This time Hana slipped quietly out of bed and crept to the door. She jerked it open quickly, turning on the overhead light in the bedroom at the same time. Light streamed into the quiet, empty living room. The wave of fatigue and frustration that washed over her made her realize how tired she was. She closed the door, turned out the light. In the abrupt darkness she couldn't see, and she stubbed her toe. She tumbled into bed this time and pulled the covers over her head.

With determination she closed her eyes. She would make friends with the sounds of the house as Grace must have done. The scrapings were . . . made by squirrels? She pictured them building nests to hide fluffy-tailed squirrel babies. She thought of the squirrels in the trees at Blue Spring Hill. Of walking there on summer days when even the air of her woodlands was green. . . . Gray. Now they looked gray.

Hana fell into a restless sleep.

She dreamed she moved into the picture on the desk and took up the summer picnic the second after the photograph had been snapped. One moment she was surrounded by flat photographic people and the next they were swelling, filling out, becoming real. Some returned to the softball game. Jimmy Klopp, wine bottle in hand, came up to her as she talked with Mel Rosen and offered them drinks. Grace, munching her fourth or fifth hot dog, ran over from the pavilion. Grace loved picnic hot dogs. Jimmy filled thin plastic glasses for them.

Grace giggled. "One more glass of wine and I'll have the courage to tell you about this incredible dream I had."

She was saying the words again, telling about

the deal on the books and the casket, her voice lifelike, low and pleasant. Then, as Grace's words continued, the picnic faded and Hana stood in a dark place. Finally the words ceased and she found herself walking toward a casket. She felt her breath rising in gasps out of her chest. A smiling man, holding a volume of an encyclopedia in one hand, stood at the head of the casket. He beckoned to Hana. She didn't want to go toward that casket, didn't want to look inside. But the man's eyes turned red, burning into hers, compelling her. She reached the side of it. She looked down.

Grace Urich lay there, a faint odor of decay rising from her. Mold was forming on her face. Her hands, folded on a frayed coverlet, looked soft. Very . . . soft. . . .

Rotten.

Feeling sick, Hana backed away.

That was when she saw the other coffin. It was empty.

Still smiling, the encyclopedia salesman started toward her.

Hana awoke with a scream.

The rest of the dark night she lay there listening to the sounds of the house. She was afraid to go to sleep again. She knew she would dream. She knew one did not say no to that particular encyclopedia salesman.

Chapter Two

TEPID WATER DRIBBLED from the shower in uncertain spirals. It was not relaxing, hardly even cleansing. Hana decided she'd have to get a plumber—soon. She wondered why Grace had never complained.

Pulling on dark slacks, topped with a green turtleneck and brown cord jacket, Hana thought regretfully about the full breakfast Mr. Fred always made for her. It wasn't until she was outside in the sunny morning, bright with the promise of a wonderful autumn day, that she began to feel almost normal. She paused, noting that sheltered trees on the cobbled road had only begun to turn gold.

Her first stop was the souvenir shop beneath the apartment. Robie Holmes, the proprietor, was a good buyer who knew her business but was unfortunately inclined to strange punk styles and dark glasses.

Robie remembered Grace Urich very well.

"Oh, yeah, sure. Sometimes— Well, you know, like Columbus Day and— Oh, I don't know—but she'd stop by when she didn't have to work. Just to talk. So I knew her. Maybe not well—but—like I said—you know—"

To stem the flow of phrases, Hana said rather loudly, "You do know she's disappeared, don't you?"

Robie seemed to be squinting through her shades. "Man. Do I know? Do I ever? Everybody around here. Scary. You know? You get thinking—could be me." She touched an orange stream of hair that nearly reached the bridge of her nose.

"There are weird people around. Know what I mean?"

"Do you recall the morning she disappeared?" Hana asked patiently.

"When was that?"

"Two months ago."

"Two months? Summer. Was that summer? I think I was away. Maybe. My lover took care of the shop for me. I just fell off the end about then. Went to L.A. Yaaahoooo! L.A.!"

Whether the half-gurgle, half-scream was positive or negative for the city of Los Angeles Hana didn't even want to know. She glanced about the shop with its handwoven sweaters, shell-shaped soaps, and brass incense burners. It was the astrological jewelry and misshapen bottles that gave her a déjà vu of the sixties. Perhaps the sixties were still alive and well in little courtyards and up strange alleys, existing inexplicably and anachronistically inside Colonial restorations.

"You know where she ate, don't you?" Robie asked irrelevantly. "Right on the corner. Every morning. The Feathered Duck. You know?"

"Thanks. I'll find it."

"Find it. Find her. I miss her."

"Oh?"

"Ummmm. Well. You know. Great to talk to. Fantastic woman. Just—like—could pick up thoughts. Even half-spoken ones."

"How convenient for you. How much did *she* talk?"

"Just told you. Didn't I? She talked to me. *Talked to me.*"

"But did she ever say anything about herself?"

Robie blinked as if that were a unique idea. "Herself? Oh. You know. I'd kind of— What I mean, she was so easy to talk to. She'd just sit there and— It was like that."

Hana suppressed an urge to double Robie's rent.

Maybe beneath the fringes of orange hair she did mind reading, too, because she added uncomfortably, "I did find out one thing—"

"Yes?"

"She used peach-scented douche."

Triple the rent.

Robie continued dreamily, "See, we got talking about it one day. I make my own out of crushed herbs and seawater. . . . That's when she told me —said the whole bathroom smelled of peach orchards in springtime."

Hana left in despair before the disjointed sentences had run to their conclusion. If somewhere in that scattered consciousness lurked information about Grace Urich, she was afraid it would remain hidden forever.

However, The Feathered Duck stood right on the corner, a place of polished wood and coffee in thick white china mugs. Brown earthen bowls of coppery mums decorated the tables. Hana chose one near a window where she could observe the assortment of people gathering for the day of the city.

She needed some of that fragrantly brewing coffee. An interview with the manager or whoever could wait. A young waitress, in brown skirts to midcalf and enveloping white apron, handed her a menu. After she had ordered scrambled eggs, toast and coffee, Hana asked, "Can you help me? I'm trying to locate a friend of mine who was a regular customer here, I understand. Her name is Grace Urich."

"Sorry."

Hana began to describe Grace. The woman grabbed at a stray curl that had escaped the pile on top of her head, then interrupted nervously, "I haven't worked here all that long. I see loads of people. I'm really sorry."

She darted away. Yawning discreetly, Hana decided she must not become too paranoid about those who didn't want to get involved. What the waitress said was logical. Sleepily her thoughts wandered to the strange-seeming nonviolence of disappearances. No corpse. No blood. Just a vacuum where someone had been. The awfulness of expecting them any moment. And they never came again. Except Grace would.

The food, served rapidly by the darting waitress, was delicious. When Hana paid her check at the cashier's station, she asked about Grace again. This time she received a better response.

"Why, of course I remember Grace. Came in here all the time. Always sat over there near the window."

Hana tried to keep her voice calm, professional. "Then she had the same waitress I had?"

"That's right. I saw in the paper Grace was missing."

"Do you recall the last time she came in?"

"Well, I don't know. . . . Seems like ages—"

"She disappeared two months ago. August thirteenth, to be exact. Can you recall if she ate breakfast here that morning?"

Another customer moved in. The cashier took care of him, then beckoned a waitress to take over.

"Let's go to my office," she suggested.

It turned out to be a cubbyhole upstairs, above

the kitchen. Even though its one window had been propped open to the morning air, odors of food clung to its surfaces. The trim, handsome woman introduced herself as Jill Devon, assistant manager.

"Are you a relative of Grace Urich's?" she asked, watching Hana carefully.

"I'm her employer. Also her friend. The police don't seem to be doing much, so I'm trying to find out what happened to her."

Devon nodded, then picked up an engagement calendar through which she paged rapidly. "Well, you picked some job for yourself. The trail must be pretty cold by now."

"I have to try."

"Guess I'd feel that way myself." She paused, eyeing August 13 on her calendar. "I'm the kind of person who makes volumes of notes. People laugh at me, but it's just the way I am."

Yet, Hana thought, certainly not a note about a regular customer paying her check.

"August thirteenth!" Devon exclaimed. "Dentist appointment. Awful date to make a dentist appointment, right? Root canal. I was really upset. And Grace Urich noticed something was wrong. I told her all about it. I don't usually talk about things like that to customers. But Grace was special."

Excited, Hana asked, "Then she was here that morning? She ate breakfast here on August thirteenth?"

"Yes. I wondered why she didn't come around after that— Well, you know she was a regular— then I heard the stories. And saw that picture in the paper. Did she disappear from work?"

Hana shook her head. "She never got that far.

Her car was still in the parking garage. The police investigated, and it's their opinion it wasn't moved that morning. No special fingerprints—just the usual blur. Did you actually see her leave the restaurant?"

Devon snapped shut her calendar book. "Of course she left the restaurant."

"But did you see her?"

"I think—yes. Yes, I watched her go out. She gave me a kind of reassuring little wave from the doorway."

"Did anybody follow her? Was anybody right behind her in line to pay their check?"

"I really don't recall—"

"You have large windows in this place. Perhaps you looked out. Perhaps you saw something. Anything."

"I saw nothing else," Devon said with finality. "Now, I really must get back to work."

As Hana followed Jill Devon back to the restaurant she tried a few more questions—What time had it been? How was Grace dressed? Did she seem different in any way? But either the woman had told all she knew or had decided further involvement of The Feathered Duck was not in her own best interests. It apparently had not been a pleasant thought that a customer had disappeared on the way from the restaurant to the parking lot.

She wondered if Jill Devon would have talked more if she hadn't told her that Grace vanished that day. Perhaps Hana had come on too strong, since Jill seemed to feel threatened. She decided to be more reticent in the future. But at least she had established that Grace had been alive and well and following her usual routine that morning.

Hana stepped out into the fresh air as Grace must have done, then paused uncertainly. One had to assume, without evidence to the contrary, that she had intended to go to work as usual.

Hana turned in the direction of the CarPark, where Grace had rented a space by the month. She walked slowly, looking about. Three doors down she saw a magazine shop. She couldn't recall whether or not Grace ever brought a newspaper to work. But it was worth a try.

The man behind the counter waved away her questions. "Lady, I got trouble remembering what happened yesterday, so don't go asking me about two months ago."

Methodically, Hana stopped in each place of business to ask if they knew Grace or had seen somebody answering her description. The answers were all disappointingly similar to that of the man in the magazine shop. It was slow, unrewarding work. She was still in the restored area where narrow beds of rust and yellow mums separated the trees.

An elderly woman who had been admiring the flowers moved slowly toward a contour bench. Hana followed and sat beside her.

"Pardon me. . . ."

The woman eyed her suspiciously.

Hana said hastily, "I'm trying to locate a friend of mine who—Well, frankly, nobody seems to know where she's gone. She lived alone near here. I'm trying to find people who may have seen her."

Carefully the woman surveyed her, then asked, "What's your friend look like?"

Hana described Grace again, wishing Jill

Devon had been able and willing to tell her what Grace had been wearing.

The woman shook her head. "Sounds like a hundred other girls going to work in some office or other. The older I get, the harder it is for me to tell one from the other."

"Were you here on August thirteenth?"

"I'm here every day. Well, every day as is fit to be outside. Won't find me setting out much in January. Like to eat lunch in town. It don't cost much if you get the daily special with the senior-citizen discount." She added quickly, "Don't get the idea I'm always here alone. Got lots of friends, you know."

"Yes, of course." Hana smiled reassuringly as she handed the woman her business card. "Please. Try to think back. Any information might help."

The woman stared at the card. "Shaner? One of *the* Shaners?"

"The only one left."

She nodded sympathetically, carefully slipping the card into the pocket of her coat as if it were something precious. Then she frowned, concentrating on the bricks of the walkway. "Let's see now . . . middle of August, you say? Pretty hot this year. August. I remember. Hate heat. Still, can't stay inside in air conditioning all the time, can you? What day of the week did you say that was?"

"Friday."

"Friday, you say? Right before the weekend." She sat straighter. "Sure! That was the weekend I went to Harborplace in Baltimore—Saturday the fourteenth was when Annie Boyer and me took that bus trip. Friday—right before the trip . . .

uh-huh. I was setting right here on this bench all morning. Thinking about the trip I was going on. We really enjoyed that, let me tell you. You ever been to Harborplace?"

Hana admitted to this flaw in her geographical education and listened to a ten-minute lecture on the wonders of the famous aquarium. As the woman launched into a description of some sort of sailing ship anchored nearby, Hana interrupted, "I'm so glad you remember the day. Now, can you recall anything that was different about it?"

"Different? Nothing's different since I retired from Woolworth's. Every day's the same. Unless I'm taking a bus trip. Going to Vermont to see the colors next week."

"Did anything unusual happen that day? While you were sitting here? Anything at all?"

"No."

Hana sighed and started to rise.

"Unless you count the actors," the woman added.

Hana sat down again. "What actors?"

She grunted. "From the playhouse, I suppose. Where else would they come from? In my day we kept actors on the stage, where they belong. Not all over the place like they are today. They belong in a theater, right? Am I right or am I not right?"

"Well—"

"Sure. You bet. But here they were like all the world was their stage. All over the street here. Not that there's any traffic on it, mind you, since they closed it off and built this mall—which was a good thing in my book."

"What were these actors doing?"

"Acting."

Patiently. "Acting what?"

"Oh, history. Making out like they were people who lived here way back when. Women in long skirts. Men in stuff made them look like they just come in off the farm."

"How many of them were there?"

She looked upward, as if a number might be printed on an old chimney. "Well, now, it's hard to tell. They moved around a lot, so it looked like more than it was, I expect. But maybe there were ten. Yes, now I think, about ten."

"And there was a lot of activity? A lot of people watching?"

"There's them will watch anything, long as it's free."

So there had been something unusual that morning. And that something was a lot more activity as the morning crowds moved toward their cars or offices. Things could happen under the distractions of a crowd. Especially if the focus was on actors.

After she left the old woman, Hana asked questions of pedestrians. Most hurried away without answering. A few regulars remembered the actors. A few shopkeepers, too, remembered the actors. Nobody remembered Grace Urich.

Hana pulled into the driveway that leisurely circled her acres of azalea bushes now slipping drably toward winter hiatus. She acknowledged that it felt good to be coming home. Good to know her own safe parking space would be waiting. Not that one couldn't vanish, she supposed, between the car and the side door of the mansion. But it did seem so much more unlikely. As she passed the woodland that separated azaleas from the lawns and house, her mind drifted wearily. First thing she had to do was talk to Mr. Fred. Then pick up more clothing. Maybe she'd come back every day or at least every other day to take a good shower. God, she'd have to get somebody at the office to call a plumber about that bathroom in the apartment. . . .

Snapping wide awake, Hana slammed on her brakes.

Damn! He was at it again.

She left the car in the middle of the drive and strode along a border of boxwood toward a group of people happily digging up her lawn. Mr. Fred, happiest of all, was directing the abominable activity.

Since the day when her father had given him charge of overseeing the estate, Mr. Fred had not changed either in appearance or attitude. As a child, Hana—who was Hannah Elizabeth Clara in those days—had looked upon him with superstitious awe. He seemed like the giants in the old-world tales Aunt Sissy read to her on winter evenings when they sat before one of the great fireplaces. He had an unfortunately large head that looked incongruous on his thin body. His eyes were dark and very alive, and if giants didn't have eyes like that they should have. His hair, too, was dark, and since he was now at least sixty-five, Hana suspected that it was dyed. Most of the time he wore a black suit. Today he was in jeans and T-shirt.

"Mr. Fred!" Hana shouted.

She was no longer afraid of him, as she had been as a child. When you wrote out a person's paycheck you knew he was no giant.

She clearly heard him order the dozen assorted

young people to continue digging before he quickly came to her.

She began angrily, "If I've told you once—"

But somehow she was following him back toward her car. Somehow he was explaining with the enthusiasm only Mr. Fred could summon for digging trenches in private gardens that this was a very special archaeological class from the college. That they'd been doing research in the Shaner archives at the Historical Society and were convinced that during one brief period of the Revolutionary War the mansion had been used as a hospital. A cryptic sentence in an ancient letter led them to believe at least two soldiers might be buried beneath the lawn—sodded just two years ago and totally free of dandelion, crabgrass, and slugs, according to Bottinger's Lawn and Garden Service, to which she paid a fortune every spring.

"Perhaps that was what made the boxwood so lush and full," he enthused. "The dead beneath the soil. The border was put in just around that time and—"

"I don't want them digging here!"

"You never minded before you fell in that trench last year. And if you had been more careful when I told you we were looking for the original cold cellar that had been covered over by your parking lot—"

"Out of here! I want them out! Did you think you could get away with this because I'm staying at the apartment?"

He opened the car door. Crossly Hana slid behind the wheel.

"I would never do anything behind your back," he stated with great dignity. "Remember, your father always said one holds a historic building such as this in trust. It is an obligation to preserve it and—"

"I suppose you call digging up the grounds 'preservation'?"

"And finding out all one can about its past. We are adding a chapter to the history of the house. Someday when there is a museum in the 1812 Annex, bones may be displayed there."

"I don't want a museum in my home! Particularly one full of bones!"

Hana slammed the door and roared the rest of the way to her parking lot. That same parking lot that had required complete repaving after the debacle of the last incursion of archaeological students. Hana had a dozen boxes of pottery shards and one crock of seventy-five-year-old pickles stored in the 1812 Annex as a result of that venture into history.

She was inside the house before she realized she hadn't asked for his help in searching Grace's apartment. She paused, closed her eyes for a moment, allowing the mood of the old building to wash over her, calming her. Perhaps Mr. Fred was a giant after all. He was certainly right about the house and its preservation. From the carefully collected Colonial furnishings to the authentic shades of woodwork and the warm stain of the wideboard floors, Blue Spring Hill belonged to the dead as much as to her. The dead and their spokesperson, Mr. Fred. "The Family" was still here in portrait and spirit.

Ghost, the shaggy white dog who, very unlike Shaners, was of uncertain ancestry, barked a greeting and came jumping toward her, followed by Crumb, a small beagle type with enormously sad eyes. With more decorum, confident in their feline superiority, Penelope Baskin and Kitty Fisher sat on the wide staircase waiting to be petted.

Sal Nunemacher came down those stairs, then stopped to stare at her.

"What're you doing here?"

"I live here," Hana told her irritably.

The trouble with wonderful servants—if one could call them that—like Mr. Fred and Sal Nunemacher was that they did take over. It was a relief to have a home run efficiently, of course, but there were times the efficiency became rather . . . relentless.

"Well, now, I thought you were going to be living in that apartment house for a while," Sal said, turning to follow as Hana and the animals went upstairs. "Penelope Baskin! Don't you dare use that banister as a kneading post! You go right on down to your logs in the conservatory!"

Hana scooped up Penelope Baskin, who looked over her shoulder to purr smugly at Sal Nunemacher. "Just here to get a few things."

"Ja, ja," Sal murmured wisely, lapsing into her familiar German.

"What do you mean by that?"

"All I know is I wouldn't want to stay there by myself neither. Not me."

Sal trailed Hana into the master bedroom with its canopied bed, then went to the closet to get out another suitcase, which she apparently had not returned to storage.

"Thought you'd be needing this. All the clothes you got."

"Thanks. I'll do it myself," Hana told her as Penelope Baskin sprang from her arms to land deftly, claws extended, on a velvet chair. "I'm not sure how much more I want to take."

Ghost and Crumb unhappily sniffed the suitcase. Sal, smiling a little, plopped it on the bed.

Damn her. She'd guessed it had gone badly. In fact, Sal had predicted it would go badly.

Hana said meekly, "I'm going to need you and Mr. Fred to help me at the apartment."

"Ach, no!"

"For just one afternoon! You know about houses—housekeeping—and I don't. I want you to help me search the place."

Penelope Baskin and Kitty Fisher meowed impatiently. Hana opened a small drawer where their catnip toys were stored. Looking uncertain, Sal petted Ghost, who had decided to sit on her feet.

After all, Sal was Old Order Mennonite, although Hana often forgot the fact. She no longer even noticed the severe dress, apron, and little cap of Sal's sect. Since Sal had long ago come out to work for "the English" in order to help her widowed mother and a large number of younger siblings, she had acquired much of the talk and some of the attitudes of that world.

"It's a house of death," Sal said.

"You don't know that. Grace could still be alive."

"Then it belongs to her, and we got no rights to be in there."

"We have every right to help somebody in trouble. More than a right, Sal. Isn't it a duty?"

Leaving Sal to think that over, Hana wandered to the window to watch the digging up of her lawn.

"Well . . . guess it wouldn't hurt to clean up

the place while she's away," Sal grumbled reluctantly. She pushed Ghost off her feet and quietly left the room.

Penelope Baskin and Kitty Fisher had selected a catnip mouse and were tossing it about on the sunburst patchwork quilt that covered the bed. Below, a young woman dropped a small spade with which she had been working, then squealed with a glee Hana could hear from where she stood. The others came flocking to her, staring down into her section of the trench.

Just what Hana needed—the bones of a Revolutionary War soldier beneath the front lawn. It would mean TV cameras and more archaeologists. The history-in-the-making taking place reminded Hana of the historical charade the group of actors were performing the morning Grace disappeared.

She flopped onto the bed and looked up the number of the old theater. Kitty Fisher dropped the catnip mouse on her lap. Penelope Baskin rescued it and dashed into the hall. A woman on the other end of the line soon assured Hana there had been no group of actors from their company performing in the streets this summer. Nor did she know of any other groups so engaged. And no, the Historical Society hadn't been involved, because they always called for a consultation if anything theatrical was planned.

Hana hung up. If the actors were not really actors, what had they been doing that morning? Had the charade been expressly for the purpose of waylaying Grace?

She felt suddenly cold. From the first she'd been afraid for Grace, but her fears had envisioned a haphazard crime, a kidnapping by an addict perhaps. She had never even considered a well-laid plan by desperate people who would commit a crime in public. Maybe the sounds she'd heard in the night could not, after all, be explained away by logic. And perhaps there had been more than one person following her to the alley.

Hana got up and ran to the window, spurred by a new sense of urgency. She forced up the protesting old sash and bellowed, "Mr. Fred!"

Beaming, he came forward.

"We've found it!" he shouted. "We have found one soldier! Wonderfully preserved skeleton!"

She knew when she was defeated. "How delightful. Tell them to just keep digging, but I want to see *you*. Now!"

It was hard to think fondly of a blackmailer, but Hana, sitting on the floor and nibbling at one of the pimiento cheese sandwiches Sal had brought in the picnic basket, did think fondly of Mr. Fred.

Really, he was so efficient he could be forgiven almost anything.

His expert eyes seemed to take in the entire apartment. Sal moved more slowly, insisting upon cleaning everything as she went. The lunch had been her idea, because she was doubtful of the sanitary conditions in the kitchen.

For Mr. Fred the price had been unlimited archaeological digging as long as Revolutionary War corpses could be found. Sal's conscience would not permit her to demand extra favors. But from past experience, Hana knew that one day soon something would be needed by Sal's large family. This would be mentioned humbly, and the fact that it would be provided was always greeted with glad surprise.

They had already been through the bath and bedroom, where the shocked Sal had insisted upon clean sheets. The bath had yielded nothing more than bottles of sinus pills properly prescribed by a local doctor. Hana had called the police immediately and asked them to check it out. There had been some snickering and the suggestion that nobody disappeared because of a bad sinus. They had noted the pills in their own search, but the medication had been dismissed as unimportant.

The bedroom turned up clothing with labels removed. And a photograph Sal had found because she considered it indecent for Mr. Fred to rummage through the lady's underwear. It had been slipped into the very back of the smallest drawer. The find confirmed what Hana had suspected—that the police search had been perfunctory and not at all thorough. She took a sip of fruity wine—Sal could be so thoughtful at times—as she stared at the picture.

The background was a suburban street where trees hid blurred houses. Could be anywhere in the Western world. The fuzzy image of a car that looked to be about twenty years old—an American make. In the foreground, quite sharp, stood three people—a girl about eight, flanked by two smiling adults, man and woman. The styles, too, seemed to be those of about twenty years before. Summertime certainly. The child had ribboned pigtails framing her wide smile and wore a pretty, sleeveless dress. The adults looked middle class yet strangely flamboyant. Hana couldn't put her finger on it, but the woman's dress was more like a costume than streetwear.

Grace and her parents? There was nothing written on the back, not even a developer's date or name. But the time seemed right. A child of about eight, yes, and twenty years ago. And the eyes were right. This girl could grow up to look like Grace. Nothing sinister about it. So why had it been hidden? Hana hesitated. She considered taking it with her, but since her intent had been to keep Grace's possessions intact, she carefully placed it in a desk drawer beneath a neat stack of notepads. Restlessly she moved into the kitchen.

Sal was muttering to herself in the Germanic dialect still spoken among the Plain People. Hana understood enough to know that Grace's housekeeping did not meet Sal's standards.

Water was splashing in the sink as Sal began to sing in English. "Now you see her,/ Now you don't./ You can't find her,/ Bet you won't!"

Shocked, Hana asked, "Sal—why are you singing that?"

She paused guiltily. "Why, it just came to me is all. We used to sing it when we were kids."

Sal turned her attention to vigorous scouring. Mr. Fred, who had been searching beneath an old gas range, wriggled out and scrambled stiffly to his feet. He was smiling as happily as if he had succeeded in having the entire lawn at Blue Spring Hill dug up.

"I have found something," he announced as he ceremoniously handed Hana a slip of paper.

"It's just a receipt for a blouse," she said, wondering if Mr. Fred was losing his grip.

He sighed pityingly. As a child, Hana had hated

that sigh. It meant that in his eyes she had been incredibly stupid.

She carried the receipt to the window to inspect it closely, looking for hidden messages. Then she noticed the date—*September 8.* Mr. Fred smiled superciliously.

"She must have been in this apartment after the date of her disappearance," he purred, a habit he had picked up from Kitty Fisher.

Because she felt annoyed, Hana refused to go along with the idea, even though she knew Grace patronized this particular shop. "More likely it was dropped by a careless cop or one of those great private eyes I hired. After all, everybody was in this apartment at one time or another."

He sighed again, then turned his back to continue searching with silent animosity.

When they had finished, the apartment was squeaky clean and anything that could possibly be there had been discovered. In addition to the photograph, the sinus pills, the missing clothing labels (which she decided had to be called a non-clue), and the receipt was an item of even more dubious importance.

It was an unmailed postcard, a freebie handout that proudly proclaimed the attractions of a restaurant offering "genuine Pennsylvania Dutch cooking." Hana supposed she should go there, but somehow she doubted anybody would remember Grace Urich.

She finally admitted to Mr. Fred that the receipt seemed to be the most promising clue.

He was getting ready to go. *"Really?"*

It must have been hell to live in Olde England with a houseful of family retainers, all recalling one's sins as a child and never forgiving them.

Hana was always willing to admit she had been a curious girl and perhaps she had, uninvited, inspected Mr. Fred's bureau drawers on occasion. But she had outgrown all that.

Surely he wasn't putting her search for Grace down to idle curiosity.

After Mr. Fred, Sal, and the empty picnic basket had gone, Hana dressed carefully. The boutique from which the receipt came sold very fine clothing, and it might be necessary to masquerade as a customer. She selected her most flattering layered outfit—beige slacks, gold blouse with a rust and gold sweater, a brown-patterned scarf—then tucked the receipt into her shoulder bag and left the apartment.

Sal's wine and sandwiches, coupled with lack of sleep, had given her a lethargic feeling. She desperately needed coffee. Besides, it wouldn't hurt to inquire at The Feathered Duck if anybody had noticed actors in the area the morning Grace vanished.

Jill Devon smiled in wary recognition.

Yes, she had noticed them. But only briefly as she was on her way to the bank for change. She recalled wishing she'd had time to stop, because she thought street theater was fun. No, she hadn't seen Grace with them. She hadn't recognized any of them or knew how long they stayed. There had been quite a crowd gathered around. She thought there were about a dozen actors.

Not much help.

Hana said, "The waitress I had this morning—I don't suppose she's still on duty."

"Yes, as a matter of fact, she is."

"Long hours."

Devon said coldly, "Somebody called in sick. She's filling in."

Hana let it go and took the same table she'd had before. It was some minutes before the young woman came.

"Hello again!" Hana said brightly. "What's your name?"

"Debby," she mumbled.

Tired? Or nervous? Probably tired, Hana decided charitably.

"Well, Debby, all I need is coffee."

"Decaf?"

"Regular. Black. And the stronger, the better."

Debby looked offended, as if she had been called upon to dispense harmful drugs. Again it was some time before she returned, obviously reluctant to be the bearer of the brew.

Hana slipped a two-dollar tip into her hand.

"Two months ago," she said, "do you remember actors doing street theater near here?"

Debby shook her head. "I usually do breakfast, so I start pretty early in the morning. Not many people around when I come down through."

"Perhaps you heard about them? Or looked out the window? Grace Urich was here that morning —Did she mention them?"

The waitress shrugged impatiently. "I told you before I don't remember this Grace whoever. I mean, who remembers customers and what they talk about? 'It's nice weather'—so who cares? And I think it's dumb when actors dress up and go around pretending to be dead people or something. I go for music—videos. That's what I like. Forget the other junk."

Maybe it was the caffeine generation who enjoyed history and drama, Hana thought sadly as

Debby hurried away in a swirl of skirts. She took a long swallow of her coffee. Very hot and faintly bitter. Should wake her up. Slowly sipping, she realized she no longer felt resentful of either the police or the private detectives. Even with her personal interest—Mr. Fred might say her personal curiosity—she wasn't doing much better.

Disquieting to realize that she might finally have to admit Grace Urich had gone into a dark void and nobody would ever know what happened to her. She thought of the picture of Grace as a child. Perhaps she should have taken it to a safe-deposit box and not left it in the apartment. Yet, what could that old photograph have to do with the woman's disappearance?

Hana's eyes wandered to the leaves outside the window. They would turn to more vivid gold, then fall. Die. Disappear. Blow away like all the other generations of dead leaves. Not really unlike people. Wasn't there a story she'd read long ago . . . about this bride who disappeared during a game of hide-and-seek and a hundred years later they'd found her bones in an old chest?

Cooped up. Not able to breathe. Horrible.

She felt a little cooped up and breathless herself. She took another sip of coffee as she watched a leaf turning in slow downward circles as it fell from a maple tree. She thought she saw it float right through the glass window to land on her table, but when she looked down it wasn't there.

Wow. She really did need sleep.

Hana took another swallow of her coffee. The cup felt so heavy. . . . As she set it down she noticed that her table had fuzzy edges. Not solid wood the way it had been but . . . soft-looking—like velvet . . .

Maybe Debby was right. Maybe caffeine rotted one's brain. Another victim of caffeine. She could see the headlines now: "Prominent Local Manufacturer ODs on Caffeine While Having a Cup of Coffee In the . . ." What was the name of this place?

Hana tried to grip the velvet edges of the table to hold on. No, it wasn't caffeine or lack of sleep. Something was wrong. Even velvet shouldn't be this hard to hold.

She turned, spilling the coffee. "Help—!" she cried. "Help me!"

The last thing she saw before she passed out was the cashier's frightened face.

Chapter Three

HANA STRUGGLED TO sit up, found she couldn't, then realized Jill Devon was holding her down.

"Please, lie quietly—we've sent for an ambulance."

Nausea swept her, but it was nothing compared to the aching of her head and the shot of pain that jabbed her shoulder when she tried to move her arm. Even though her eyes were still slightly out of focus, she recognized the small office of the restaurant.

"How long have I . . . ?" she began dizzily.

"Not long. But it seems—Oh, I wish they'd get here."

"I'm all right . . ." she said weakly.

"You're *not* all right! You passed out cold, knocking over chairs and spilling everything."

They could hear the siren now, to Jill Devon's obvious relief. Feeling rather ridiculous, Hana closed her eyes again.

Feet hammered on the stairs. When Hana opened her eyes, Jill had gone. She felt too weird to object to the ministrations of the two paramedics hovering over her. She did object to the stretcher and the ride to the hospital. The pair was pleasant but firm. It was best.

Later, in an emergency room, where nurses first took samples of blood then pumped her stomach, Hana became aware that she'd been drugged. She didn't know why it had taken her so long to figure it out, except that whatever she had been given had done things to her head. A doctor who wanted to admit her asked impersonal personal questions, but Hana insisted on signing a release and calling her lawyer, Mel Rosen, to come for her.

As soon as she hung up, she realized she should have called Mr. Fred instead. Or Elsie. Or even Bill Longenecker. It was embarrassing to realize that when she needed help, it was still Mel she thought of. My God, it had been so long ago—those dates in high school, the first college summers when they were together all the time.

For just a little while back then, she had thought he would always be there.

But when Mel arrived at the hospital, his obvious concern made it all right. She was given instructions about seeing her personal physician the next day, then Mel was permitted to wheel her out to the emergency entrance to his parked blue Volvo. On the way, she decided he was still the best-looking guy she had ever met. Or maybe it was just that his looks suited her. He had kind brown eyes, a strong face, and thick dark hair just turning gray at the temples.

When they were safely away, Hana said lamely, "I'm sorry I called you, but—"

"Don't be foolish, Hana. I was glad to come. You know I would. Any time. It's a nice change from defending our nuclear power industry against all and sundry. Want to tell me what happened?"

"I was drugged."

"Oh, come now—"

"I was! Either in The Feathered Duck or by the food Sal brought to Grace's apartment. We had a picnic for lunch. But I don't think it was in that. I'm pretty sure that whatever it was, I got it in the restaurant."

"The Feathered Duck?" He sounded scandalized. "I've eaten there hundreds of times. Why would anybody—"

"Why would they pump my stomach if I hadn't been given some pretty rotten gunk?" she demanded as she rubbed her shoulder. They said she had struck something when she fell and would be black and blue by tomorrow.

"It could have been tainted food. If your Sal brought things from home, maybe they were out of the fridge too long."

"I was drugged!" she insisted.

"How can you be sure?"

"Well . . . it felt that way."

"Oh? And how many times have you been drugged? From your vast experience of people slipping illegal substances into your food and drink, which time does this most resemble? Out of the, say, hundreds of times it has happened?"

She had often heard that bantering, teasing tone he used. But then the smile, spreading from an early uncertainty, became broader until it crinkled the corners of his eyes. That very same smile she remembered. Damn. Being drugged was crappy—mentally and physically. She'd gotten over Mel Rosen years ago. There had been a quarrel, hardly remembered now. Strange how small, unimportant things change one's life. . . . That last college summer. They had both worked out at the old barn that had become a short-lived strawhat theater. A time apart from the rest of their very sensible lives. Hana recalled even having fantasies of going on the stage, much to Aunt Sissy's and her father's horror. Both she and Mel had walk-on parts in the last show. He was so awkward that she had laughed at him. He had become very angry, things had been said . . . and then it was time for them to return to their respective colleges. The next summer he had traveled, then gone on to law school. Their relationship had never been the same. That wonderful summer of fantasy had been their last time together.

Regression.

That's what the drug had done to her. She was almost afraid what she might do next. She remembered one very special day when they'd been in the car together and had driven out to the lake and . . .

"I've read a lot of mysteries," Hana said coldly, turning to look out the window.

But she could still feel his smile. Like sunlight.

He reached over and patted her hand. "It's

okay," he said softly. "You've been through a lot, but I'm here now."

Hana was startled. Since his return to Conover they had kept their relationship strictly professional. Had she conveyed some of her feelings . . . ?

"I could stop the car," he went on. "There's a pulloff up here under some trees—"

"No!"

"Just to talk, Hana. Relax for a while. Like old times."

"Not today," she told him unsteadily.

And suddenly she wanted to cry. Not because she hurt and felt washed out but because she missed that young girl who had been herself. Who had been in love. Before she had taken over Shaner Industries. Before she had become forty and set in her ways.

Except, of course, that somebody truly set in their ways wouldn't be living in Grace Urich's apartment and putting herself in danger. The thought eased the dim threat of tears and brought today back into focus. Hana began to rummage in her bag.

"Lose your wallet?" Mel asked with concern.

Frantically she dumped the contents on the seat between them.

"It's not here!"

"Your wallet?"

"Not my damn wallet! The receipt!"

"What receipt?"

"We found it in the apartment—Mr. Fred did. A receipt for a blouse."

"I don't see what possible connection—"

"It was dated September something. *After* her disappearance! She was back there, Mel. She went back to that apartment for something and dropped a receipt."

"My. How convenient." He swung the car onto the road that led to deeper farmland beyond her estate. "I'm sorry, my dear, but I just cannot turn off my lawyer's mind. Sure, it sounds like a nice clue. But why would she drop something like that for you to find if she doesn't want to be traced? Unless somebody planted it to make you think . . . well, that she's still alive. Or was, long after August twelfth."

"But if that's true, why would somebody have me drugged to get back the receipt?"

"You don't know that's what happened," he said reasonably. "You were rushed to the hospital—it could simply have been lost. Which is probably what happened, because I can't see that one could logically connect an ordinary receipt with Grace Urich's disappearance. It would be insanity to drug somebody for something like that. Or have you the idea that it might be Grace herself who had it done?"

She hated when he got into his reasonable mood. She always had.

"Must every conversation with you end in a cross-examination?" she snapped.

They pulled into her parking lot. Hana wanted to jump out and run into the house, but her legs refused the directions. Mr. Fred came to greet them, followed by Sal and Elsie Hardinger.

"I was afraid you'd insist on going back to that dreadful apartment," Elsie said. "I really was."

"How did you know—?"

"I called her," Mr. Fred reported grandly. "After Mr. Rosen called me."

They trooped upstairs together, followed by the

animals of the house. Mel and Mr. Fred supported Hana, even though she kept insisting she was perfectly all right. She was tucked into bed by Sal, who was staying beyond her usual time to make milk toast and bread pudding for the invalid. Of all the foods of all the world, Hana loathed bread pudding most.

Even worse, after Mel and Sal left, Elsie Hardinger remained to read aloud from a travel book about the islands of the English Channel. Hana and the animals, who had crawled into bed with her, fell asleep at the opening of the second chapter.

Chapter Four

HANA AROSE EARLY the next morning, rather surprised to discover that, other than a painful shoulder and a dull headache, she felt very nearly alive. She did not risk going to the kitchen because she was sure Mr. Fred would be there, intent upon looking after her. Instead, she ate the dish of bread pudding Sal had left on her bedstand. It was the consistency of library paste but felt surprisingly good going down.

She splashed rubbing alcohol on her shoulder, patted each animal, then crept from the house. As she nosed down the driveway, she thought she heard Mr. Fred shouting. If he'd made a doctor's appointment for her, he was going to be disappointed. Hana had too much to do to waste time being checked over.

Mel Rosen's thinking about the stolen receipt was logical, but suppose somebody had taken it to call her attention to the boutique? Surely they must realize she would remember the name of the place once she had seen the receipt.

Before she had fallen asleep in the middle of the English Channel the night before, she had been thinking. It was really obvious who had taken it. And who had drugged her.

Her first thought had been to get over to the little shop where the blouse had been purchased. But it was rather too early for that, and besides, there was another stop she wanted to make.

The Colonial glass of the windows at The Feathered Duck was steamed by the warmth inside and the snap of the autumn cold without. The attractive aroma of brewing coffee again filled the place, but failed to arouse Hana's appetite. Jill Devon looked startled.

"I thought you'd be in the hospital," she said. "How are you?"

Hana shrugged her good shoulder. "Where's Debby?"

"Our waitress?"

"She does work this shift, doesn't she?"

"Normally, yes, but—"

"Is it her day off?"

Jill turned to a customer standing with check in hand. Hana grabbed her arm. "My lawyer picked me up at the hospital yesterday. I was drugged, you know. Now, if you don't want legal action, you really should cooperate with me. You suspect

Debby put something in my coffee, don't you? *Don't you?*"

"I don't know."

Jill took the startled customer's money, automatically rang up the bill, handed over the change with a wan smile, then turned to Hana.

"Yes, all right. She was acting strangely. But maybe she was just frightened. We did everything we could to help you. Debby, too—"

"Who carried my bag upstairs after I collapsed?"

"I'm not sure. There was so much happening—"

"But you didn't carry it."

"Two customers helped us—somebody was saying we shouldn't move you, but it seemed we really ought to get you out of the restaurant. I thought—Well, anyway, Debby has worked here for six months. We've never had any trouble with her. What's missing? Something must be, or you wouldn't—"

"Give me her name and address."

"But I just don't—"

"Your choice. My lawyer, the police, or me."

Jill Devon flushed, then scribbled an address on the back of an unused Feathered Duck check. Satisfaction warmed Hana. She had sounded almost like Mike Hammer. Tough.

Driving through a decaying neighborhood on the other side of town, Hana decided that, in addition to toughness, a detective needed a good car and a full tank of gas. How did economically deprived private eyes manage? The waitress lived in an old apartment house that looked as if it would soon sag into its vacant neighbor. A cab idled in front. As Hana pulled up across the street, a young woman with two suitcases ran out and got into the cab. In her navy peacoat and knit hat she could be . . . anybody.

Hana hesitated.

The cab pulled away. It was now or never.

Hana followed that cab.

Visions of TV car chases with screaming tires entertained her as suburbs and traffic lights slowed their progress practically to a halt. After the cab reached the bypass, however, the speed increased to a dizzying fifty-five miles per hour. Hana soon realized they were headed for Conover's small airport. One couldn't really go anywhere from there (unless you counted Pottsville, which hardly anybody did), but one could get commuter planes that connected with large planes in Philly and Pittsburgh.

If Debby and the cab driver were awake and even reasonably intelligent, she was sure they must know by now they were being followed. At first she tried to keep other cars between them, but that wasn't as easy as it looked on TV. An actual chase with Debby driving her own vehicle might be easier, although Hana wasn't at all certain now.

There were awkward moments at the airport. Hana frantically searched for a parking space while the cab swung into the terminal to deposit Debby at the door.

If it really was Debby.

The parking lot was a snakepit booby-trapped by automatic arms demanding various amounts of change for the robotic favor of opening to permit her car to get through.

By the time she had run from a parking lot at the edge of a field of winter wheat, she was feeling sick and, even worse, seeing leaves growing out of a metal lamppost that could not possibly have leaves. For a moment she wondered if, after all, she should find time to see her doctor. Her sore shoulder throbbed from a bump she had given it while feeding the maw of an automatic arm. She paused outside the automatic doors to get her breath, then, trying to look like a casual traveler, followed a man with a briefcase inside. Little of the frenetic bustle of big-city terminals was to be seen at Conover. Seated on a plastic chair, looking worried as she stared through large glass windows at empty runways, was Debby, the waitress from The Feathered Duck.

Thank God there was an empty seat beside her.

Trying to look in charge of the situation and not as if she badly needed to sit down, Hana plopped into the chair harder than she intended. Despite the jar, she noted thankfully that the wave of dizziness had passed.

Debby stared at her for a startled second, then began to rise. Hana put a restraining hand on her arm.

"Maybe if you talk to me, it won't be necessary to go to the police."

Madonna-sullen, Debby said, "Go blow it out your ass, lady."

A number of people looked at them curiously. Hana leaned closer and hissed in what she hoped was a tone dripping with malice, "I'm a rich woman. I can be very helpful to people—or very mean. Did you see that man with the briefcase who came in with me? He's a private eye, and I can have him call the police any time I raise my little finger. But maybe I won't have to do that if you come with me for a private little talk."

Hana struggled to her feet. To her surprise, Debby rose and followed. Down a corridor, near the baggage claim, Hana found a quiet corner where she could lean against the wall. The waitress stood in front of her, clutching a very full flight bag that Hana had not noticed before. She'd apparently checked through the suitcases. Without the full skirt and efficient apron she seemed younger and very vulnerable.

Hana hung on to the wall. "I know you put some sort of drug into my coffee, Debby."

"Try and prove it."

"I already have. Someone saw you." She assumed the positive attitudes and expressions she employed in her TV spots for Dutch Blue carpets. "You know you're in a lot of trouble, even if it wasn't your idea. Or was it?"

Debby blinked, said nothing.

"All I want from you is information," Hana went on. "Cooperation and information, and we'll keep it between the two of us."

Letting the carry-on slip to the floor, the waitress began to play with a strand of her hair, twisting it around her fingers. Finally she mumbled, "Okay, so I dumped some pills in your coffee. Some kids take that stuff all the time. Won't hurt you."

"I very nearly had to spend the night in the hospital."

"Yeah, well, I notice you're up and around now."

"Did you ever have your stomach pumped?"

"Shit, no."

"I did last night. It's lots of fun."

"Want me to say I'm sorry?"

"I want you to tell me why you did it."

"Because I need money! You wouldn't know about that, would you? I bet that blouse you got on cost seventy-five dollars."

Debby threw her hair back over her shoulder as if it were the cause of all her trouble.

Hana had received such challenges before and usually ignored them. So she was rich. Most people who challenged her about it would love to be in her shoes.

"Who paid you?"

"I don't know."

"Oh, really?"

"I don't! They called me—on the phone."

"When?"

"A long time ago. I don't remember exactly. I was supposed to get thirty-five dollars a week."

Hana stared at her. "To do what?"

"What'd you think? To keep an eye on Grace Urich. Like I said, I needed the money and it didn't seem like it was anything serious."

"An anonymous person paid you to spy on Grace, and you didn't think it was serious!"

"I just thought maybe she was fooling around with some woman's husband and they wanted to see if they could catch her at it," Debby told her defensively. "All I was supposed to do was keep an eye out to see who she was with. Walk past her apartment on my way home. Hang out at that stupid gift shop downstairs a little. Watch her when she was in the restaurant. That kind of stuff."

Hana felt sick again, but not from the drug. So somebody had been after Grace Urich for a long time. Was Debby the only spy? That seemed unlikely. Suppose somebody in her own office had also been watching Grace . . . ?

The waitress said miserably, "So anyway, every

Friday there was this envelope in my mailbox with the cash inside."

"How long did this go on?"

"Maybe about three, four months."

Hana wanted to howl with anger. "And you never told anyone? Knowing she might be in danger, you continued to spy on her—"

"I tell you I didn't know she was in danger! I didn't even think about that. It was only after she disappeared that I got . . . scared."

They'd been talking loudly. Hana took a deep breath.

"Did they contact you after she disappeared?"

"Uh-uh. Everything just stopped. Well, that is . . . until yesterday."

"And what happened then?"

Debby was punishing her hair again, twisting it wildly. "Another call. At work this time. Weird. About this business—giving you the pills."

"And how did you know those pills weren't poison? How did you know you wouldn't kill me? After all, you knew the woman you'd been spying on had vanished and might be dead."

Debby stuck the twisted strand of hair in her mouth and sucked on it. "I didn't want to. Really I didn't. I even said at first I wouldn't do it. But they threatened me. All I had to do was this one thing and then I'd never hear from them again. That's what they said. And they told me it wasn't dangerous—that nothing would happen to you or to me. I needed that five hundred dollars!"

"Five hundred—?"

"Yeah."

"And they told you to take a receipt out of my bag while I was out?"

"No— I was just supposed to get your bag and

look for any papers . . . pictures—anything I could find fast. It didn't seem to matter much. Just so I took something."

"That's strange. How did they deliver the drug?"

"You mean the pills? Little package. Just like the money. It was put in my locker at work. That was kind of scary."

"I'm sure it was. How did they know I'd be in the restaurant?"

"They said you'd been there before and would come again. I was to do it whenever I had the chance. So then you got there almost right away, and I thought I'd get it over with."

"Do you have this package? Or any of the envelopes?"

"They told me to burn the stuff, and that's what I did."

"You've been saying 'they.' Did more than one person call you?"

More hair chewing. Hana longed to grab the hair out of her mouth.

"I don't know."

"You said 'they'!"

"Because I don't know!"

"My God, you heard a voice—"

"Muffled. Always— Oh, you know. Like they held something over the phone. Like on TV."

"Was it a man or woman?"

Passengers were moving, going through the metal detector, which was now staffed and operating. A Voice of God from somewhere announced the arrival of a plane about to head out over the mountains to Pittsburgh.

Debby looked at the activity, then at Hana. She took the hair out of her mouth to ask, "What are you going to do?"

"Man or woman?" Hana asked again.

"I tell you I don't know!"

"You must have an idea—"

"I don't know!" It was a wail.

"Is that the plane you were planning to take?"

"Yeah."

"And after Pittsburgh?"

"I got this brother in Seattle. He's been wanting me to come and all that. He and his wife work. I can take care of the kids for them for a couple of months. Then maybe come back here if I— Oh, I don't know."

"Did these people—whoever they are—tell you to get out of town?"

Miserably the young woman shook her head. "I'm scared. I'm just scared. I'm . . . sorry."

The Voice became more persistent. Debby looked as if she was about to cry.

"Give me your brother's address," Hana told her. "Then get out of here."

Debby rummaged but found nothing to write on. Hana pulled out her own notebook. The waitress scribbled an address, then grabbed her carry-on and ran down the corridor toward the metal detector. Feeling like a lousy detective, Hana watched her go.

Chapter Five

LATER, HANA WAS headed for the boutique when her car telephone buzzed with a frantic call from Jimmy Klopp, as excited as only he could get about business emergencies. Had she forgotten she was scheduled to make a TV commercial that day?

Hana had. Completely.

Grace Urich, always on top of everything, would never have allowed it to happen. What a hole Grace had left. Big enough for Hana to fall into. She didn't like the thought.

The commercials had been one of Grace's special interests. Locally, only she and Hana knew the secret of the flying-carpet spot. And it wasn't all trick photography. Hana's favorite, and the first to be distributed nationally, was the padded cell completely covered in Dutch Blue with Hana as an inmate cured by staring at the carpet. Small rainbows had descended upon her and the carpet. That *was* trick photography.

She promised Jimmy she would call the TV station.

His voice still crackled at her. "You ought to be here. Your office staff doesn't know what it's doing without Grace. And I cannot make all these decisions myself. Why a person in your position has to fancy herself a detective when she's got a business to run . . ."

Hana assured him she would check in at her first opportunity, then hung up, wondering again how somebody with Jimmy's neuroses could be so good at his job. Perhaps she should make an appearance at the office even though she was on an official leave of absence. Anyway, there were other reasons for going.

As she swung onto the bypass she dialed the TV people. Like Jimmy, they too were frantic. Hana was always amazed how people reacted to an inconvenience like one missed appointment. Carpets were always dyed, commercials made, business conducted. And if none of the above happened for a twenty-four-hour period, the world continued to turn.

Her aunt, serenely presiding over the living and the dead of Blue Spring Hill, had taught her that.

Hana spoke soothingly to the TV people, made an appointment for the morning, then got off at the next exit and drove to her office.

Shaner Carpets, set back from the highway behind a forest of evergreens, had been described in *Business for America* magazine as having a park-like atmosphere. Even some of the famous azaleas had been replanted here. The article had glorified it as a model plant whose few emissions had been taken care of in the sixties by John Gunter Shaner.

As she drove along her private road, Hana felt a familiar thrill of pride. It always came when she had been gone for even a few days. This was something worthwhile, substantial and important. For a moment she wondered if Jimmy Klopp might not be right. Why was she playing amateur detective when she was responsible for all this?

Jimmy came rushing from the office building even before she got out of the car. Were spies everywhere? Hana shook her head, hoping paranoia was not about to set in. So a curious person happened to glance out the window and had told

Jimmy she had just pulled up. Reasonable enough.

He cried, "I'm so glad you're here! There's a major problem about the new shipment of Wyoming wool . . ."

Patiently Hana stood on the macadam parking lot listening to Jimmy's harangue about Wyoming wool. The air was sweet even if he was not. There had been a rough period in his life right after his divorce five years ago when she had altruistically gone out with him a few times, mostly to let him cry on her shoulder. But he had wanted to rebound right into her bed. He was good-looking in a strange puppy-dog kind of way (a lot like Crumb at home), but she didn't believe in mixing business with that kind of pleasure. He had been quite persistent.

She suggested a suitable substitute for Wyoming wool, then went inside. The next half hour she devoted to reassuring everybody that the company was still prospering despite her absence and reassuring herself that it really was so. She gave Jimmy an enthusiastic pat on the back, because he was doing extraordinarily well.

Finally she was free to go to her own office. It was a small suite—her large, well-appointed room, Grace Urich's smaller one, and the sunlit, glass-surrounded reception/work area, decorated, like all the rest, with living plants, well cared for and thriving. Mary Hafer, the receptionist, looked up with a warm smile. But then, that was her job.

"Welcome home, Ms. Shaner! We've missed you."

Just as her instincts for selling carpets were ninety-eight percent sound, so now her instinct told her that one of these people, her office family, had been receiving money from an unknown source to spy on Grace. Mary Hafer? Seemed unlikely. She'd been with the company since Hana's father's time, except for furloughs for a honeymoon and one pregnancy. Now nearing retirement, Mary seemed too stout and placid to be any kind of spy.

Kathy Evans and Jane Padesky ran the computers. Kathy was a possibility, Hana supposed, since she'd only been with them for six months. Of course, she'd come with good recommendations, but she was inordinately fond of clothing and jewelry. Jane was plainer, divorced, with two kids to support. She might need the money, but would she do anything to jeopardize her job?

Cindy Hefflefinger and Carl Reid ran the word processors. Carl was the grandson of an old friend of her father's. The family had money and position and Carl was there more or less as an apprentice in the business world. So was Cindy Hefflefinger, except that she had gone to a community college rather than Ivy League. Her mother, a janitor in the plant, had appealed to Hana to give her daughter a chance.

Cindy was ambitious and impatient. Of all, she seemed the most likely candidate. Hana greeted each, then went into her own space to sit wearily at her desk. God, but a detective's life was hard. The carpet world was simple compared to it, even counting Jimmy Klopp's crisis level. It was one thing to suspect that somebody had been hired to watch Grace, but another to prove it. Even if she returned after hours to go through their desks, it seemed unlikely incriminating evidence would be left here. Especially considering how careful Debby's contact had been.

Still, she had to do something.

Thoughtfully Hana rubbed her shoulder as she considered her own physical condition, then called Cindy Hefflefinger into her office.

"Sit down, please."

Warily, Cindy sat.

"How's your mother?" Hana asked.

It was established that the elder Hefflefinger was still cleaning.

"Are you happy here?"

Cindy was sitting up straight now, her eyes hard and bright. "Look, I wish you'd tell me what's wrong—instead of asking about Mom and if I'm happy. I got a job. Sure I'm happy. I like working here. And I think I'm doing well. I'm sure trying."

Hana smiled. The janitor's daughter was not about to be intimidated by the head of the company. She studied the young woman for a second, then made her decision.

"Somebody in this office was spying on Grace Urich."

Apparently whatever Cindy had been expecting, it wasn't that.

"Spying?" she repeated. "Wow. But—why pick on me?"

"I don't know," Hana admitted.

"I do," Cindy said with sudden bitterness. "I'm not in the same class as Carl baby. So why not pick on Hafer? She's not in the same class either."

Hana held her temper, glad that Cindy had not also noted that Mary Hafer was black. She wasn't sure she could have taken that.

"You seem impatient, anxious to get on."

"Well, why not?"

Why not indeed.

"Have you noticed anything . . . unusual going on around here?"

"You're asking me to spy on them for you?"

Hana sighed. "You may go back to work."

"Yes, Ms. Shaner."

She said it straight enough, but there was a hint of mockery in her eyes. The thought of questioning any more of her own people disgusted Hana. Another day. Or maybe never. Maybe she didn't have to know who was spying on Grace.

But she knew she did.

She considered going over Grace's résumé again, even though the private detectives had looked into it and their report had shown no irregularities. Information on the form had been sparse, but enough to get her the job in the first place.

A union representative arrived, eager to bypass Jimmy Klopp and deal directly with Hana. By the time she was finished with him, she knew she barely had time to get to the boutique before it closed.

Chapter Six

IT WAS A small shop, specializing in what was called "The Pennsylvania Dutch Look." Mannequins were autumn scarecrows. Blouses were draped over pumpkins and a corn shock wore designer overalls. There were few customers at this hour, although Hana knew the place had a large following. A woman raised contact-blue eyes from a notebook in which she was writing.

Sounding awkward to herself, Hana explained why she was there. About a receipt she had lost. For a blouse bought a month ago.

The woman blinked as if a soft contact had hardened. "A month? That's a long time."

"Perhaps you keep a record of sales?"

"Not cash sales."

Hana described Grace Urich as the possible purchaser.

She shook her head. "Maybe if you described the blouse."

"I don't know what it looked like."

"Wait a minute— Hey, are you talking about that young woman who disappeared? Grace . . . odd name."

"Urich. Grace Urich."

"It's funny you should come in here asking about her—"

"Why funny?"

"Well, about a month ago—isn't that when you said this blouse was purchased?—the daughter of a friend was filling in because my regular saleswoman was on vacation. We were so busy with the last of the summer sale items! I mean inexpensive. I was practically giving clothing away.

Anyway, Karen—my friend's girl—had this customer she claimed looked just like the woman who disappeared. You know, there were pictures in the paper—even some posters on the kiosks in the Square. I didn't pay much attention to Karen. I thought it was her imagination."

Hana hoped she sounded reasonably calm as she asked, "Where can I get in touch with her?"

"You can't. She's returned to school in New England."

When Hana insisted, she called her friend and got Karen's phone number at the college. Feeling encouraged, Hana returned to the CarPark and Grace's cobblestone street.

As the autumn day faded, so did her elation. She ran into the apartment, clicking locks behind her. Inside the door, she stopped.

In the heavy silence, she knew something was wrong.

Slowly she moved forward, turning on lights, looking about. The lamp—had it really been in the center of that table? The crystal sleeping cat she had given Grace last Christmas—had it been so close to the lamp? How could she be sure after Mr. Fred and Sal had been stirring about? Yet the feeling persisted that once again someone had been here in her absence.

Damn! It was too late to change the lock tonight. But first thing in the morning . . .

Trying to put it out of her mind, she went to the phone. As she reached forward, it erupted into shrill ringing. Hana screamed.

She forced herself to take a few deep breaths. People who went to pieces when a telephone rang were good candidates for therapy. Perhaps some people were not emotionally equipped to be detectives. Maybe she was one.

Scooping up the receiver, she said briskly, "Depending upon who it is, this could be a recording."

"Ms. Shaner?"

Cautiously Hana admitted her identity.

"This is Cindy Hefflefinger."

Uh-huh. "Yes, Cindy?"

"I've been thinking about what you said this afternoon," she said breathlessly, as if she'd jumped into cold water. "And I don't like to talk about people—I don't like to spy on people—yet . . . Grace Urich *did* disappear. . . ."

She waited, but Hana decided not to help her.

After a beat, Cindy continued, "Well, you know I work pretty close to Carl Reid. For a while there I thought he might have a thing for Grace. He was always finding excuses for going into her office. Kind of like he was watching her. I thought it was weird, but I'd never have said anything. You're right about me wanting to get ahead, and I think most of the time you can do that best by minding your own business."

It was about all Cindy had to say. Hana thanked her carefully, then hung up. Carl Reid? It seemed so unlikely. Could be Cindy was simply diverting suspicion from herself.

What a mess.

She groaned aloud, then tried to call Karen, the seller of the blouse. It took twenty minutes of dialing and holding before she got through to a student center on the girl's dark New England campus. During her wait, Hana closed her eyes, letting her mind wander back to college days, to those exciting autumns of colored leaves and semester beginnings.

A girl's voice brought her out of the past.

"Hello? Hello! Is anybody there?"

As Hana explained, she heard a background of talk and laughter mixed with rock music. Karen apparently was not only having trouble hearing, she had difficulty understanding. Summer was obviously light years away. Hana began all over again. It wasn't until she got to Grace Urich's name the second time that she struck a chord. Karen stopped her, telling her she'd call back from another phone in a few minutes.

Hana had no choice but to hang up when the precious connection was abruptly broken. As soon as she was off the phone, oppressive silence returned to the room. She wasn't sure this Karen would even bother to call back. And if she did, would it mean anything? Hana rose, moved to the window. No fog tonight. Very dark. If anybody watched, the watcher was hidden.

The phone rang.

This time Hana ran to answer.

Bless her. It was Karen.

"I couldn't figure out at first what you were talking about," she said. "Then that name—Grace Urich. She's the woman who vanished, right? I always think it's so scary when people drop away like that. I guess I must have read everything they wrote about it, and they had lots of pictures of her in the paper."

"There weren't a lot of pictures," Hana corrected. "Just one. It was a photograph enlarged from a group picture taken at a picnic."

"Well, it was good enough for me to recognize. Anyway, I thought I did. Except her hair was different. I said to Tracy later—she was my boss—that I was sure I'd seen the woman who vanished. But Tracy was busy and she said people often look alike and what can you tell from newspaper pictures anyhow? I guess she was right. I guess I never really saw Grace Urich at all."

"But at the time you did think it was she?"

"Sure. I told you. Hey. How'd you find out about it?"

"The receipt for the blouse was in her apartment."

"Then I did see her? After she disappeared?"

"It would seem so."

"Wow— Who'd you say you were?"

"Her employer."

Disappointment. "Oh. I thought maybe you were a detective. A woman detective, like on TV."

"Well, I'm playing detective right now. And you can help me. I want to know everything this woman said and did."

"Umm," Karen said thoughtfully. "Let's see . . . it was pretty late in the day. And not long before I had to quit to come back to school. We were busy because of a big sale Tracy was having. Do you think maybe that's why she came in? Because it was so busy and she could get lost in the crowd? I don't usually say much to customers, except about the clothes. Tracy doesn't like it. Of course, I'm not a regular—I just help out, so I can do more what I want."

She went on to describe how she had felt tired of the job and tired of the bargain hunters, so she had talked to this particular customer. The woman had been sympathetic—just like Grace. She'd taken Karen aside—to give her a chance to unstress, Karen thought. There was nothing personal in their conversation. Why should there be?

"Did she say where she was going?"

The question was routine. Hana did not expect an affirmative reply.

"Well, we were standing near the window. Maybe you noticed the shop is near that row of houses they're restoring? I said to her how I thought the sample house looked nice. It was the only one they had done at the time. And she said, yes, it did look really awesome. Only, I'm not sure she said 'awesome,' but she did say she was going over there to take a better look. They were still digging around, you know. Maybe they still are. I kind of laughed and told her not to fall in any of the holes. I really did. Maybe that's why I got so stressed when I thought about it later."

"Did she take you seriously?"

"Hey, I don't think so. Because I wasn't serious."

"When did you get the idea this woman might be Grace Urich? It wasn't right away, I gather."

"Oh, no. Not until right before she left. I looked up at her as I was giving her the change, and it was like I was looking at the picture in the paper."

After she thanked Karen for calling back and had hung up, Hana sat still, thinking. Had Grace really said she was going to see the restored house? Had Grace even been there? Could have been somebody else.

Could have been somebody deliberately trying to point the way to Grace's body.

No, no, no . . .

She wanted to believe Grace had been shopping a month after she supposedly disappeared. Because it would mean, for whatever reason, she had gone voluntarily.

A sudden restlessness was like an itch in her legs, an urge to rush down to the restoration project even though she knew it would be ridiculous at this time of night. There would be nobody to question. And if somebody had drugged her to steal the receipt, what might they not do to keep her from finding . . .

Finding nothing. There was nothing to find in those ditches. So there was no hurry.

She put on her robe, flipped on TV, and settled down to an uneasy evening. She had four calls during Prime Time. Mr. Fred phoned to inquire how she was doing and inform her that the archaeology students had unearthed an arm for which there was no body. Perhaps it had been amputated by a surgeon. . . . Hana hung up on him as he was launching into details of amputation proceedings during the Revolutionary War period.

She sat back and thought about Mr. Fred. In the confusion of the past days she'd had little opportunity for quiet thought. Or—she had to face it—maybe she didn't want to go where some thoughts would take her. Only two people had known about the receipt—Mr. Fred and Sal. They had left the apartment rather fast, as she recalled. There would have been time for either of them to make a call. Unthinkable that either of them would—Absolutely. Unthinkable.

Wasn't it?

Of course, Debby had declared she hadn't been told to get the receipt—just papers or pictures. But the fact remained it was the receipt that had been removed from her bag.

When the phone rang again, she gladly snatched it up. A Sergeant Kochen was calling to tell her that Grace's sinus medication had checked out. Nothing remotely suspicious there. He also mentioned that Hana had been drugged by what he familiarly referred to as yellowjackets, as if they were old acquaintances of his. When pressed he came up with pentobarbital sodium, which had undoubtedly been slipped into her coffee. Afterward, Mel Rosen phoned to discuss some legal matters that needed her personal attention. Since he could as easily have contacted her during business hours, Hana knew he was also making sure she was all right.

The fourth call was from Elsie.

"Want to go out to eat? I was just sitting here and I said to myself, I bet Hana hasn't even thought of dinner despite what happened last night—"

Hana declared she had stopped on the way home. She chatted with Elsie a little more, then wandered to the kitchen to eat some of the picnic lunch Sal had thoughtfully left in the refrigerator. It tasted better than the bread pudding, yet she had little appetite.

As she nibbled a cold sandwich, she realized the apartment had imprisoned her as she had never been imprisoned before. Her own fear kept her there, preventing her from escaping through the alley below.

Better to stay behind locked doors—bolted, so that even if someone had a key they could not enter. To curl up in this comfortable chair, engulfed in her quilted robe. Safe. She wondered how many other women—and men—in this city felt that way when darkness came. It was all so sad. Worse than sad, really. She felt as though she were coming out from behind her thickly rolled carpets and seeing a foreign place, outwardly the same, perhaps, but what were these fine Colonial facades now hiding?

An autumn rain began, drumming against the window. The house creaked. The enemy was all around. Maybe those under her own roof could not be trusted. Even in her chair, Hana no longer felt safe.

Chapter Seven

IT WAS, HANA thought with a smugness that after a moment's hesitation she forgave herself, convenient to be a Shaner. She felt a strong urge to hurry, but haste in itself had not only ruined relationships, it had, she was sure, obscured trails of mystery so they could never be followed.

She and Mary Hafer made deliberate, dignified phone calls. They ascertained the point at which the restoration had been a month before. Long-overdue favors were called in. She phoned Melvyn Rosen and requested that he accompany her. After all, a person in her position had to be careful digging for bodies as well as at company picnics.

Everything arranged, Hana kept her appointment at the Fur and Feather Refuge to film the commercial. This animal group had grown out of her and Elsie's campaign to spay farm cats in Conover County. Its main thrust was education and consciousness-raising for humane causes, but there was also a kennel, office, and large cat house on a bit of Shaner-owned land off the Fruitville Pike.

When she arrived, the camera crew was already there. Hana knew she had been fortunate in finding a young woman from the community theater who had a real flair for directing commercials. Her name was Nancy Reilly, but because she hated the name Nancy, she called herself Pocky. Hana had never been able to figure out why anyone would consider that an improvement.

A massive section of Shaner Morning Red carpeting was spread between the buildings of the shelter. A fence had been constructed around it, and inside roamed a motley assortment of creatures in various stages of impatience. A particularly mean-looking large gray cat swiped at Hana as she entered the enclosure. A dog that had been sniffing tentatively backed away from the cat. The carpet was already showing signs of use.

Hana told Pocky, "I want to do this fast. I've got business in town."

The unflappable Pocky eyed the animals and shrugged. "I think we'd better do it fast or that carpet will be shit."

The scenario had Hana, in jeans and Animal Rights T-shirt, telling the breathlessly waiting world about the cleanability of Shaner carpets. She had chosen Morning Red because of the golden trees rising above the buildings. As she spoke, smiling at the video camera, leaves floated down to land like small golden hands on the red.

The mean cat strolled over and decided to use her leg for a kneading post.

Pocky had the good sense to keep the camera rolling.

Hana scooped up the cat. He looked surprised but held his peace for a few minutes while she finished her exultant carpet prose. Then, as if on cue, the cat glared down at the carpet and hissed contemptuously.

"Cut!" Pocky cried. "It's a print!"

Volunteers paraded the animals back to kennels and cat house, respectively. A battery of vacuum cleaners descended on the carpet. Hana had refused to shoot the last scene first. Certainly it would have been easier, but it would also be unfair. Shaner carpets *were* the easiest in the world to clean, and she intended to prove it. Pocky's own white Persian had been chosen for the second scene. Quickly Hana changed in the rest room. Now she wore a white ball gown, with a rhinestone tiara on her white hair and a white wand in her hand. The film would be cut so that she would magically appear with the white Persian and a clean carpet.

The bored Persian sat in the middle of the carpet sniffing disdainfully. Golden leaves cooperated, continuing to fall as Hana floated about, showing off the almost clean carpet.

"Cut!" howled Pocky. "My God, Puff, did you have to pick that moment to wash your ass?"

Puff, insulted, sat up straight. It wasn't until the tape was rolling again that she returned to her interrupted ablutions. Five takes were necessary. Still, Hana decided, looking at her watch, it wasn't too bad. She located the mean gray cat again, had him taken home to Mr. Fred by a volunteer who was into dogs, not cats—and especially not that cat—got back into her jeans, and drove to town.

Looking uneasy, Mel Rosen hurried up to her. "Hana, do you know what you're doing? Have you cleared all this through the proper channels?"

"Every detail."

"But . . . what do you hope to find?"

She knew by the look on his face that he knew well enough what she expected to find. *Hope* was certainly the wrong word.

"I'm sorry," he said awkwardly.

Hana gave the order to begin.

The city, which was always peeling layers from its face to look beneath—and often surprised at what it found there—had no trouble peeling away one month of restoration. What Karen and Grace had seen that day as they looked through the shop window was pinpointed.

They moved carefully.

A foreman came over to them to explain the exact work that had been done that morning a month ago. He was really into restoration and remembered it like the face of a loved one.

"We were doing trenches along here—putting in new water lines. When these places are finished they'll be good for a couple hundred years. Really good. Those are *pipes.*"

Hana looked into the reopened trench. Yes, indeed, they were pipes. She supposed pipes were as important as carpets to some people.

Dirt piled up. Heaps of it.

The foreman finally said, "Can't be anything else down there."

Mel looked at her quizzically. "Hana, are you sure—"

"Keep going," she ordered. "Farther back. Back toward where you were the day she disappeared."

The foreman hesitated.

"I'm paying for it," she said evenly.

He shrugged. The backhoe, methodically scooping bricks and clay, continued. Tensely, Hana watched. If it was there, she wanted it found. And somehow she felt it had to be.

It was.

They discovered the body beneath water pipes laid down two days after Grace Urich disappeared. The woman had been thrown into the ditch, faceup, then covered with dirt so that the pipes would be laid above her by unknowing workers.

Hands clenched into fists, Hana stood watching as men lowered themselves into the trench to carefully uncover her. Mel tried to pull her away, but she refused to go.

Police came. Spectators. Blinking lights. Voices. Official people doing official deathly things.

Mel remained at her side, fielding unnecessary questions, answering some, telling her to reply to others. Hana forced her mind to focus on the moment, on necessary trivia. She knew she could have done it without Mel, but she was glad she didn't have to.

"Is this Grace Urich?" a detective asked.

Hana wanted to scream at him that it wasn't the Grace Urich she knew. The Grace who laughed and told funny stories couldn't be this woman with dirt for eyes.

Instead she said quietly, "Yes. At least I think— Yes. It's . . . really . . . hard to tell. Maybe it's not . . . maybe—"

"We'll want you to come down to the morgue later," he told her, then added, "We don't need you here anymore."

Hana shook her head. Watching. From a distance, but watching. A crew from the TV station arrived. They shot pictures of everything, including Hana. Mel firmly took her arm.

"Let's get out of here," he said. "You can read the police reports later."

Docile now, she went with Melvyn to a bar near the CarPark.

He didn't remember what she drank. Or maybe he did but thought she had changed. In films men always remembered, and it meant a lot to the woman.

Damn.

She ordered a Bloody Mary—with extra hot sauce. Maybe if she felt the burn of it, she wouldn't feel anything else.

He was watching her. "You can't be sure that's Grace Urich, you know."

"I found her through that receipt—the receipt somebody stole from me. . . . How could it be anybody else?"

"All I know is that in law you cannot accept the obvious. I think detective work must be something like that."

"Perhaps. The girl in the shop thought she saw Grace a month after she disappeared, but this body seems to have been buried right after she vanished. Karen—the girl—must have been mistaken."

"But if Grace didn't buy the blouse, who did? Who took the receipt to her apartment?"

"I don't know!" She sighed shakily. "It has to be her, Mel. Who else is missing?"

"My Lord," he said. "There are millions of people missing."

Chapter Eight

THE MORGUE WASN'T just a place as other places are. One could go into a store, a theater, a house, but when one went into a morgue . . . The word MORGUE, black lettering on thick, swinging double doors, seemed to fly toward her, making her want to duck. Her breathing became shallow, as though her body rejected the air, full of faintly unpleasant odors. Smooth walls of institutional green and shiny floors of terrazzo. In some ways it looked like an operating room. But death was the only anesthetist.

The white-coated woman said her name was Dr. Ralles. She seemed pleasant, content, and spoke almost affectionately of her corpses.

Elsie tightly gripped Hana's hand as Dr. Ralles pulled out a long, body-size drawer.

"We've cleaned her up to some extent. She really cleaned up well, considering. Beautiful hair. Long and healthy."

Hana swallowed hysterical laughter. How could the woman describe this hair as healthy?

She looked down. The face was composed. The eyes closed.

"Oh, dear God," Elsie whispered. "Poor Grace."

Hana continued to stare, feeling herself grow rigid. It was an odd sensation, starting along her backbone.

"Is this Grace Urich?" Dr. Ralles asked.

Elsie spoke through the tissue she held pressed against her lips and nose. "Yes. That's Grace."

"You're a friend?"

"Yes."

The doctor turned to Hana. "And you're her employer?"

Like rigor mortis the rigidity was leaving her.

"That is not Grace Urich," Hana said.

Dr. Ralles blinked.

"Hana—" Elsie began.

"It is not Grace Urich!"

"We often encounter this sort of reaction," the doctor announced cheerfully. "You must understand she cannot possibly look as she did in life. But she will by the time the funeral directors are finished with her. I am always amazed that— Well, I assure you, Grace will look just like herself at the memorial service."

Hana said doggedly, "Grace's hair was never that long."

"It was long," Elsie said.

"Not that long! And there's . . . just something about her. She looks younger—"

"Death soothes away cares. So often they look years younger."

Hana suffered a brief urge to kill the doctor.

"I still think it's Grace," Elsie declared.

"You didn't know her as well as I."

Dr. Ralles inquired gently, "Isn't there a relative

somewhere? We don't mind keeping her as long as necessary."

"There's no one," Hana said flatly. "At least there was no next of kin listed on the forms she filled out when she joined our company."

"Won't you look at her again now that you've had a few moments to collect yourself?" the doctor urged. "And bear in mind the altered state of her appearance."

Hana did look again. It was not altering or change she saw. It was a face folding in on itself. The rot of fallen leaves in February. Buzzing of flies on a dead animal left too long by the roadside.

She heard herself asking as if from a distance, "What killed her?"

"Not to worry. We've got it all in our reports."

"Damn it! What killed her?"

"A knife. Good sharp thrust . . . I'm sure she died before the shock was over."

"Was it— The knife—did they find it?"

"I think not. Now, then, *is* this Grace Urich?"

Was it, after all, Grace? How in God's name could she tell for sure? How could she look at that face another second?

"Fingerprints," Hana said too loudly, her voice bouncing off the sterile walls. "Grace's fingerprints are on file at my office."

"Fine," Dr. Ralles said heartily. "The fingers are in pretty bad shape, but we can inject them to fill them out again so that the decay . . ."

Elsie tugged at Hana's arm.

In the parking lot, Hana's spine felt anything but rigid.

"Are you all right to drive?" Elsie asked suspiciously.

Hana nodded. She wanted to drive. Anywhere away from there.

To save Elsie's nerves, which she suspected were as fragile as her own at this moment, she handled the car with extreme caution, pulling into the tree-lined suburban streets beyond the hospital. The brown smell of autumn came through the open windows. Leaves were crisp, colorful.

"You looked a little green back there," Elsie said.

"I'm all right."

"It really was Grace, you know."

"Do I? We'll see what the fingerprints say."

"Be reasonable, Hana. She looks like Grace—you know she does. And she was buried there right after Grace disappeared."

"I traced her through a young woman who saw Grace long after that."

"Who thought she saw Grace. You know how kids are today. Think about it, Hana. That restoration project was a convenient place to toss Grace's body if she was killed anywhere in center city."

As Elsie continued to be relentlessly realistic, Hana speeded up, glad when they reached the travel agency. Bill Longenecker came out to say a few words of condolence. He kept asking questions. Elsie called the dead woman "Grace."

Hana escaped as soon as she decently could.

She decided she didn't want to go home. How could she face another body covered with soil, even one dead for hundreds of years? Or just that arm. At Shaner Carpets people might be curious, but there she was boss. If she wanted to be alone, all she had to do was tell Mary Hafer to keep everybody out of her private office.

She'd get the fingerprints ready for the police. Maybe look over Grace's résumé again. Or just sit quietly behind her desk.

It was a unique experience for her not to trust the people who worked most closely with her. It had been a Shaner canon—a sacred commandment to create a team and go with it. Her father had always said a team will do better than a group of individuals all going in different directions. A good employer will create trust, and in return the employer must trust the team. She always had.

Was that really Grace?

She couldn't get the face out of her mind. Barbaric custom. Did they always do that? Bring the nearest and dearest there to identify the body? She wished Mel Rosen hadn't been in court. Elsie meant well, of course, but— Damn. It wasn't Elsie. It was death. A friend killed and thrown into a public trench, covered with dirt, waiting for pipes to be installed over her so she might not be discovered for hundreds of years. In a time when whatever small war Grace had been fighting was forever gone. Like the soldier buried beneath her lawn.

At the office she ignored Cindy's questioning eyes and asked Jane Padesky to bring her Grace's file.

Surprised at finding how grateful she was for the security and safety of her own office, Hana opened the cover slowly, as if something evil might arise from it.

Nothing did.

Her private detective's report was there. All of

this was on the computer, of course, but Hana had long insisted on keeping some old-style files. Can't teach an old dog, and all that. She considered that she had gone with the times very well—she even liked Bruce Springsteen—but there was something comforting about physically holding a file in her hands. Lately she had been slipping everything relating to Grace's disappearance into it. There was even the address in Seattle that Debby the waitress had given her.

Carefully she reread the report on Grace her detective had given her. Yes, everything had checked out. At least, the computers had. Strange new world. These people had done a job of detecting while seldom leaving their computer and the phone. And probably they had talked to tapes rather than people on the other ends of the phones. Maybe that was why so many individuals disappeared. They dropped down between the weird lights of computer screens, through the centers of tapes, and were never heard from again. And nobody noticed because the machines were in control.

No family, no next of kin.

Well, she'd known that. What she had glossed over before, near the end of the report and dismissed by the detectives as unimportant, was a record of a phone interview with a real person. When Grace was twenty, she had worked for . . . um . . . Plastic Communications, Inc. Whatever that was, it was located in the small city of Shamokin, Pennsylvania, about forty miles away. The woman interviewed had worked there forever, claimed she could recall every office employee and that no Grace Urich had ever been among them.

Hana dialed her detectives.

A secretary, respecting affluence and importance, immediately connected her with Mr. Ralph Sensenig.

She interrupted his hearty greeting. "I've been reading over your report on Grace Urich's background."

"Um," he said, and she could hear the whir of his computer as he brought said report to the surface.

"This woman in Shamokin—she swears Grace Urich never worked there."

"Uh-huh."

"Is it possible she's telling the truth? Your detective dismissed the possibility."

"Rightly so, Ms. Shaner. Senile. Obviously senile. And under the influence."

"Drugs?"

Shocked. "At her age? No way. Alcohol. Totally unreliable witness. Believe me. Totally unreliable."

"But you didn't interview her in person?"

"No need. The interview was conducted by phone, and we then proceeded with a computer check of her background. Suspicions confirmed. Too old to be considered reliable. Habitué of local taverns."

He was so sure of himself, Hana gave up. Then, as an afterthought and because she was looking at it, she gave him the name of Debby's brother in Seattle. Again she heard the click of his computer. She wondered if the long minds of the computers reached Seattle. Yes, they did. No, there was no one of that name living at that address. Nor anywhere else in Seattle.

She'd been had.

That little twit of a poisoner had played her for a fool. The detective asked if she wanted him to turn his computers on this brother. Hana refused the offer and hung up. There probably was no brother, and Debby, whoever she was, had long gone somewhere.

But the woman in Shamokin was still there. Still working, so she couldn't be as senile as the computer suggested. Anyway, what did they know about the human mind? Hana wrote down the name and phone number on a desk pad.

The intercom buzzed. Carl Reid wanted to see her.

Instinctively, Hana slipped Grace's file into a drawer. Carl entered, his manner breezy, youthful, and attractive. Hana had often predicted he would go far even without the push from his family.

He came right up to her desk, friendly as always. Then casually he glanced down at the name on the pad, making her wish she had swept that, too, into the drawer.

Jimmy Klopp had given Carl order forms from the West Coast. Carl did not understand the long list of numbers accompanying the forms. Companies were always trying new systems these days. It took her only a few minutes to straighten out his confusion. He thanked her cheerfully, made a comment about beautiful weather, said fall was his favorite time of the year, and left.

Surely a bright boy like Carl should have been able to figure out those numbers. She knew he sometimes called attention to himself with legitimate questions to which he might or might not have the answers, but before she had found that rather endearing. Now she wondered if ambition was the only reason for these special visits to her inner office. Was Cindy Hefflefinger right? More disconcerting, could he have been the shadowy form that followed her that first night?

Suppose the body in the morgue really was Grace. Suppose the detectives were right and nothing out of her past had killed her, nothing even in her present. Except a psychotic individual working for Shaner Carpets who had eliminated Grace for his own crazy reasons and now meant to eliminate Hana herself. It really made more sense than any other way she looked at what had happened. People were flipping out all the time these days. The eighties might be called the Decade of the Flip-Out. Worse than the sixties, she thought. Back then, there had been a manic kind of hope.

But maybe she herself was flipping out and Carl was simply the pleasant, ambitious son of a family she had known all her life. To even talk about these unfounded suspicions could ruin the young man's career.

For the next three hours she tried to concentrate on carpets. With no success.

Pocky Reilly called, excited. She had the videotape of the new commercial, and it was the best yet. The gray cat was so very special. That shot of him hissing at the carpet was priceless. Certainly good enough for national distribution. When would Hana like to see it?

Glad for an excuse to escape, Hana went to the studio. For moments she forgot Grace Urich entirely as she watched the bright colors of the commercial with wonderful close-ups of the mean cat.

"Another Morris in the making," Pocky boasted.

Later, while heading for Blue Spring Hill to give the new cat the good news about the commercial and his possible future stardom, Hana thought again of Carl Reid. She would get him. Trap him. And certainly, if he had done this horrible thing to Grace, he deserved it. But Hana hated traps, either for animals or humans.

Coming up her drive, she saw that although the trench across the lawn was bigger, surprisingly nobody was working in it. In fact, everything looked peaceful, the way she expected Home to be. Except that it was now no longer the refuge it had always been. Maybe the best thing to do would be to talk to Mr. Fred and Sal. Get it out into the open. They must have told somebody she was carrying that receipt.

She parked and entered her house.

Chaos.

Sal had lost her cool, which was unusual because she apparently felt cool to be part of her religion. Frantically using a hand-held vacuum, she scurried about the feet of some dozen archaeology students, who were muddily celebrating with cola and artifacts in hand. Ghost and Crumb barked about, running in excited circles. Mr. Fred, carrying what looked like somebody's arm bones, dashed through followed by a mean-looking gray cat.

Hana backed out the door and closed it firmly.

She returned to her car, zipped down the drive, then headed out of town. Logically, the detectives' report about the woman who claimed Grace had never worked at Shamokin Plastics wasn't even important anymore. Grace was dead.

She had seen the body.

Worse, she had smelled the body. Why was this thing inside her head refusing to believe the obvious? That wasn't how you sold carpets. Nor was it how you solved mysteries.

So what possible reason did she have for driving to Shamokin to interview this person?

None.

Hana headed for Shamokin.

Chapter Nine

SHAMOKIN, PENNSYLVANIA, CURLED beside its creek, still colored by acid from the coal mines, with anachronistic charm in late-afternoon sunlight. An anthracite Brigadoon, no one had cared enough either to destroy or to restore, leaving workers' homes and owners' mansions to survive with haphazard grace. On all sides mountains, now bright red and yellow, appeared to close off access to anywhere beyond. Higher than these, a bald gray lifeless pile dominated one end of town. This was the highest mountain of culm, or coal debris, in the country, if not the world. In the bars, Shamokians took a perverse pride in it.

The narrow road by which Hana had come into town had been designated as the permanent detour around Centralia, a town collapsing into its underground mine fires. When she stopped for gas, she had been told of a shortcut. After becoming lost in a maze of mountain roads, she reached

Shamokin just in time to locate the plastics company before closing time. With the passing of the Age of Coal, a small number of other industries had moved in to take advantage of area resources. Plastics Communications was one.

Sophie Sidowsky turned out to be a woman of sixty who moved like thirty and obviously drank agelessly.

With the promise of "I'd like to talk to you over a couple . . ." Hana lured Sophie to a tavern near the railroad tracks that took up half of the main street. Sophie flopped into a chair at a table beside a curtained window and ordered scotch. A surprisingly good brand, Hana noted, as she paid for their drinks. Hanging out at the bar were blue-collar workers and out-of-workers, in a uniform of jeans, flannel shirts, and heavy shoes. They knew Sophie; she knew them.

"Nice place," she said, waving her drink around. "No rough stuff. A lady doesn't have to be afraid to come in here."

Skeptically, Hana looked at the work crew and wondered how a gentleman would fare.

"Nice town, Shamokin," Sophie continued. "Beats Hazelton all hollow. Where'd you say you were from?"

"Conover."

"That's a nice town, too. If you like flat. I'll take mountains."

She drank to the mountains. Hana poured her own shot into a glass of soda water.

"That spoils the taste," Sophie said disapprovingly. "Now, then. What's all this about a girl who disappeared?"

Hana had decided to be entirely truthful. Polluted waters and stark banks of gray debris belonged to people who knew truth could be ugly.

The woman listened quietly while she had her second Scotch. Yes, she remembered the call from Hana's private detectives.

"Computers," she snorted. "They said I was wrong because the dumb computers said so. What the hell are computers anyhow? Robots. No better than the jackasses that program them. Or maybe—ha!—somebody put in something that shouldn't be there. Huh? Today people come and go, not like the old days where you latched on to a job and stuck with it. So after a couple of years who cares or even knows who did what?"

"You were here eight years ago?"

"You bet. Same room, same desk. And she'd have been right there in the room with me. Right across in the other corner. If she'd been there at all. But she wasn't. Eight years, you said. . . . Uh-huh. That was Sarah Rogers and Bett Fanelli working with me then."

Hana brought out her picture of Grace. "Have you ever seen this woman or anyone who looked like her?"

Sophie motioned to the waitress and ordered a double this time while she seriously studied the photograph.

Finally she shook her head. "She's never been around here that I know of. And I've been all over the place. Well, I mean all over Shamokin."

Hana believed her.

"Aren't you having another?"

Hana shook her head. "I have to drive back over these mountains."

"Yeah, it's best to be careful. Listen, don't take shortcuts no matter what anybody says. Especially on dirt roads. A whole car full of kids went right through when they were joyriding on one of those old roads last year."

"Right through?"

"Road collapsed over an old mine shaft. Swallowed the car and the kids. Hundreds of feet down into a flooded mine."

Feeling a little sick, Hana lifted the edge of the curtain to look at the city, slowly moving toward its suppertime.

Sipping her drink, Sophie said musingly, "Funny different ways people disappear, isn't it? Those kids disappeared into a hole in the earth. This woman . . ."

"Grace Urich."

"She disappeared on a city street. You say her name was Grace Urich? I say there was no such person as Grace Urich."

"I knew her!"

"You knew somebody all right, lady. But her name wasn't Grace Urich. I'd lay odds on that. Somebody invented her and fed her into computers. Bet they could invent politicians that way, too. Bet I could do it myself. Imagine electing a president that doesn't even exist."

She laughed about that, then loudly repeated her idea to friends at the bar who laughed with her.

Their loudness hurt Hana's ears. It had been a long, exhausting day, starting with a visit to the morgue. Her shoulder, now in vivid autumn shades of bruised flesh, gave her a twinge. Still looking through the window, she was glad to see Carl Reid coming along the street. Perhaps she would ask him to drive her home.

Carl Reid?

Drowsiness vanished. There was only one reason for him to be here—he had seen Sophie's name and number on her desk. So obviously he had been snooping. Spying. He had guessed where she was going. Or—

Had she put Sophie Sidowsky in danger? Somebody at the plastics company must have told him where Sophie was. The image of the body in the morgue flashed through her mind, followed by an abrupt memory of Carl she had tried to forget. One day she'd overheard part of a story he'd been telling to a couple of salesmen. It had been a sadistic, sexual story, supposed to be funny but to Hana's mind only brutal. His laughter at the end of it had been cruel.

Hana let the curtain fall.

"Sophie, will you do something for me?"

"Huh?"

Hastily Hana explained about Carl Reid.

"I'm sure he's coming to find out if you talked to me. Do you mind lying a little?"

The woman grinned, lifted her glass in a toast.

"Good," Hana went on. "Tell him I know he's spying in my office and I also know who's paying him to do it. Tell him I'm on my way to see that person now. Make sure to say *you* had no idea what I was talking about. If you want, tell him what you told me about Grace. I think this will distract him from you. But just in case, don't leave here alone. You seem to have a lot of friends around to help you."

"Sure do," Sophie said largely. "Don't worry about a thing. Hope you find the missing girl."

"Is there another way out of here?"

"Through the kitchen. Just say you know Sophie if somebody asks."

Hana dropped a twenty-dollar bill on the table, then quickly hurried toward the rear of the large room. As she ducked through a swinging door, she heard Sophie ordering another drink.

A stout woman busily chopping onions at a wooden table looked up in surprise.

Hana smiled and used Sophie's magic name, which brought a grin and a nod. The alley beyond the kitchen stretched gloomily between old factories toward a narrow side street. Hana ran, turned the corner, and headed for the seedy downtown hotel where she had parked her car.

She knew Carl's red sports car from his joy at its purchase six months before. Risking losing him, she drove around nearby streets looking for it. When she was about to give up, she spotted one on a public lot opposite some shops. Even though she realized there were probably other new red sports cars in Shamokin, she pulled in and parked. After all, that blue-and-orange afghan on the back-window ledge could only have been crocheted by Carl's mother.

As she sat waiting, she hoped the short autumn day would not end too soon. It would be impossible to follow anything on these mountain roads in the dark. Or would it? In daylight, surely he would finally notice her sedate Chrysler sedan, but at night if she could just learn to recognize his taillights . . . Maybe instead she should have confronted him in the bar.

Debby the waitress had been so eager for money she had been willing to work for an anonymous, mysterious whoever. But Hana couldn't see the Carl Reid she knew doing anything so wild. He was too ambitious, too conservative. If he, too, had been doing spy work—and the fact that he had come to Shamokin proved that in her mind—then he knew well enough who and what he was working for. But she couldn't imagine *who,* and even *why* eluded her.

The man himself, seemingly intense and preoccupied, came hurrying into the parking lot and got into the car without looking around. Hana pulled out of the lot seconds after him. Her confidence increased as they traveled one way streets, stopping at traffic signals, always heading in the direction of the mountain road that led back to Conover. As far as she could tell, he was unaware he was being followed.

As soon as she realized where he was going, she dropped back. This seemed much easier than following Debby's cab. Perhaps, she thought smugly, she was becoming accustomed to routine detective work.

When they reached the mountain road, Carl picked up speed. Despite relatively light traffic, Hana confidently paced him, enjoying the sensation of skill as she swung around curves, climbing higher.

They passed a plunging, narrow waterfall after which the road leveled off. Carl slowed to fifty. Hana braked. They were now the only cars on the road.

Abruptly Carl accelerated, tearing around a curve with tires screeching. Hana followed. She saw the flash of his brake light as he turned onto a dirt road that circled the mountain.

He had spotted her. So much for Super-Detective.

Angry with herself, she swung after him. It wasn't until she was careening along through low-growing trees that she realized this had to be an old mining road. Exactly the kind Sophie Sidowsky had warned her about. Hana slowed to twenty, cautiously looking for a place to turn. If Carl Reid wanted to fall into the center of the earth, she had no wish to join him. Abruptly the road dipped toward a plateau. Through the trees, at this height nearly bare of leaves, she saw gray barren acres of culm from an abandoned mine. There, she hoped, she would find an area wide enough for a turn.

The road had become deeply rutted. If Carl still drove at the same speed, his precious sports car would be a wreck.

She reached the culm field to find heaps of the stuff oozing over the road, obscuring it. Her hands sweating on the wheel, she peered through the dusty windshield. Headlights didn't help. The road was disappearing under her wheels. Carefully she crawled the car around a small mountain of culm and nearly skidded into Carl's automobile. Hana braked and turned off her motor. She sat still for a moment, listening to the silence around her. She wished she had a weapon. God, she must be miles from nowhere. Somehow she would have to turn around and get back to macadam. The nose of the red sports car was deep in clinging culm. Carl must have spun out of control.

Wondering what to do, Hana opened her door and got out. She would have to find a stick—something—and test the firmness of this crap at the side of the road. Maybe Carl could help. They would forget other matters until they were back in civilization.

His car was empty, the ignition turned off.

The sun had dropped below the mountain. Twilight made the scene even more desolate. Cautiously she moved around the sports car and down the road to where weathered boards created a kind of sluice box over which a small falls poured, the water as gray-black as the surrounding debris. From the sluice box outward as far as she could see were rolling hills of culm, that drab material like no other on earth. No plants grew. It was an alien landscape, the ultimate ruination of earth.

Hana shivered, thinking of what it would be like to be trapped here in the dark. She started back toward her car.

He screamed.

The cry was so full of terror that for a moment she thought of the demons rumored to dwell beneath this desolation, deep in the mines. It had come from someplace in that abandoned scene of hell in front of her.

Carl.

Of course it had to be Carl. Surely nobody else was in this mess with them. Nor could she believe he had planned to meet anybody here. But she could believe that if he had gone into that culm to get away from her, he had run into trouble. She moved a few feet off the road, keeping near the thick running water, where the ground—if one could call it that—looked more solid.

"Carl—?"

"Help me!"

Old boards used for whatever purpose had fallen away near the sluice. She picked up two of them, then again moved forward, wondering what in the name of heaven she was doing here. The culm rolled under her feet like gritty, clinging sand. It poured into her shoes, and at places she sank to her ankles. Walking was exhausting. Her shoulder ached.

"Keep calling, Carl!"

He did. She slogged onto what almost seemed like a path, but even here it was like wading in the sands of hell. She moved slowly, expecting the awful stuff to collapse under her at any moment. Carl's frantic voice was close now. She crept around a mound of the filth and saw him. He had left the path—perhaps to hide. Culm had shifted beneath him, and he was buried in it to his waist.

Hana stopped, staring at him.

In that moment she would have given anything to be back in Conover in Grace Urich's apartment. Even if one was scared to death there, it was a place with solid floors.

This was . . .

"God, help me!" he cried.

He struggled desperately, sinking another inch, the fine grains sliding closer about him.

"Don't do that! Keep still."

The two boards she had brought reached only a short way. She dropped them, then turned.

"Don't leave me!" he screamed.

"Shut up!"

As she returned to the remains of the workings around the sluice, she wondered if she should go for help. Sophie would know what to do, but Shamokin was a long way on the other side of the mountain. Carl was panicking. And even if he was as calm as Mel Rosen addressing a jury, whatever hole he had slipped into might suck him farther down at any time.

And she wasn't even sure she could turn her own car.

She made five trips before she had enough

boards to form a reasonably solid path to Carl. The last ones she had to rip off the sluice while water slopped over her shoes and her shoulder nagged with pain. She placed the boards carefully, crawling on hands and knees. Her own clothing was filthy and torn. Finally she decided it was the best she could do.

"Now, Carl. Put your elbows on the boards and pull yourself slowly out."

During her last trip he had been quiet, almost somnolent. She suspected he might even be making his peace with God, whatever God meant to Carl Reid. He said nothing as he moved his arms until his elbows were on the last board. It tilted toward him. He screamed again.

Hana slowly inched forward. It seemed to grow darker very abruptly. Or maybe, she considered, it was just that she was . . . slightly terrified. She lay along the board, panting, holding it down with her weight.

He strained. "I can't—"

"You've got to!"

He strained again, reaching toward her. Gritting her teeth, ignoring her own hurt, she took his hands, pulling. The boards settled more deeply into the culm. She had a shocking vision of sliding headfirst into a deep hole. She and Carl tumbling into forever together . . .

Then she realized he was moving forward, onto the boards, out of the muck. She slithered backward to give him room.

It was probably, she decided later, only five minutes until they reached the path where he collapsed on all fours. He was filthy, with black streaks across his face through which his tears had washed pale tracks. Hana supposed she didn't look much better.

He began to whimper like a hurt animal. Hana slapped him hard across the face.

She was sorry the moment after, but tension and frustration suddenly cramped her abdomen. She felt she had to go to the bathroom more desperately than at any time in her life.

"Stay here if you want," she snapped. "I'm going back to my car."

She moved fast then, but somehow he came stumbling after her. All defiance and charm were gone from him now. She hated to look at him. If he staggered off the path she was damned if she would save his butt again.

He moaned when they reached the road and saw his precious automobile. Hana opened the passenger side of her car. He looked wildly uncertain for a moment, then came forward and tumbled into the Chrysler. Hana stepped to the rear of the car, where she could have some privacy.

Darkness was oozing across the barren landscape, as if it came up out of black holes that led to blacker mine shafts. The western sky looked greenish, as it does in the mountains during the last of the daylight.

"Hold on," she breathed to it. "Just stay light a little while longer."

She hurried into the car, nearly died with relief when it started right away, then slowly, doggedly, maneuvered back and forth, an inch at a time.

But finally it was around, the lights were on, and they were crawling upward on the pitted road. She didn't look at Carl again until they were back on macadam and once more headed toward Conover. His eyes were staring straight ahead, unblinking even when other cars came toward them, headlights glaring.

"You knew I was following you?"

He nodded dumbly.

"That's why you turned onto that awful road?"

Another nod.

"And you skidded because you were going too fast. But why did you get out of the car and run away into that . . . glop?"

He took a deep breath like a sigh, his voice cracking when he answered her. "I was going to hide. Thought you'd go away."

"All right. Now tell me where we're going."

"Huh?"

"The name and address of the person who hired you to spy on Grace Urich."

"But you know. That old woman back there at the bar . . . she said you knew—"

"We lied, Carl. But you're going to tell me, aren't you? You're going to give me the name of the person who persuaded you to violate the trust I put in you. You tell me. Then maybe—just maybe—I won't blackball you in every industry in Conover. And you know that's not an idle threat. I can do it."

He mumbled a woman's name and address, then curled sideways on the seat in a half-fetal position, as if he had retreated to a simpler time in his life.

Hana drove the dark miles in silence.

It was an impersonal apartment complex in one of the better suburbs of Conover. Mock-Colonial, deeply carpeted halls, landscaped grounds. Carl hung limply beside Hana in the small vestibule. There was no name in the slot beside the number of the apartment he had given. There was no answer to her ring.

He held out keys.

Hana used one of them to open the vestibule door. He padded silently after her down the hall, as if sleepwalking. There was a hollow sound when she knocked on the apartment door. As she fitted another key into the lock, she knew what she would find.

An empty room.

That much was obvious even before she turned on the light. Blinking, Carl moved to the center of what must have been the living room, then stood still, mouth open, looking about. Hana quickly closed the door behind them and bolted it.

Avoiding Carl, she closed the drapes. It wasn't the coal dirt smeared all over him—after all, she was in the same condition. Nor was it the fact that he had obviously wet his pants sometime during the evening, although she dreaded to see the front seat of her car in daylight. It was the way he had crumbled. Without courage.

She went through the rooms, turning on lights. Nothing had been left except marks on the carpet where furniture had stood. Everything was clean, even the bathroom. Nowhere to hide anything.

When she returned from her search, he was exactly as she had left him.

She forced herself to look at him as she said quietly, "The woman has gone. Tell me, was she reluctant to give you a key to this apartment?"

"I loved her. . . ."

"Did she make any trouble about giving you a key?"

He shook his head. "No, no. She insisted. It was better, she said— Hey, she can't be gone!"

"Carl. I'm sure this wasn't even her real home."

"What do you mean? What're you talking about? She lived here! I ought to know."

Hana almost felt sorry for him. This man was no murderer. This man was a fool.

"You were coming to warn her I knew about her?" she asked gently. She waited for his nod, then went on, "Where'd you meet her?"

"Singles bar."

Poor little rich boy, Hana thought. It must have been easy to pick him up, if you were good. And this woman, whoever she was, had been good. She'd have covered her tracks well, so it was pointless to try to find her. She had existed only for this time and in this place. Like the actors the morning Grace had gone . . .

"What did she want you to find out about Grace Urich?"

"Anything . . . everything—"

"Like what? Be specific."

He shook himself as if trying to awaken from a dream. "Hey, it was no big deal. She just said . . ."

"What, Carl?"

"Well, she wanted to know how Grace got along with people. What she talked about at lunch. Just stuff like that. I thought—you know—maybe Gracie was looking for another job."

"But she's been gone for two months. Why were you still snooping?"

"I wasn't—"

"Spying, if you'd rather."

"Oh, shit."

"There's a body in the morgue, Carl. Is it Grace Urich?"

"I don't know. . . ."

"Okay, this woman was interested in Grace. What was she interested in after Grace disappeared?"

His eyes were darting around, as if trying to find a way out of the room. "I was just . . . supposed to . . . keep an eye out—to see if she got in touch with you."

Hana drew a deep breath. Somebody besides herself believed Grace was alive after she vanished.

"When did you see this woman last?"

"Oh, I don't— Let's see . . . two days ago. She said she was going to be busy for a couple of days and I wasn't to come around."

"Busy with what?"

"She didn't say."

"What did you think?"

"I thought she might be married or something. Boyfriend."

"Did she ever mention a boyfriend?"

"No."

"She must have told you something about herself. Even if they were lies, she must have said something."

"Well, she didn't. So what? I knew everything I had to know!" he cried. "She wasn't like any other woman I ever knew. She was . . . wild. Wonderful. I mean, you talk about sex. She was . . ."

"What, Carl?"

He sat on the floor.

Hana sighed. "I don't suppose you have a picture of her."

He shook his head, then began to cry, sobs shaking his dirty shoulders. Hana dropped his keys on the floor beside him.

"Carl," she said, "you're fired."

Chapter Ten

HANA, ANNOYED NOT only with Carl Reid but with herself, spent the next two days being the efficient executive she was. She gave Cindy Hefflefinger a temporary promotion to executive assistant and arranged that another young man be hired to replace Carl. She began the first exploratory steps toward the production of women's clothing in Dutch Blue. She even found time for a checkup with her family doctor.

While a burglar alarm and a new lock were installed in Grace's apartment and plumbers worked overtime to put in a new shower, Hana stayed at Blue Spring Hill. After some deliberation she instructed her private detectives to investigate Carl Reid's woman. It took them only hours to come up with the answer she suspected. Whoever the woman was, she, too, had dropped out of sight. Hana also had them check out the postcard found in Grace's apartment. Again the answer was expected. It was a tourist card dispensed by the thousands each year. Nobody in the restaurant recalled or was interested in Grace Urich.

Feeling herself again in command, Hana decided she was ready to tackle Mr. Fred. She had worn her best gray suit to the office that day. A suit so perfectly tailored it looked as if it had cost a fortune, and very nearly had. The skirt was long and just full enough. Pale-gray stockings, gray shoes, and a severe high-necked black blouse shot with red threads completed the arresting outfit. It would be an advantage.

It successfully intimidated even the TV teams crowding about the digs on her lawn when she reached home. The news of the Revolutionary War bones had apparently been announced through the head of the university department that had sent the diggers. Bones and fragments of other matter had been spread on plastic and were being immortalized on evanescent tapes. The students were all there, along with older archaeologists, sagaciously peering into the trenches. Mr. Fred beamed over it all with Tolkienesque speeches that sounded as if he were speaking of Middle-earth.

Since there was no way to prevent the inevitable interview, Hana consented to it, graciously. Graciously, too, she thanked (on videotape) Mr. Fred for his interest. She even managed to be gracious to the students, who wagged about her like Ghost and Crumb. Those two canine beings joined the party before the interview was over, since they shared a love of digging with the eager students.

The interviewer, a fuzzy young man with an anchorman's professional smile, stared into the cam facing them and asked, "Would you care to also comment on the latest development in the Grace Urich case, Ms. Shaner?"

Anger, which had been nibbling at Hana since the mess with Carl Reid, popped to the surface. No one had called her office. No one had informed her there were late developments.

And no one was going to throw Hannah Elizabeth Clara Schoener off-balance in front of the media.

"I'm so very sorry," she said with sad graciousness. "My office will give you a statement on that matter tomorrow."

Still gracious, she placed a hand briefly on the

interviewer's arm as if they shared a special secret, smiled just a little, and turned away. The anchor was left to conclude the business at hand, facing his cam alone. Through smiling teeth, Hana gritted at Mr. Fred. "I want to see you."

"Of course, of course," he agreed, but first there were introductions to celebrity archaeologists on hand. It was another twenty minutes before Hana could graciously retreat into her home. Ghost and Crumb remained to represent the family.

Inside, however, everything was blessedly quiet. Penelope Baskin and Kitty Fisher cast a purr at her as she went by the wide windowsill on which they were perched to view the human commotion on their lawn.

"Sal!"

The dignified ticking of the grandfather's clock in the hall was Hana's only answer. She went to the back of the house and down two stone steps into the old kitchen, which had been a separate building at one time but had been joined to the house sometime during the years right before the Civil War.

Sal was seated at the scarred pine table peeling potatoes.

In the center of the table sat the large gray cat, occasionally extending a paw toward a dangling peeling.

"You know cats are not allowed on the table," Hana said.

"Tell *him* that," Sal grunted, not looking up from her work.

"Bad boy! You are not to get on the table," Hana announced imperiously, lifting him down.

He hissed and leaped back up. Sal grinned.

Hana tried twice more.

"Well, we'll have to work on it," she finally said with dignity. "You must help. And we'll have to name him. Something nice."

"Nice?"

Hana saw what Sal meant. The cat stretched and scratched himself.

"A bath," Hana ordered.

Sal groaned.

Quickly Hana changed the subject. "Sal . . . the receipt we found in Grace Urich's apartment. Did you mention that to anybody?"

"It had nothing to do with me. Why should I talk about it?"

"Somebody did."

"Well, now, it wasn't me," Sal said uneasily.

Hana believed her. The exuberant Mr. Fred seemed a more likely candidate. When she returned to the sitting room, he was waiting impatiently.

"You said you wanted to see me," he reminded her accusingly. "We have guests outside, and I must get back to them."

"You have guests."

Hana sat on the still-original tapestry of an 1824 love seat. Mr. Fred glared. Penelope Baskin and Kitty Fisher slipped from the windowsill and slunk toward the kitchen.

"Who did you talk to about the receipt we found in Grace Urich's apartment?" Hana asked.

"Why, no one—"

"Mr. Fred! Somebody knew I had it. It could only have been you or Sal who talked about it."

"Perhaps," he said with dignity, "somebody figured it out—knew we were searching. If it was planted, they'd assume we'd find it."

"And you didn't mention it? Not to anybody?"

There was just a second of hesitation.

Hana pounced. "Tell me who you talked to."

"Well, Sal and I discussed it between ourselves."

"Where?"

"On the way home that day. And . . . after we got here I may have mentioned it in passing to one or two of the students. I was justifiably proud of the discovery. I think I should be commended rather than questioned."

She stared at him. He stared back.

Finally he said irritably, "All right, I shouldn't have said anything. But this whole affair is fantastic. Who could have dreamed you'd be hurt because of that old receipt?"

"Grace Urich was hurt."

"But you are a Shaner!"

Although the argument was irrefutable, Hana doggedly persisted. "You must have broken all speed records getting back here to spread the news of your brilliant find."

"What do you mean?"

"It didn't take me long to get to The Feathered Duck. Which means somebody worked very fast."

"I see. Well, yes . . . I was anxious to return to our dig. Perhaps I did exceed the speed limit."

"And did any of your students exceed the limit getting to a phone after you told them?"

"Of course not! What are you suggesting?"

"I'm suggesting that one of your industrious diggers arranged to have me drugged that morning. Who was here? Do you have a list of their names?"

He cleared his throat. "Yes— Well, no. The regulars, yes. But, you see . . . it was such a fascinating dig, and being here at Blue Spring Hill made it even more special . . . different young people were showing up all the time. Regrettably I didn't check them all—they just seemed . . . like college kids. Really inoffensive. Harmless."

"What you're saying is that there's no way to check who was here that morning?"

"I'm afraid that's true. I'm sorry. I was interested in our work. I never thought . . ."

He looked so uncomfortable, Hana sighed and dropped the subject. As he turned to go she asked, "What's the latest development in the case? The interviewer said there was one."

"The fingerprints from your office files—they did manage to get prints from the body. . . ."

"They matched?"

"They matched."

Hana sat very still. Mr. Fred waited another moment, then softly left the room. Somewhere at the back of the house were sounds of cats fighting and Sal hollering. The clock in the hall chimed sadly, as if it had spent many years recording news of deaths.

So.

Grace Urich really was dead. The body had been identified, and the lonely hope Hana had held had been futile. Now that the police had her murdered body they would be more interested in Grace. They would probe and investigate with official authority. Hana could return to her home, her office, take up her life where it had been before this terrible tragedy.

She felt weary, unworthy of the gray suit.

Slowly she went upstairs to her room, where she changed into slacks and baggy sweater. At least she had found the body. At least Grace could be buried. She wasn't being held prisoner somewhere, God knows what being done to her. At least Hana knew.

She'd have to find out when the body would be released. Arrange a funeral.

But later. Now she wanted to be alone. She wanted to return to Grace's apartment. She had to go back there. She scribbled a note for Sal, which she dropped on the hall table on her way out. Mr. Fred and company were still busy, although the TV van had gone. Hana drove away fast.

Later, having experienced the new shower and bolted the door, Hana picked up the picture of the company picnic. Grace's young smiling face stared out, and finally Hana wept.

The phone rang several times during the evening, but she did not answer. After her tears were spent she sat for a long time thinking about what she was going to do now that Grace was definitely dead. Her first reaction, that it was over for her, became less certain. She had never subscribed to the philosophy of an eye for an eye. If Grace were standing here in front of her, right here in the apartment, would she want her killer found? Would it mean anything to her? *Did* it mean anything?

If Grace Urich could get through and speak, what would she say?

Hana tried to see through Grace's eyes. Restlessly she rose and moved about the apartment. Suddenly she was seeing the place in a new light. She thought back to that day when she herself had brought Grace here for the first time. Grace had lived in an apartment with which she was clearly dissatisfied. Hana had told her about this one, which had just become available, and after some questions, Grace had expressed definite interest.

The questions . . . Had they all been about the security of the place? Hana thought so. And Grace had looked out the windows, yes. Had inspected the bedroom windows, barred where the tree outside might provide a means of getting into the apartment.

Hana now stared at these bars, then opened the window and touched them. In her new awareness, for the first time she realized the bars were quite new, close-set, cemented into the wall. Some old bricks had obviously been removed for this purpose. Thoughtfully, she closed the window again. When the house had been restored the old window bars had been deemed good enough. But she recalled they had been thinner, more ornate. At some time Grace had, without permission and at her own expense, installed these new ones.

All the other windows were high off the courtyard, making the apartment a small, safe fortress. And the old bolts and locks on the door had been very sturdy. Only the thought that other keys might be around had prompted Hana to change them. So Grace had sat up here reasonably safe. Reasonably protected. And if she had a weapon—a gun perhaps—it might explain why they had to kidnap her in public.

Maybe that was what Hana had sensed the first night in the apartment. Grace's fear. A fear so terrible it had created nightmares—like the one of the caskets she had told about at the company picnic. All the time Hana had known her, Grace had lived alone trying to protect herself against . . . What? Who?

Hana threw herself across the bed.

"I'm going to get them, Grace," she whispered. The intensity of her resolve shocked her. She wept again for her dead friend, then fell asleep and didn't waken until morning, when all the noises of the night were gone.

Chapter Eleven

THE CORONER'S INQUEST was a blur of TV cams, confusion, and questions through which Mel Rosen guided her. The verdict was hardly surprising: murder by person or persons unknown. Afterward she and Mel argued about the necessity of holding inquests. She felt they were a waste of time. They had certainly wasted her time when she wanted to get on with the business of finding Grace's killer/killers. Mel had declared himself astonished at her legal ignorance.

It wasn't until the day after the inquest that Hana managed to get an interview with Sergeant Kochen of the Conover police.

The police station was like most police stations of small, relatively law-abiding cities. It occupied part of the basement and a great deal of the first and second floors of an old Victorian city hall, comfortably surrounded by maple trees, their leaves now yellow-brown.

Sergeant Kochen greeted her as if he dreaded the interview. Looking more like a scholar than a policeman, he had a sensitive mouth, slender nose, and dreamy eyes accentuated by oddly-sixties metal-framed glasses. Beneath his suit he wore a maroon turtleneck sweater. He looked to be, surprisingly, only in his late twenties.

His office, if one could call it that, was a desk partially surrounded by an eye-level divider covered with what appeared to be Dawn Gray carpeting.

He leaned back in his chair as Hana eyed the Dawn Gray, recalling that another of Grace's ideas had been to push the use of carpet for wall covering.

"So," he said carefully, "what can we do for you today, Ms. Shaner?"

"At the inquest it was definitely stated the fingerprints proved Grace Urich was dead. But I wondered . . . isn't there any chance at all a mistake could be made? Could they get good enough prints from the—from her?"

"Forensic medicine is quite an exact science. The prints matched. Absolutely no doubt."

Hana took a deep breath before she asked, "So what are you going to do about it?"

He looked surprised. "Find the killer, naturally."

"Oh, good."

They bared their teeth briefly at each other in what passed for smiles, then he asked, "Ms. Shaner, have you something to tell me?"

She explained about Carl Reid and the mysterious woman. He listened wistfully as he took notes.

"We'll check it out, of course, but—"

"I understand. Were any policemen around the downtown mall the day Grace disappeared?"

He switched a button on an intercom. "Send Officer Alcorn in to me, will you, please?"

"You've questioned him about that day?"

"We are not amateurs."

"Sometimes it's hard to tell," she murmured.

His glasses were slipping; he pushed them back in place. "I've found your obsession with this case quite curious."

Hana did not give him the satisfaction of showing annoyance. "I'd hardly call it an obsession."

"Really? To move into a dead woman's apartment, track her every move—where she ate breakfast, all of it. Even relatives of murder victims seldom go to those extremes."

"I'd do the same for you, Sergeant Kochen. *If* you were a friend."

"One could wish for such friends as you, Ms. Shaner, especially if one has the misfortune to be murdered." He was looking at the wall carpet behind her. "Do you know much about the history of crime in Conover?"

Hana did not really care to learn about the subject in depth, but Sergeant Kochen proceeded to tell her anyway. His special emphasis seemed to be on arsonists who set fires in order to experience the excitement of helping put them out.

Finally Hana interrupted. "If it weren't so preposterous, I'd think you suspected me of killing Grace."

"Oh, did I give that impression?" he inquired as Officer Alcorn came around the room divider.

Kochen introduced him and invited Hana to ask any questions she wished.

Yes, Officer Alcorn had seen the actors that morning. No, he didn't ask if they had a permit for street theater. He presumed they were from the repertory company and everything was as it should be. They seemed professional and were doing no harm.

"Did you recognize anyone in the troupe? Did anybody look familiar, as if you might have seen them before?"

"I don't get to the theater much," he said regretfully.

"Perhaps you saw them somewhere else."

"I don't think so."

"Can you remember what any of them looked like?"

"Well, one of the lead guys was real tall—fine-looking man. But they all had on wigs and makeup like actors do. It'd be hard to recognize any of them in regular clothes, even the tall guy. I watched for a while. It was comical." He glanced uneasily at the sergeant. "Not too long, of course."

"Did you notice the women? Could any be described as very sexually attractive?"

The officer's eyes gleamed, but Sergeant Kochen said dryly, "It would be the worst kind of ID. What's sex to the officer here may not be sex to Carl Reid."

He was right, of course. Officer Alcorn hastily switched the subject from sexy women with an assertion that he had seen nobody who answered Grace Urich's description in either the cast or audience.

Hana gave up and turned to Sergeant Kochen to ask about the funeral. He told her it could be any time. Since no relatives had come forward, the body would be released to her as requested.

Hana left the police station feeling she had encountered another dead end. The only thing she had learned was that she herself was a suspect. The thought was slightly frightening. Surely they would not persist in such an outrageous idea. But if they did, she would have to speak to Mel Rosen.

The only real progress she had made lately was the moment of truth when she had tried to see through Grace's eyes and had realized the apartment was Grace's little fortress. With physical clues so scarce, maybe this was the only direction she could take. It had nothing to do with psychic powers, because, heaven knows, she'd never had those. But if she concentrated hard enough perhaps she could experience another insight into her friend's mind.

Grace had gone to that restaurant—the one that gave out free postcards. Hana felt sure of it. And even though her detectives had checked it out, they hadn't looked at it through Grace's eyes.

She phoned Bill Longenecker and invited him to lunch.

As Hana drove through the mellowing, harvested countryside, Bill, sitting beside her, complained, "I don't even know why I agreed to come. I mean, after our last date."

"You did it because you're nice," she said lightly.

"Damn right. Too nice for you. But I wanted to find out what you were up to, since you hate this kind of 'exploitation' so much."

The restaurant was on the Philadelphia Highway near a pseudo-Dutch farm and villages devoted to crafts for tourists. Bill took a professional interest in it all, noting out-of-state license plates, numbers of automobiles parked at various attractions, and whether these attractions were keeping themselves polished and painted.

Grace must have driven here, pulled into this parking lot. She would have noted the large beds of flowers, yellow and orange marigolds, scarlet sage. Had she come because she loved flowers? Hana didn't think so.

It was a large restaurant with a gift shop on the second floor. The main room overlooked a flower and vegetable garden at the rear.

"Let's sit near the windows," Hana suggested.

Grace liked to sit near windows.

It was crowded but not inconveniently so, and the hostess found a table in a corner where Hana had two windows.

"The food here is pretty good," Bill said enthusiastically. "It's really one of the better places in the area. Gets crowded. Lucky you called early."

Hana stared at the menu. What would Grace have had? No intuition came. She finally chose shrimp because she knew Grace liked shrimp and they were the daily special.

Bill was watching her.

"So what are we really doing here?" he finally asked.

She told him about the postcard.

"My God," he groaned. "They're all over the place. We even have some in the office. No way does it mean she came out here."

"She did," Hana said stubbornly. "And she kept that card for some reason. Maybe to remind her to come back again."

He appealed to the ceiling. "Give me strength."

"Bill . . . didn't you like Grace?"

He hesitated. "Yes, I liked her."

"But?"

"Oh, it's nothing really. Okay. *But* I always had the feeling there was a lot cooking just beneath that calm surface. She made me tense is all. Like I was near a volcano."

"I never knew that."

"Well, who goes around saying such things about somebody unless they're—I mean, while they're around."

The meal was good. Bill returned to his favorite topic—tourists. He was seriously contemplating Elsie Hardinger's suggestion to do a tour of Conover County crime scenes. He'd been looking into it, and there were more than he'd suspected.

Any other time the subject would have irritated Hana, but today she let him talk while her mind drifted. Had Grace met somebody here? It wasn't the sort of place Grace usually went, so there must have been a special reason.

Later, Hana went to the rest room, but she found no graffiti that said "Grace was here." She saw Bill busily making notes about the proposed crime tour as he drank his coffee, so she slipped upstairs to the gift shop. She was surprised to find it specialized in toys made by the Dutch, featuring Dutch theme and clothing. It was the best display of its kind Hana had seen. Around a corner, behind glass, were shelves of carefully dressed Amish dolls with hand-painted faces.

This was it.

The thought came in so strong that for a moment Hana was shaken. She wasn't sure she really wanted this method of detection to succeed. As Bill had said—weird. Maybe not even true. Maybe she was reaching, because why on earth would Grace Urich buy an expensive Amish doll?

She hurried back to the table, for the moment not interested in seeing anything else through Grace's eyes. She supposed she should ask around among their mutual friends to find out if Grace had given a gift of a doll to one of the girls.

No. That didn't feel right.

Damn!

This really was no way to solve a mystery. Sergeant Kochen had been right to call her an amateur. No clues, so make them up. Pretend an intuition you don't have, and all kinds of answers will come into your head.

"I'm not even going to ask what you think of this idea for our crime tour," Bill said on the way back to the city.

"You're right. Don't ask."

"You're snappy enough now that you got what you wanted out of me again. Remember. Someday you may not have good old Bill to kick around."

Hana sighed. "I'm sorry. Really. It's just that I found out this morning the police actually think I may have killed Grace."

"Well, did you?"

She looked at him, swerving the car. A passing van blew its horn angrily.

"Hey, watch out!" he cried.

"Are you serious?" Hana asked, ignoring the horn.

"Would I be here if I were?"

"You could be doing research for your tour."

He chuckled. "I could at that."

She dropped him at his office. Elsie was out. Autumn was always a busy time in the business. Without a conscious decision Hana drove to the CarPark. The way between it and the apartment had become very familiar. So familiar that she hardly noticed the buildings she was passing. But Grace . . . was this a path of danger to her? Did she look warily about every day, wishing she were safe inside the apartment? Whom did she look for? Man or woman? Or was it possible she didn't even know?

Somehow, Hana had to get into Grace's past. Nobody else seemed able to get there. But surely there must be conventional ways. . . .

Suddenly Hana could feel Grace's fear. She might have been tempted to run. No, she would restrain herself. She would go forward cautiously.

Glad that it was afternoon and not a foggy night, Hana inserted a shiny new key into the gleaming lock of the front door. A crisp click and she was inside, carefully closing the door behind her and making sure it was secure.

She climbed the steps as Grace had done. She put another key into the bright brass lock of the apartment. She paused.

Somebody was in there. Now. This minute. Somebody waited.

She heard nothing, saw nothing. None of her five senses was involved in the knowing. Her knees felt weak. She wished she had a gun. She'd have to get one, learn to use it. She knew she should go quietly down the stairs, leave the building. Get Mr. Fred. No, the police. And if nobody was inside? Or even if they were there now and had gone by the time help came? Would Sergeant Kochen call her worse than an amateur? She was a suspect, so should she risk having them think she was crazy?

She realized time was passing as she stood before the apartment door doing nothing. Abruptly Hana turned the key in the lock and opened the door of Grace Urich's apartment.

Her instincts were right on target. There *was* somebody in the apartment.

Chapter Twelve

SHE SAT ON a chair, staring straight in front of her, large eyes on Hana's face. It was almost too much. For seconds Hana felt breathless, drained, and afraid she would faint. Anxiety had propelled her forward, but she had not expected this.

It was a child, a girl of about eight.

Coldness crept along Hana's spine. The girl was dressed in a style reminiscent of twenty years earlier. She had pigtails tied with ribbons, like Grace Urich in the old picture. She looked like Grace. . . .

Automatically Hana closed the door behind her. The click of the new lock brought her out of her daze.

"How did you get in here?" she asked, surprised to hear herself whispering because her intent had been to speak with loud authority.

The girl continued to stare at her.

Suppose Grace had come back—somehow—as a child? A ghost child? Suppose she had been roaming this apartment at night and those were the sounds Hana had heard.

My God.

She could never tell anybody about this. Never. They'd take away all her carpets, lock her in a padded cell for real, and this time she wouldn't have Dutch Blue to effect a recovery. That only happened on TV.

She moved forward and reached out to touch the girl. The child blinked, drew back.

She was real.

Hana cleared her throat, trying to assume command of the situation.

"Are you alone?"

No answer.

Leaving the girl where she was, Hana explored the apartment. So far as she could tell, everything was in order. Nobody hiding in the shower stall or under the bed. The windows not barred were locked.

She returned to the living room and bolted the door.

"What's your name?"

No smile, no sense of recognition in the eyes, no flicker of expression. Hana hesitated, then waved her hand in front of the child's face. She blinked again.

"Are you all right? . . . Damn it! Answer me!"

But she didn't.

Hana sat on the sofa. That was when she noticed the small suitcase beside the chair. She grabbed it. Not locked. The girl made no move, didn't even watch as she rummaged through. Two small dresses, slacks, blouses, a skirt, pajamas, underwear. No identification, no tags—nothing.

The dolls in the gift shop.

Hana was sure now why Grace had gone there.

"I was in a shop today," she told the child, trying to force her voice to be calm, normal. "They were selling very pretty dolls dressed like the Amish people who live around here. They had black bonnets and black aprons, but the dresses were pretty colors like blue and lavender and even orange. Did you ever own a doll like that?"

The eyes turned in her direction.

Encouraged, Hana asked, "Did your mother give you one?"

The eyes slid away again. She looked small, defenseless in the chair. Her feet, in anklets and Mary Janes, didn't reach the floor.

Hana tried to recall if Grace had ever spoken about children. Even other people's children. Had she talked to Jane Padesky at work? After all, Jane had two kids. Maybe Grace and Jane had talked when Hana wasn't present. If Grace had brought the child here . . .

Could a dead woman do that? And Grace was dead. The fingerprints had said so. Somebody else *must* have brought her.

"Will you please say something? Speak to me?" Hana rose and stood in front of the girl. "All right, so you won't talk. But will you do me a favor? If you can hear me, will you just nod? What can it hurt if you move your head a little for me?"

She waited, staring at the child. For seconds nothing happened. Then the head tilted forward in an almost imperceptible nod.

"Now we're getting somewhere," Hana said with pseudocheerfulness. "Let's try another question. Did your mother bring you here?"

But there were no more nods or shakes, no matter how Hana coaxed and cajoled. She knew she should call the police, let them make of it what they would. Yet . . . amateur though she might be, Hana had the girl and the girl was a key to Grace Urich's fate. And a kid can't sit in a chair forever.

Hana went to the kitchen.

Not, she thought dismally, that there was much food to find. Or much ability on her part to create a meal.

Eggs. What a favor chickens had bestowed on the human race.

In the course of her college career, while sharing an apartment off campus, she had mastered the art of scrambling eggs. She managed now, and even created toast. Balancing paper plates, she carried their lunch in to the girl who had not moved. Wordlessly she pulled a small table in front of the child, placed the plate on it, then sat across the room. Without looking up, she ate her own eggs with unnatural relish.

At first Hana thought she had failed. Then slowly the girl picked up the fork and, leaning forward, took a bite. Once started, the child gobbled every scrap of food.

They finished at about the same time.

"Did you have enough?" Hana asked.

Her hope that the food would change things vanished when the girl leaned back, assuming her deadpan expression.

"Look, sister, if you don't cooperate with me, I'm going to have to call the police."

Still no response.

Hana went into the bedroom, closing the door behind her. She dialed Mel Rosen on the bedroom phone. Fortunately he was in his office.

"You're kidding," was his unprofessional response when she told him about the child.

"She looks like Grace," Hana whispered. "Like that picture of Grace as a child."

"Oh, Hana!"

"It's true, Mel."

His voice went cool and legal. "I wish I could come over, but I've got an important appointment in twenty minutes, so there's just no way. But I'll tell you what I want you to do. Take that girl to the police. Immediately. Tell them where you found her and what the circumstances were."

"But suppose Grace had her sent here to me? Suppose—"

"Hana! Grace Urich is dead. Let the police handle it!"

He was waiting for her promise. She stared at the closed door. When she opened it, would the child still be there? Would the apartment door still be locked, bolted, and the child gone?

He sounded impatient now. She really couldn't blame him. "If I must, I'll cancel my appointment and take you to the police myself. In fact, maybe that's what I'd better do."

"No. It's okay. I'll do it."

"Will you? Promise me you'll take that kid to the police. Right now. Not half an hour from now."

"Yes, all right."

"Promise, damn it!"

"I promise!"

She hung up and returned to the living room. As far as she could tell, the child had not moved an inch. Hana hesitated, then went to the desk and got the photograph of what appeared to be Grace and her parents. She was almost surprised to find it, but there it was, in the drawer exactly where she had left it.

"Do you know any of these people?"

The child stared straight ahead.

"Will you at least look at the picture?" Hana said slowly, articulating carefully. She held the photograph higher, right in front of the girl's eyes.

Nothing.

She put away the picture, got her shoulder bag and the small suitcase, then said briskly, "We must leave now. Get up, please."

She had not expected cooperation. But to her surprise, the girl rose and took the hand Hana held out.

They left the apartment in silence. When Hana opened the downstairs door and peered out, she half expected a mysterious watcher, perhaps even shots. Instead she stepped out into a serene afternoon. A gust of wayward wind brought a few fallen leaves into the alley, but otherwise it was still.

The gift shop was open. She paid Mel Rosen a great deal of money to give her good advice, and usually she took it. But this was different.

"Come," she said, pulling the girl toward the shop.

Robie Holmes was playing a tape of mesmerizing music. At least it appeared to mesmerize her. She leaned on the counter, glazed eyes on a voodoo mask. Fake, Hana hoped. With a shock, she saw that Robie's head was now shaved except for a bright pink fringe from forehead to nape of neck.

"Robie? . . . Robie!"

Hana waved her hand in front of the woman's eyes before they focused and Robie smiled a greeting.

"Landlady, welcome. I want you to hear this. I want the whole world to— I mean, listen . . . like water, isn't it? Like wine. Like liquid sugar. Like melted rock. . . . Think of it . . . rock-bleed . . ."

Hana pushed the child forward.

"Robie, this girl was left in the apartment upstairs. Whoever brought her must have passed by the shop. Did you see anyone?"

Continuing to sway to the music, Robie smiled

vaguely down at the child. "Like large people dwindling in time to become small people," she sighed dreamily.

Hana walked behind the counter and switched off the tape.

"It has all run away," Robie sighed. "Into the eyes of the mask. Holes absorb music. Eyes of masks absorb the music." She spoke to the child. "But you know that, don't you? Of course. You do. The landlady doesn't. The rest of them don't."

Hana resisted a desire to slap Robie, settling for seizing her arm.

"Did you see who brought this child to my apartment?" she asked tightly.

"Hey, ouch! Hey, woman. I owe you rent or something? Not nice. Violence is not nice. I get all black and blue and yellow. I mean . . . yellow. Umm . . . love it. Yellow. Tattoo that yellow bruise all over my arm. . . ."

With a sigh Hana gave up, took the girl's hand, and headed for the door. She looked about carefully, but apparently the alleyway was still empty.

Just as they stepped outside, Robie called.

"Nobody brought her. She came alone. Floating up the alley on the wind. The wind blew her. Like it blows the leaves. Blew her to the top of the roof and in a window. I saw her blowing about up there. Across the roof. Leaf-child. Child of the trees—yellow trees—poor, bruised, yellow trees. . . ."

Hana kept walking.

All the way to the CarPark she tried not to act nervous, not to attract attention by looking behind them. She thought a few people did stare pointedly at her, at the child. But nothing was said, nothing done. She felt thankful when she had the girl sitting in the passenger's seat with the door securely locked. As she drove directly to police headquarters, she decided Mel had given her sound advice.

She pulled into a space reserved for a police car.

Still obedient, demure, carrying her own small suitcase, the child followed Hana into the Victorian building. As the door closed behind them, cutting off the autumn wind busily removing color from the trees, Hana let out a slow breath. They were in the hall where marble steps ascended to the second floor and where the old-fashioned rest rooms were located. Through swinging doors which led to offices, a young policeman entered and stopped to stare at her. A policewoman in uniform followed, merely glancing at Hana and the child as she moved toward an exit.

"Ms. Shaner?" the man asked respectfully.

He was good-looking, handsome even. A boyish admiration shone in his eyes as he told her how much he liked the commercials she made. He especially went for the ones with the animals, and he'd heard she had already made another. He laughed about the group of dogs who had followed two men carrying a rolled-up carpet because a bone was inside it. How when the men stopped, the dogs had ripped and torn at the carpet to get the bone. How little damage they had done, proving again how really good Shaner bindings were. He asked her to send him an autographed picture for his kid sister who loved animals. Her name was Meg. His was Ed Kochen.

"Kochen?"

"The sergeant's younger brother."

He was so enthusiastic. He was so good.

The child who had been standing beside her so docilely was no longer there.

"The girl!" Hana exclaimed. "The kid I had with me—where'd she go?"

He looked surprised. "Why, to the rest room. Right over there. I saw her go in a couple minutes ago."

Hana ran to the rest room. It was still furnished with the original 1910 fixtures and tiles. One frosted window, dusty and obviously painted shut years ago. Three booths. Two empty. Beneath the door of the third she saw heavy legs and solid black Oxfords. Hana knocked on the door of the booth.

There was silence. Then a cautious voice said, "Yes?"

"Is a child in there with you? A girl of about eight?"

She hadn't considered how weird the question would sound. She banged on the door again before a frightened voice said, "I'm in here alone, lady! This is a police station, you—whoever you are. So don't try anything!"

"I'm sorry!"

Hana pushed at the window, but it was unmoving. She ran back into the hall. No sign of the girl or the young policeman. She looked outside but saw nothing except a different young cop putting a ticket on her car. She dashed back inside as a stout middle-aged woman came out of the rest room, looked about suspiciously, stared at her for a moment, then quickly left the building.

Hana hurried upstairs to Sergeant Kochen's office. Even to herself, she sounded hysterical as she told her story. There was this child who had appeared out of nowhere. Except she could produce no such child. Nor even a witness that the girl existed. Except Robie Holmes, and somehow she didn't want to mention Robie Holmes.

"Your brother saw her," she told Sergeant Kochen. Even before the words were out of her mouth, she knew he had no brother.

But Kochen and his assistant solemnly took her description of the child and the supposed policeman. Too solemnly, she thought resentfully, the way one might if faced with an emotionally disturbed person who must not be excited. She even told them about the woman in the rest room.

This was too much.

"Did you see the kid with her?" Kochen asked wearily, shoving his glasses back into place.

"No."

"Could she have hidden the kid? Like under a long cloak or something?"

Miserably Hana shook her head. "The woman was definitely alone. She seemed to be frightened of me."

"Yeah," Kochen said dryly. "A lot of weird people show up in public lavatories."

Then he suggested she go home.

But when she insisted that the rest room be searched, he sent his assistant with her. More as an escort out of the building, Hana suspected, than with any hope that evidence of a child would be found.

The assistant was young, not nearly as good-looking as the bogus Ed Kochen.

"Does he think I'm weird?" Hana asked as they went down the marble stairs.

"No, Ms. Shaner," he said politely. "Just worried."

"What do *you* think?"

"I think when somebody gets killed, their friends can get funny ideas. See, if there was a— What I mean, this kid could have been any runaway that hid in the apartment. Maybe she wanted to steal something. There's a lot of that going around."

"She couldn't have been more than eight!"

He grunted. "You should see some of the stuff we've caught eight-year-olds doing. They grow up fast today."

He knocked on the door of the ladies' room; then they went in together. He checked the window, confirmed her opinion that it hadn't been opened for years. The stout woman had left no clues in booth 3. All toilets had been flushed. All paper towels discarded properly. There was nowhere to hide. At Hana's insistence, the receptacle for the paper towels was removed and thoroughly searched. Hana waited for the results, aware of the grumbling references to Her Royal Highness and the attitude that if anybody other than a Shaner had demanded this it would not have been done.

Triumphantly the assistant gave the paper towel receptacle a clean bill of health and returned it to the rest room.

Hana had no choice but to leave, taking her parking ticket with her.

Unhappily she drove back to the CarPark. She knew she had to return to the apartment. Despite what the frog-headed Robie had declared, somebody must have brought the child. Her sense of logic rebelled at the idea expressed by Kochen's assistant that the girl was totally unrelated to the Grace Urich mystery.

As she walked along the mall toward the alleyway, shops were closing with the setting sun. The wind had turned colder. Leaves scudded along the bricks and a few tattered petals from the mums followed them. The child had been brought to her . . . to help? As a threat? But if there were no notes, no way of understanding, how could she possibly get the message? Unless . . .

She remembered the first frightening night she had walked this way. No less frightening now as she thought of the strange way the girl had appeared. Almost as if she were living in some sort of time warp.

Long ago—high school? college? sometime—she had read a book entitled *Portrait of Jenny* in which a girl appeared first as a child, then as a teenager, her life relived rapidly, much as a camera speeds up in time-lapse photography. The story culminated in the girl's untimely death.

If Grace could come back as a child . . .

No. Better to believe she had imagined the girl.

Was she going mad? Maybe that's what this was all about—somebody wanted to drive her crazy. To take over Shaner Carpets?

The gift shop was closed, although Hana suspected Robie might still be there because she heard faint Indian-type music.

Cautiously she opened the downstairs door, cautiously went up the stairs, listened at the apartment door before she cautiously opened it. Her senses told her it was empty. The phone was ringing as she went inside.

It was Mel Rosen. After his appointment he had called the police and had been told the whole story.

"Did you call anybody else?" she asked.

"What are you trying to say?"

"Nothing, really. Except they seemed to be expecting me, since they had that fake cop planted there and you were the only one who knew where I was going with the girl."

"Hana, I said nothing to anyone. Not even here in the office. But somebody could have figured it out. It really was the only logical thing to do, and people know how logical you are."

She swallowed a hysterical desire to laugh. What logical person thinks she's living *Portrait of Jenny?*

Mel was just leaving the office. He insisted on stopping by on his way home. She didn't want him to. There were still those old emotions that had been so inconveniently revived. Besides, she knew what he was going to say. But Mel declared he was coming, then hung up on her.

She searched the apartment thoroughly, looking for clues, for notes. She even poked beneath the kitchen range where the receipt had been. She called home and talked to Mr. Fred. Nobody had shown up there except a well-known archaeologist from Washington, D.C. Hana didn't want to hear anything about bones.

She was expecting Mel, but his arrival startled her anyway. Trouble was, he knew it. She couldn't meet his eyes.

He sat in the same chair the child had used and stared at Hana until she was forced to look at him.

"This has got to stop," he said calmly.

"I don't see how it can."

"You must return home to Blue Spring Hill. Come here during daylight hours if you insist, but don't stay. Not overnight, and not by yourself for long periods." Now his own eyes dropped. "And . . . Hana, I think you should see your doctor."

"You think I'm becoming mentally unstable—"

"Damn it, no! Certainly not. You know me better than that. And I know you. But what I do think is that your nerves are shot. You need something to calm you down. Look at you."

She went to the mirror. He was right. Fear and sleepless nights were telling. Circles, which had never been there before, had appeared under her eyes. Even with makeup, she looked pale and tired.

He said it softly. "I care about you."

"Do you?"

He did not move except for a nod. Looking at him in the gathering twilight of the room, a lot of years were washing away from her. The sense of warped time she had experienced with the child was with her now. They were young again. . . .

He rose and came to her, put his arms around her, and kissed her gently. The kiss was a pain inside her. No one else in her life had ever meant so much. Would there be the same joy? The same contentment? She relaxed against him, euphoria filling her. Then fatigue began in her legs and moved along her back, as if they were growing older by the second as they stood there. They had reached middle age and in moments more would be . . . seventy. Then eighty . . .

Before it happened, Hana fought her way back to today. Mel was now stroking her hair, his hand wandering to her neck, massaging, caressing. She pulled away and moved across the room. He did not follow, but she could feel his eyes on her.

"Have you forgotten how close we were?" he asked quietly.

"No. No, Mel, I haven't. But why now? Why not a year ago? Two years ago? Or right after you came back to town?"

He had returned to Conover about five years before because he wanted to relocate after a bitter divorce that had given him full custody of his two children. He never mentioned his wife. He dated, but as far as she knew he had not become serious with anyone. She suspected he might be afraid of another close relationship.

"I don't know," he said frankly. "I . . . really . . . don't know. Maybe I'm afraid of blowing it again."

He turned on a lamp.

She blinked. "Why'd you do that?"

"I want to look at you. Did I ever tell you how becoming I think your white hair is? I really love it."

Inexplicably, she felt embarrassed. "Nobody really loves white hair."

"I do. On you. Your face looks so young. . . . It's such a contrast—"

It was too complicated, too unnerving on top of everything else. "I'm sorry, Mel," she said. "Maybe we can resume this conversation another time. It's just . . . bad timing, I guess."

He, too, suddenly seemed embarrassed. "Yeah. . . . It's been a rotten time. Okay—all that aside, I really don't want you staying here tonight."

"I'm staying," she told him flatly.

He ran an agitated hand through his graying hair. "What am I going to do with you?"

"It's not your problem."

He looked hurt. "Maybe it is, Hana. Humor me. As an old friend. Go back to Blue Spring Hill tonight."

She waved that away. "I would like your opinion on something."

"Sure. I'm good at giving opinions."

"You always were."

He laughed, and the atmosphere in the room lightened. "What do you want to know?"

"If some fellow dressed up like a real cop, do you think he could move around city hall without anybody noticing?"

"If he was careful, I don't see why not. Not everybody knows everybody else down there. Want me to try it?"

"No. That's okay."

He contemplated her. "You're going to stay here no matter what anybody says, aren't you?" She nodded; he sighed. "Then what about Sal? Or Mr. Fred? Maybe one of them could stay with you if you insist on this foolishness."

"Somebody has to take care of Blue Spring Hill."

"Somebody should take care of you."

"I can take care of myself. I've been doing it for many years."

They stared at each other for a moment, then his eyes dropped. "Well, that's that."

As he moved toward the door, she said quickly, "Don't you understand? There's a child involved in this. I have to be here in case she comes back."

"Hana," he said impatiently, "that girl probably has nothing whatever to do with Grace Urich."

She hurried to get the picture. "She does. She must. This is the girl I saw."

She thrust the photograph into his hand. He studied it before he said, "Quite an old picture by the look of it. Where did you find this?"

"Here."

"It could be—"

"It is! I know it's Grace."

"But Grace as a child. Not the Grace we know. The girl you took to the police station this afternoon couldn't possibly be this one. Think what you're saying, Hana."

"Yes, I know. . . . Of course you're right. It couldn't be this child. But why couldn't it be Grace's daughter?"

"I didn't know Grace Urich had a daughter."

"Neither did I. But the girl looked just like her, and she had to come from somewhere."

Mel handed the picture back to her. "None of this would stand up in court."

"What a dumb thing to say! Honestly, Mel. . . . Do you always retreat behind law books when you don't understand something?"

"I'm not the one under discussion, Hana. Do you want to tell me how you think this girl got into the apartment?"

She hesitated. "Somebody brought her."

"Like who?"

"You want me to say it, don't you? You want me to say that I think Grace brought her."

He dropped onto the arm of the sofa and sat there looking at her for some seconds before he said, "Grace Urich is dead."

He waited, obviously wanting her to say something, anything, to convince him she hadn't gone mad. Or had proof, of which he knew nothing, that Grace was indeed still of this world. Or perhaps even proof that she had visited from some dimension of the dead. Hana sought for words but found none. None that Mel Rosen would want to hear, at any rate.

Finally he rose. "Will you call if you need me?"

She nodded.

Still he hesitated. "Are you sure you don't want me to get in touch with Mr. Fred? Elsie, or even Bill Longenecker? Anybody?"

"I'm sure," she said emphatically.

Looking defeated, he left the apartment. She went to the window to watch him walk away. Below, street lamps were coming on. The wind seemed to have died with the sun. Mel didn't look back. She pushed home the bolts on the door, then sat in the large comfortable chair to wait.

Time was such a strange thing. Like water. You couldn't hold it. Rip Van Hana. Sitting here for a hundred years. Or was it twenty in the story? Didn't matter. When she looked at the clock only an hour and a half had passed. She listened to the silence of the apartment, wishing she could put on a tape.

But if they/he/she heard music, they might not come. Finally she had to go to the bathroom. When she returned she almost expected to see the girl sitting in the chair. What she should have done was taken a picture. It at least would have proved the existence of the child. She paused, staring again at the window that overlooked the alleyway. It seemed to be the focal point of the room. She had been drawn to that window the first time she entered the apartment, and it was the place to which she always returned. She went to the window and looked out.

With a kind of weary resignation, she stared at the figure below. As before, it was in shadows. She felt no surprise. The surprise would have been if no one had been watching. It could be someone Mel had sent to keep an eye on the apartment for her protection, but she didn't think so.

Two days ago—even yesterday—she would not have gone down alone. She wished again she had a gun, a camera, anything that could be used as a weapon. But there was no weapon, not even a broom.

Taking keys and purse, Hana ran from the apartment, clattered down the stairs, and burst through the front door. The figure turned, fleeing before the onslaught of her approach. As she ran, Hana could see the figure well enough to realize that whoever it might be, the person was smaller and shorter than she. But that hardly mattered. She wanted to get her hands on somebody—*that* somebody. Wanted them real under her fingers, even if she had to scratch and strike out and bite—

They burst onto the mall, leaves flying beneath their feet. Into pools of light and dark. Hana was gaining. The mall was intersected by many small alleys similar to the one that led to Grace Urich's apartment. Some went to shops, some were short-cuts to other streets; all were narrow, Colonial, bricked. The somebody she pursued ducked into one, to become swallowed in the walled dark.

Hana plunged after.

Her breath now came in gasps. She scraped against sharp, uneven bricks, ripping her sleeve, momentary pain from a brush burn on her arm slowing her. Light from a street at the end of the alley was the only illumination. She saw the shadow of her prey moving in that direction, like herself, slower now.

Her eyes on the dark movement ahead, she ran faster, aiming herself like an arrow between the walls. Closer. Gaining again. They were almost at the next street. The prey ran faster too, then, reaching some uneven cement, crashed into the wall with a cry.

Hana grabbed.

She felt the plastic jacket in her hands. She felt the thin arm beneath it. There were moments of struggle as the person tried to wrench out of her grasp. Hana hung on, digging in, shoving the figure off-balance toward the street. She spun the person around in a macabre kind of dance as they emerged into the brightness of a street lamp. A shadowing hat fell from the head; long hair spun out. The face was fully visible now.

Hana dropped the arm. She opened her mouth. She thought she was screaming.

But only harsh mumbling sounds were coming out.

Chapter Thirteen

SHE SAW THE face of a teenage girl. A face that had matured from the rounded one of the child she had found in the apartment but had not yet become the face of the Grace Urich she knew. Yet Grace's eyes looked out at her from that face. The girl, now free of Hana's grasp, darted to another alleyway and disappeared.

This time Hana did not follow.

She was hyperventilating, shock numbing her. Feeling too weak to stand, she groped toward slab steps of a house and sat down. *Portrait of Jenny,* she thought dizzily. Yes, that's what it was. The girl had grown years in just a few hours. . . .

At that point Hana, holding on to a wrought-iron railing, pulled herself to her feet. She had to get back to the apartment. Now there was no way she could take Mel's advice and see a doctor for her nerves. They would think she had really gone over the edge. There was no one she could talk to about this. No one to call or confide in. There was only herself with God knows what or who on the other side.

Staggering a little, she entered the alley through which she had followed the girl. When she reached the mall she paused. Some distance away a group of teenagers joyously celebrated their youth. In the other direction two people walked a large dog. Chilly now, Hana crossed to the Urich alleyway. She prayed it would be empty. Another such chase would probably kill her.

It looked empty, felt empty. Even the music of the gift shop had ceased. Hana had left the downstairs door unlocked.

Carefully she entered, looking about, then locked and bolted the door, hoping she was not penning something inside with her.

The stairs were well lit, nonthreatening. She had pulled shut the door to the apartment itself, thank heavens. Even so, once inside, she made a thorough search of places where a human being could hide. Then she zipped herself in with bolts and closed the drapes. She would not look through that window again tonight; nor would she leave the apartment.

And in the morning she would pack the few belongings she had here and move back to Blue

Spring Hill. Retreat was definitely in order. After all, if she were dead or driven out of her mind, there would be nobody to find out what had actually happened to Grace Urich.

Hana was passing the bookshelves on her way to the bathroom to look for something to put on her brush burn when she noticed the set of encyclopedias. She was sure they'd been there before —yes, Sal had dusted them—but now one book was out of line, protruding as if inviting her to lift it down. She ignored it, went to the bathroom, and sprayed antiseptic on the sore before she returned to the living room and took down the volume. It fell open automatically, because a photograph had been used as a bookmark.

The page was illustrated with a picture of a coffin. The photo was that of the child she had found in the apartment. It was a Polaroid flash picture taken when the girl was seated here on the chair. Hana experienced an irrational fear of touching it, but forced herself to remove it from the book and put it in her handbag.

She nearly changed her mind about waiting until morning to leave. Obviously someone (something?) had easy access to the place despite the new lock and bolts. She could call Mr. Fred and have him come to get her, but she did not want to give anybody—including Mr. Fred—the idea that she had run in the middle of the night because she was afraid. Afraid to go alone to the CarPark. But, most of all, afraid to stay. It was bad enough she was going home tomorrow, but at least she would go with dignity. She could cover herself with a story.

In the kitchen she found an aerosol cleanser whose label indicated it was irritating to the eyes.

She would hold it and use it on whoever she had to. And of course, she would stay awake all night.

After taking down the encyclopedia volume again, she turned to the page where the picture had been. There she found a brief but morbid article about children and death. It stated children had an instinctive fear of death even before they were aware of it in realistic terms. In drawings, play, and dreams they lived with this primitive fear.

Chapter Fourteen

SUNLIGHT BRIGHT ENOUGH to penetrate the drapes awakened her. For seconds she couldn't recall what she was supposed to do that day. Then she groaned and stiffly stirred. The encyclopedia volume she'd been reading slid to the floor. She had often wondered how TV and book private eyes suffered all sorts of assaults and kept going. She herself felt twenty years older. Sleeping in a chair all night hadn't helped, of course.

She had intended to shower when she reached Blue Spring Hill, but her body dissuaded her from waiting. After ten minutes under the hot needling water, she felt more like facing what could be a difficult day. She dressed, packed, locked the apartment, and hurried to the CarPark, glad to be driving home. She would check in, then go to the office. If she got her life back on course maybe she could think sensibly, something she hadn't been doing much of lately.

White clouds banked against blue sky above the harvest fields gave her a sense of her own place again. This was her land, and these were her people—Mel, Elsie, Bill, Jimmy Klopp, and, of course, Mr. Fred and Sal. Even Carl Reid, now fired and disgraced. Grace Urich had come as a stranger. She had become a stranger again. The woman Hana had known as Grace had not existed.

People were still digging up her lawn. Hana hoped they would not notice her. They didn't. But she could not get into the house without Ghost and Crumb noticing. They came yelping and wagging in an ecstasy of welcome. The noise brought Sal, Mr. Fred, Penelope Baskin, and Kitty Fisher. Behind them slunk a gray figure in jungle-crouch position. Hana greeted everyone, including the croucher.

Sal eyed the suitcase. "Looks like you're home to stay."

"I have concluded the first phase of my investigation," Hana said airily. "I need no longer remain in the apartment."

"Ja," Sal grunted. "Sure."

"There's another bag in my car," Hana told Mr. Fred.

Mr. Fred sighed and left the room.

Sal surveyed Hana critically. "What you need is a good breakfast."

"It's late for breakfast."

"Yeah, well."

Hana had breakfast in the kitchen. Crumb and Ghost accepted dog biscuits, then went outside. Kitty Fisher and Penelope Baskin shared a dish of special-formula dry cat food from the health food store. The gray cat jumped onto the table, throwing over a carton of milk, spilling it across the floor.

"That cat's name," Sal said darkly, "is trouble."

The carton had fallen on its side. The face of a missing child stared up at Hana. Their dairy had featured missing children on its cartons for a year or more now. Advertising. As she ate and Sal mopped, Hana thought of the child in the apartment. Had fear made her silent? She had not seemed like a normal eight-year-old. Certainly not the eight-year-old Hana herself had been—open, curious, talkative.

Was she a missing child? Was Hana seeing too much resemblance? If this was not Grace Urich's child—and there was no evidence that she was—had Grace kidnapped the girl? A weird idea, but then, everything about Grace was turning out to be weird. Had someone taken the Polaroid picture because they felt Hana wouldn't be smart enough to take one and they wanted the girl found? But she *had* been found. Or did whoever brought her to the apartment want her found again? Someone else might have grabbed her at city hall.

"I wish you'd eat all that breakfast," Sal grumbled. "You're wasting away."

Hana forced down most of it. The cats followed her upstairs, where she carefully reapplied her makeup, hoping she looked more like herself. Hana agreed with Sal's name for the gray cat when he leaped onto her dressing table and knocked half a bottle of cologne on top of Penelope Baskin. Penelope B. hissed angrily before she decided she liked it.

"You *are* Trouble," Hana said as she lifted down the Gray One.

Later at the office she decided that the night's sleep, breakfast, and fresh makeup had done the trick. Nobody stared. Nobody was overly solicitous.

Cindy Hefflefinger was doing a rather good job of filling Grace's place, without Grace's flair.

"What do you want to do about this preliminary report on going into Dutch Blue women's fashions?" Cindy asked.

"On hold temporarily."

"How temporary?" Hana raised an eyebrow. Cindy said lamely, "People have been inquiring."

"I've decided I don't want to go into it until I can give it a lot more time than I have at present."

Cindy looked very competent as she nodded and made a note. But her voice was uncertain when she said, "Another thing. The police called twice to remind you that Grace Urich's body is— Well, they've finished with it. You know the funeral can be any time."

Hana had been deliberately pushing this final gesture toward Grace to the back of her mind. She recalled when her father died . . . and Aunt Sissy—there had been so much to do. So much to decide. A casket first. Maybe Elsie would go along . . .

"I asked Mary Hafer which funeral home took care of your father and your aunt," Cindy said. "So I took the liberty of calling them and arranging for Grace's body to be picked up."

Hana felt a surge of gratitude out of all proportion to the deed. She was aware that Cindy was watching her closely.

"Thank you," she managed.

"My mother works hard—as you know—and when two of her sisters died just six months apart, I did the arrangements for her. She was too upset and—Anyway, if you'd like, I'd be glad to pick out a casket, do whatever else . . ."

If not family then friends, close friends, should do those last rituals of love and service. When Hana considered the lengths to which she had already gone for Grace, her inability to walk this last mile seemed incomprehensible.

She heard herself telling Cindy to go ahead.

"I thought a single plot in the new memorial park out near the bypass—"

"She'll be buried in the Shaner plot in the Mount Conover Cemetery. God knows there's enough room. The Shaner who founded it thought we'd go on forever."

Cindy took more notes. Most efficient.

"Flowers?"

"Donations to the Fur and Feather Refuge."

"Well, that's enough to get me started," Cindy said tactfully. ". . . There's one other thing."

"Yes?" Hana sounded more irritable than she'd intended.

"Carl Reid. He's still around."

"Here?"

"Security's been on the lookout and won't let him in, of course. But . . . he called me the other night."

"What for?"

"He wanted me to meet him somewhere. Talk about what's going on in the office. He told me he misses it terribly."

Hana had dismissed Carl Reid from her mind. A fool, a dupe. The scenario called for him to go crawling away. Apparently that wasn't the way it was playing.

There was a look in Cindy's eyes Hana couldn't read as she asked, "Do you want me to see him and find out what he's doing?"

"Do you want to see him, Cindy?"

"I don't really mind—"

"Then it's entirely up to you."

A most changeable young woman. Hana smiled.

Cindy looked annoyed. "I'll get started on these funeral arrangements," she said tartly.

Chapter Fifteen

ONCE A WEEK Hana had lunch with Elsie, which sometimes included the director of the Fur and Feather. That day she lunched with Elsie alone, and what Elsie wanted to talk about was not animal issues but Grace Urich's funeral.

They had driven into town to eat at The Feathered Duck. Hana still couldn't bear to drink their delicious-smelling coffee.

Elsie arched her neck with annoyance. "I'm shocked—utterly shocked—that you are permitting an employee to make the final arrangements for poor dear Grace."

"How'd you find out about that?"

Huffily Elsie stirred her coffee. "I called your office. Told that Hafer woman I wanted to set up a time for you and me to go to the funeral home.

She informed me the Hefflefinger girl was doing it."

Mary Hafer was not exactly fond of Elsie. She had probably relished delivering the information.

"You said you had something special you wanted to discuss with me," Hana reminded her. "Was that it?"

"No. . . ."

Must be a zinger, Hana thought.

"I'd like a key to the apartment," Elsie finished boldly.

"Grace Urich's apartment?"

"What other apartment would I be talking about? You're not staying there anymore. Sal said so."

"But why do you want a key?"

"I may want to rent it."

Hana nearly dropped her soup spoon. Elsie had recently bought a condo in a new high rise and seemed happy there.

"Bill and I," Elsie added uneasily.

Hana's spoon clattered down. "You and Bill Longenecker are going to live together?"

"Don't be funny, Hana! I think that comment is in the worst possible taste. You know we're working on setting up a tour of crime scenes in Conover County."

"I know he's talked about it, but . . . I mean, *Grace's apartment?*"

"We've already spoken to that odd person you rent the gift shop to. She's all for it. I think. Have you noticed how hard she is to talk to? Anyway, it would bring tourists back there on a regular basis. Murderers' Alley—that's what we'll call it. We'd want to buy the furniture, too—keep it just as it was the morning Grace walked out."

It was almost funny. More than almost. But it also made her lose the little appetite she'd had. As Elsie kept talking, Hana looked out the window, depressed by a gray autumn day. Perfect day for a funeral. Except the funeral wasn't today. She ate half her sandwich when it came, pushed away the plate, and, ignoring Elsie's plea for an answer about the apartment, said she had to get back to the office. She had no heart to fight it out today, but Bill Longenecker's travel agency would never get Grace's apartment or her things.

Jill Devon, the cashier, took Hana's money and smiled.

Hana invited Jill and anybody else who might be interested to the graveside service. It was what she had decided upon, all she could really handle.

That afternoon she refused two calls from Bill Longenecker, sure Elsie had gotten to him and that he wanted to pressure her.

She accepted a call from Sergeant Kochen.

"Wanted to tell you there will be police at the Grace Urich service. No matter how quiet you keep it, there are always curiosity seekers who find out."

"But I haven't been keeping it quiet. I've been telling everybody. I was even considering putting a notice in the paper."

"Are you crazy, woman?" he exploded. "They'll tear the cemetery apart. This case has received national publicity. Every tabloid in the country will be there if you do that!"

"I wanted people to know about it."

"For Christ's sake, why?"

"I believe there are those who might be interested. Her family. I think that child belonged to her. Maybe somebody will bring her to the service."

"Change the time, Ms. Shaner," the sergeant snapped. "Have it tomorrow instead of the next day to confuse the curious. And leave the detective work to professionals."

Hana refused. She also refused his belated invitation to look at mug shots to see if she could spot the bogus cop. She felt convinced he only made the offer because he considered it a waste of time. These actors/murderers were too slick to be in Conover mug files. But because he insisted, she compromised by agreeing not to advertise the memorial service in the newspaper. Since she had already spread the word among just about everybody she knew who'd had any contact with Grace, she supposed the circles would widen without further effort on her part.

And if the child didn't appear at the funeral? Well, she'd worry about that later.

Chapter Sixteen

THE DAY OF the funeral was a perfect one for a picnic. The sun shone in a bright sky with all the brilliance of July. It dazzled the eye more than a summer sun as it lit the scarlet maples of Mount Conover Cemetery, turning them to the radiance of red glass. Here and there a poplar tree thrust a tower of gold into the blue. Grass, refreshed by rain during the night, spread vividly green among the tombstones. It was a day for artists and photographers.

In counterpoint was the group of somberly clothed individuals crowding beneath a canopy erected near a Victorian carved angel. Rumored to have been copied from the living face of a Shaner ancestor, the angel had stood upon her solid pedestal for over a hundred years, her stern, frowning countenance obviously disapproving of her descendants, her muscular arm holding aloft a stone flame of uncertain symbology.

Not knowing Grace's religion—another of so many things about Grace she did not know—Hana had chosen the Reverend Doctor Catharine Bowles-Richards from her own Unitarian-Universalist church to conduct the service. A liberally noncreedal denomination, it seemed the most appropriate for Grace's unknown preferences.

Not only that, but the Reverend Bowles-Richards was known to favor a long black cape for such occasions, a cape that gave the proceedings a theatrical dash Hana considered appropriate. She would have buried Grace Urich with totally private grief in some afternoon of rain except for the fact that this had to be a production.

The cast of characters stirred as restlessly as the unquiet trees above. Now and then a red leaf drifted past black coats to lie on the green grass. Cindy's carefully selected casket was closed now. There had been a brief, private viewing at the funeral home before the procession here. Shaner Industries had closed for the afternoon of mourning, and the entire office staff gathered around Hana. Jill Devon and two waitresses from The Feathered Duck were there. Carl Reid, too, had come, but hung back. Elsie and Bill stood by

Hana's side. Mel Rosen, solemnly handsome, was right behind her. Even people from the animal shelter, Pocky Reilly, and the TV crew, some of whom were working on the six-o'clock coverage of the event, came. Mr. Fred and Sal were present, along with an assortment of archaeology students. Hana hoped they wouldn't start digging here.

Sergeant Kochen and his assistant stood at one side, as sober as if they were family. Deterred from joining the group at the graveside by numbers of uniformed police, knots of the curious crept among the tombstones.

Expectantly Hana watched the children of these people, of whom there were quite a few. But no girl who looked like Grace Urich. A man with a camera began to argue loudly with a policeman.

Kochen moved to murmur to Hana, "If you think this is bad, you should see what would have happened with more publicity."

She noticed he wore a black turtleneck today. She was impressed.

Zoom lenses on expensive cameras meant national press. She looked beyond them to the higher parts of the cemetery. Trees obscured much of it. Too much to see if a child might be there peering down on them.

The Reverend Bowles-Richards began to read poetry, some of which she had written herself for memorial occasions. Her cloak stirred in the breeze; her voice lifted with it. She included a Hebrew verse and something from the Apocryphal Book of Mary. This was followed by a prayer.

Everybody bowed their heads, even Sergeant Kochen and the assistant. Probably, Hana thought, in keeping with police protocol at funerals of the murdered. She would pray later; now she was on watch. And she saw them.

Or thought she did.

It was so brief. On the hill near an ancient mausoleum, with the dazzling sun at their backs, two figures appeared. A child and an older girl, or at least a taller one. They had stepped forward to look down, then almost immediately disappeared into the shadows of trees as the sun blinded Hana, turning everything a bright silver.

The now reasonably quiet curious had been herded by police into an area on the main road that led from the gate to the crematorium. Hana slipped away between tombstones as the prayer continued, then darted behind a row of boxwood, still pungent and green.

She began to run, away from the sound of prayer. No one gave chase. Almost certainly some of the mourners had seen her, but they stayed with the prayer. She knew the place well. On pleasant afternoons she and Aunt Sissy had often visited deceased relatives. Her aunt had always spoken of them in the present tense, bringing to life their endearing idiosyncrasies. There was a gazebo up near the mausoleum where they sometimes had a picnic lunch, dropping crumbs for the birds like offerings to the dead.

Hana stayed away from the path and road, keeping trees between herself and the funeral. Finally, wearily, she reached the spot where she thought the children had been.

No one.

And what would people think? That she was acting more erratically than ever, running away from the service during prayer? Mel Rosen. God, what would he think?

Well, she could claim to be overcome by grief. She would certainly not claim to have seen any children.

She moved in the direction of the old mausoleum, intending to return by the macadam pathway. One of the more wealthy families of the canal-building era had constructed this columned gray stone monument during the early 1800s. A disastrous number of their children had died of something called canal fever, and in their memory they had erected the largest edifice in the oldest part of the cemetery. The black door, with an iron netting through which, in her childhood, Hana had looked to see the cobwebbed drawers of the dead children, had always been tightly closed. Not even omnipotent Aunt Sissy could open it.

Now it stood ajar, wide enough for a child to slip through. Hana paused. At this moment, the last thing she wanted to do was go into that mausoleum. Nobody even knew where she was. Suppose . . .

But if the child had gone in there . . .

If it was a living child and somebody had left that door open so she could go inside . . .

She walked softly, put her hand on the cold metal, and pushed. It moved with a loud, rusty squeak. Squinting, she could see the small grimy windows of stained glass that let in little light. She recalled there were three aisles, maybe four, all of marble with handles and names on each drawer. Four graves high, no way to see over the top. Cautiously Hana stepped inside.

Had she really heard a sound? Or was it a chipmunk, many of which had burrowed comfortably into graves? After the bright sunlight outside, the place seemed unnaturally dark. She moved along the clammy wall toward one of the aisles.

When she stopped again to listen, her kneecaps bobbed like yo-yos, a sensation she had felt only once before in her life. It had been in her senior year at college when she had waited in the hall for her interview that would decide whether or not she would graduate with honors.

She felt she had entered into a dreamworld—one where encyclopedia salesmen beckoned toward caskets. She forced herself the few feet to the end of the building, where she could see along the farthest aisle.

Despite the chill, she was sweating. She expected to see almost anything. What she saw was slanting gloom. Nothing. No corpse. No bones. No lurking assailant. Nothing.

For a moment relief paralyzed her. Then, as her eyes became accustomed to the dimness, she saw something she had not noticed at first. Caught on a metal nameplate was a bit of ribbon.

Somebody had been here. That ribbon . . . It looked like the one tied around the child's pigtail.

A sound began faintly, as if seeping from the walls, as if as much a part of the place as the damp odor of death. It was the far-off whimpering of a child. As if somewhere in these stacked graves a child had been caught halfway between earth and hell.

Moments later Hana found herself outside, even though she didn't remember how she had gotten there. She paused, steadying herself with a hand on the blank gray sides of the mausoleum.

Beyond the trees, an earthly voice called her name.

Forcing herself to walk, not run, she moved toward the path leading to the lower portions of the cemetery. The mausoleum with its open door was behind a screen of trees when she met Sergeant Kochen and Mr. Fred. She paused as they hurried to her.

"Are you all right?" the sergeant asked, his eyes on her face.

Hana wondered if she looked as if she had heard a ghost.

"We were worried when you ran away during the prayer," Mr. Fred said with one of his sighs. "It wasn't like you."

What he meant was, it was not good for the Shaner public image, which, like the house and digging, Mr. Fred considered to be under his guardianship.

"I was overcome with grief and felt I had to be alone for a few minutes," Hana said breathlessly. "I'm all right now."

She swept past them before Sergeant Kochen could ask more questions, which he was obviously about to do. There was a thought in her mind: Tell the police, have them search the mausoleum. But if what she had heard was a cry for help from . . . wherever, whoever . . . it was sent to her alone. The child had been sent to her, too, and only disappeared when she was about to turn it over to the police. If she ever got her hands on that girl again, she would keep her own counsel as she was keeping it now. No police.

"Just a moment, Ms. Shaner," Sergeant Kochen called after her.

A man with a motorized camera leaped from behind a bush and took a series of fast pictures. Another joined him, asking loud questions about Grace. Mr. Fred and the sergeant came up. Other police arrived, struggling with surging TV people. Even Pocky Reilly had joined the mob.

They rolled down the hill together, where the curious roamed over graves, and especially about the canopy, where representatives from the funeral home were trying to quickly finish the proceedings. The service was over. The Reverend Bowles-Richards and her cloak had already gone. Elsie fought her way to Hana and put a protective arm about her.

She said it aloud. "You look like you've seen a ghost!"

Hana laughed. People looked shocked, especially Sal, who had come over to them indignantly accusing everybody of a lack of respect for God and the dead. Hana was still laughing as they bundled her into a car while more photographs were taken and some of the curious began demolishing the canopy over the grave and trampling flowers, some of which were always sent despite a request for donations.

As they drove away, she looked back in time to see one of the funeral directors knocked down as he tried to defend a spray of silk carnations.

Chapter Seventeen

MR. FRED AND Sal had arranged for a simple lunch at Blue Spring Hill after the service. Sergeant Kochen and his assistant, uninvited, showed up, the sergeant refusing to be deterred from his announced suspicion that Hana had a prearranged meeting with somebody in the cemetery. Elsie stationed herself nearby as Hana repeated her story of running away because she had been overcome by grief. Facing the enemy, Elsie then demanded to know, for heaven's sake, what Hana could possibly have seen in that old cemetery. Were they perhaps looking for ghosts on such a beautiful day? She declared she thought the police had better things to do than harass a grief-stricken friend of the deceased on the very day of the funeral. Ghost and Crumb growled at them, glaring from the comforting shelter of Elsie's pleated skirt.

Friends from the funeral stood about the living room, forming a solid backup. One archaeology student held a shovel like a weapon, although Hana couldn't imagine why he had brought a shovel into the house unless he had unnatural designs on the potato salad. Mel Rosen then stepped forward and began talking legalese. Which he did so well, Hana thought. Sergeant Kochen and the assistant, both looking embarrassed, accepted coffee, sandwiches, and silence, soon slipping away to the police car waiting in the drive.

Despite the presence of students, the diggings were respectfully quiet today. Jimmy Klopp, rather mellow from Mr. Fred's sturdy punch, interrupted Elsie's relentless solicitude by hanging over Hana's chair while he reminisced about the summer picnic and how Grace had drunk his wine. He seemed about to cry. Hana left him to Elsie and joined Bill Longenecker, who was offering his own remembrances of Grace, tactfully not mentioning his desire to rent her apartment for a tour. Mary Hafer and other women from Shaner Industries were telling anecdotes of Grace in the office. Hafer recalled something Grace had said one time that she did not understand: "I do my best living in the parentheses of life."

Hana discussed possible meanings with them, trying to keep her mind on these people and their needs. She could not let herself think about the mausoleum and the horrible sound of the child's crying. She told them about the time, during a visit to Blue Spring Hill when Kitty Fisher and Penelope Baskin were doing their early-summer molting, that Grace had said, "Hana, your home is held together with cat hair." And in describing a saleswoman who visited the office at times, Grace once said, "She thought a hot meal was toast."

Then Hana eased herself out of the group. She spoke politely to more people, but words felt dry in her mouth. She excused herself, left the room, and crossed the hall to the snuggery, her own special place downstairs where she often watched TV or read or contemplated the gardens from the window.

She was sitting with her hands over her face when someone came into the small room. Through her fingers she saw Mel Rosen.

Hana let her hands drop to her lap. "Hello, Mel."

"I was concerned about you."

"I just needed to be by myself for a couple of minutes."

"Want me to go?" he asked as he sat in the chair beside hers.

Hana smiled faintly. "And if I said yes?"

"I'd go, of course. But not right away. I thought we'd better talk."

"About what?"

"What you didn't want to tell the police."

"You're imagining things."

"Uh-uh. I always know when a witness isn't telling the whole truth. Hana, if it's about this child you found in the apartment—"

"She disappeared. You know she disappeared."

He studied her. "Let me give you some good advice. No charge. If you have any information about a missing child, give it to the authorities. There's a lot of publicity about kids in trouble, and kidnapping is a very serious crime."

Impatiently, Hana waved away his warning. "Mel, how am I going to find her again?"

"Contact your private detective agency—"

"Assholes."

"Oh, come now. Dozens of corporations use their services. They have the finest modern computerized equipment—"

"I don't need modern equipment! I need something more personal. Would I be breaking any laws if I advertise for information about the girl?"

"No, but if you get any, you must pass it along to the proper authorities."

"Of course," Hana promised.

"I mean it."

"I know you do." She rose. "I'm sorry, Mel, but I have to get back to my guests."

He got up and wordlessly put his arms around

her. It felt good. She wanted to lean against him, wanted to draw strength from his support.

"It's okay," he said. "This is just sympathy."

"Mel . . . sometime, when this is over, we've got to talk."

"Yes," he said. "I know."

He held her for another second before they left the room together.

The lunch and punch, the condolences, the talk of Grace as dead and past seemed to go on for hours. But as her guests dribbled away, Hana noticed it was only two o'clock. She was sure Elsie would linger, but even that staunch supporter apparently had other things on her mind and hurried away with the rest. Hana went to her room, leaving Mr. Fred to attend to the last of the lingering students.

She did not know why she was so reluctant to touch the picture of the girl. Except that it was something private and almost awful, not to be shared. She forced herself to get it out of her bag, to hold it in her hand, to look at it. To remember what the encyclopedia had said about children and death. If the apartment child was a real living girl and had been kept in that horrible mausoleum—and Hana decided she had to accept the premise of her reality, because madness lay in the other direction—then a real, logical effort to find the girl in this most real world was necessary. She studied the photograph again, especially the eyes. Like dead eyes. Dazed? Drugged?

Wrong. It was all wrong. Something awful had been done to that child.

Hana sat at her desk, composed an ad that offered a reward, listed the Shaner Industries phone number, then called the newspaper office.

Chapter Eighteen

IT WAS A good, attention-getting ad. Too much so, according to Mel Rosen, who called first thing to warn her what was going to happen.

It did.

The switchboard at Shaner Industries took hundreds of calls from people who thought they had seen the girl. Sergeant Kochen phoned demanding to know where Hana had gotten the picture she had used in the ad. She told him she had taken it herself. He wanted to know why she hadn't shown it to him. Hana claimed to have forgotten all about it. After a moment of silence, Kochen groaned. His assistant came around to collect the photograph.

In the end Hana was forced to follow Mel's advice and turn over the mountain of phone data to the police, who began the routine, monotonous task of running down leads and checking the girl's picture against their files of missing children. Reporters from tabloids began sensational speculation about the identity of the father of Grace Urich's "daughter." This speculation ranged from Mel Rosen (horrified) to Bill Longenecker (all publicity is good because it sells tours), to Mr. Fred (pleased and smug), to Jimmy Klopp (hysterical), to the ghost of the Revolutionary War soldier dug up from the lawn (reaction unknown).

It was a full week before things began to cool down.

Each day Hana went to the office. She helped Pocky Reilly get the new commercial ready for national distribution, but otherwise kept a low profile. At lunchtime Cindy Hefflefinger brought salads for her to eat in the privacy of her office. Hana had not returned to the apartment.

Every day she checked with Sergeant Kochen, but no real leads had developed as a result of the ad. Impatiently he promised to inform her immediately if they had any luck. He doubted they would. Hana's life spun back into the ordinary patterns she had known before Grace's disappearance. Maybe this was the end of the trail.

Elsie showed up to share Sal's Friday-evening soufflé. Trouble had shared it, too, jumping onto the table and grabbing a mouthful from Elsie's plate.

"You'll never train that miserable cat," Elsie had grumbled.

It was a good thing Trouble didn't like coffee, Hana thought as they set theirs on the low coffee table in the snuggery. This room she kept informal, comfortable, unhistorical. A place to curl up and weep for one's sins.

Abruptly Elsie turned the conversation to what was on her mind. "Bill and I are going ahead with this crime tour."

Hana sighed. This was just what she needed.

"Whether or not you rent her apartment to us," she added.

"Well, I'm *not* renting it to you. There's been enough publicity."

"And whose fault is that?" Elsie snapped.

She was being unusually tiresome tonight.

"I did what I had to do."

"Didn't get you far, did it? Anyhow," she went on quickly, avoiding Hana's eyes, "that alley and the gift shop are public property. You can't keep us from walking there and looking at the place from the outside. Actually we don't need an inside tour. We've got this house in the country—tourists love to get out in the country—where two children were murdered by the mother's live-in boyfriend. They can't find tenants—people say it's haunted by the little children. Perfect for us."

Elsie left soon after that. Trouble slunk in and stood looking at her. He had an Egyptian face, she decided.

"You must stop jumping on the table," she told him, then patted the couch beside her.

He sat on his haunches, weighing the invitation.

"You're a house cat now, and you must begin acting like one," she told him. He twitched his tail. "Where are the others?"

He almost smiled.

"Did you chase them upstairs again? You are a bad boy."

The telephone rang.

Hana picked it up, hoping it wasn't Elsie, calling to make one more pitch for the apartment.

The voice was low, muffled, but she thought it was a woman's.

"Couldn't call before. Too much noise about that ad in the paper."

"Who is this?"

"You want the girl?"

"Yes! Of course."

"Then come get her."

"Where?" There was silence on the other end. Hana gripped the phone more tightly. *"Where?"*

The voice sounded farther away, as if a bad connection was fading. "You know where."

"How should I? . . . Is the child all right?"

"You know where. You were there the day of the funeral."

"The cemetery? Oh, God. You mean the mausoleum?"

"Two-thirty A.M. Come alone. They're all around and they're watching, but I think it'll be safe then. Nobody would suspect you'd be coming here at that time of night. Be careful you're not followed, or I'll have to take her away again."

"Grace? There's something about your voice . . . Grace, is that you?"

The woman hung up.

The last of daylight had faded now, leaving the room twilight-dark. Hana dropped the phone into place and sat very still. Trouble jumped up beside her with loud, impudent purring. Absently Hana patted his head, suddenly finding great comfort in the fact that it was only eight o'clock. She was well fed, comfortable here in her favorite room. There were hours and hours before two-thirty. Hours in which to decide not to go. Because, of course, that was the only sensible decision. Suppose this was all a plot to get at her? If she were kidnapped or murdered, Shaner Carpets could lose millions of dollars.

It had been more than a week since she had heard the sound of the child crying in the mausoleum, but she couldn't erase that whimpering from her mind. She could almost hear it now. Which was ridiculous. Perhaps she had never really heard it. She reached up to turn on a light.

Mel Rosen. She could call Mel. He said he would do whatever he could. But would he do this for her? Would his legal mind balk at trespassing in the cemetery at two-thirty A.M.? Mel would want to call the police. Then what about Bill? He wouldn't be as good, but he would do it. And use the site for his next stupid tour.

The woman on the phone—well, if it was a woman—had insisted "they" were watching. Whoever "they" were. Maybe Sergeant Kochen knew and wasn't telling her. Maybe he thought she'd be frightened.

And maybe he was right.

She thought of the child again as she had looked sitting in the chair in the apartment. So remote, so . . . hurt.

Suppose she really was Grace Urich's daughter? Suppose . . . well, somebody was trying to save her from whatever or whoever had killed Grace? Suppose the child was in danger? Suppose Hana didn't go and the girl would be found dead in that horrible place?

She actually put her hand on the phone to call Kochen. To have the cemetery surrounded by police. And then . . .

. . . the person who called wouldn't bring her. Because that person was watching as well as those other whoevers. Two sides and she herself somewhere in the middle. Perhaps the person, woman or soft-spoken man, wasn't even one of the Good Guys.

Perhaps Grace hadn't been a Good Guy.

She turned on the TV so its flicker of light could be seen in the room. She tried to take her mind off the hours between now and two o'clock. She couldn't concentrate. She muted the sound, staring at the flickering images.

For every ten times she decided she would go, there were five she decided not to. The fact that it was becoming overbalanced on the side of going frightened her. Kitty Fisher and Penelope Baskin came into the room, suspiciously eyeing Trouble. He sat up to stare at them. When he made no overt move, they finally lay down and rolled with their bellies up. Good body language. Trouble glanced away, pretending he hadn't noticed.

If only people would roll over like that. Then one would know they weren't going to do something ghastly.

Ghost and Crumb took Mr. Fred along for their evening walk. When they returned they sent him to his quarters while they joined the cats in the TV room. Trouble decided he'd fraternized enough and stalked off in the direction of the 1812 Annex.

At midnight Hana switched off the TV and went upstairs to bed. The house lay quiet. A day was ending with familiarity. All she had to do was go to sleep, pretend the phone call had never come. Who would blame her? Sergeant Kochen and Mel Rosen would probably tell her she had made a wise decision.

At one o'clock Hana turned out the lights in her bedroom and put on dark slacks and a black turtleneck sweater.

No way did this mean she was going. Or if she was, she would call Mel at the last minute and get him out of bed.

Didn't matter. She knew she wasn't going to call anybody.

At two o'clock she went into the hall, where she paused, listening. There were night lights throughout the house. Of course, she would have to turn off the alarm system to get out. Risky. Maybe that was what "they" wanted her to do. Maybe somebody wanted to get inside to steal Mr. Fred's old bones.

Oh, now she was getting hysterical.

Taking deep breaths, she padded quietly

through her house. Then she became aware someone was padding after her. She stopped in panic. But it was Crumb, awake and prowling. He growled apprehensively at her reaction.

"Shh!"

By the time Hana was in her car, passing the dark azaleas, she knew she had gone too far to turn back. Of course, she *could* turn back. But she wouldn't. And if this was it—if something happened to her . . .

Well, it had been a good life. She'd had the money to do what she wanted. She had done some worthwhile things, helped the helpless, people and animals. She had traveled, lived well. A long time ago she had even met Mel Rosen.

For some stupid reason, Hana wanted to cry.

Chapter Nineteen

FOR A LONG time she passed no other vehicles on the country road winding through somber, deserted countryside. In the city a few trucks, then a number of cars, hurried by. Nobody seemed to be paying any attention to her.

Her first bad moment came when she reached the cemetery. In recent years the high spiked-iron gate had been padlocked every night. She got out of the car, leaving its door open, to find that the gate swung quietly at a light touch.

So she could have been stopped there, but she wasn't. Recent days had been October-perfect with a harvest moon that rose red every night then paled to gold and finally bright silver as it moved across the sky. It was the kind of moon that made Hana recall night pictures of corn shocks and pumpkins that had appeared on Aunt Sissy's calendars each fall. It made her think of Aunt Sissy, buried now in this cemetery.

She slid quickly into her car again, locked the door, then drove slowly into God's Large Acres. This hill had been designated as a public burial ground in 1800, when it was outside of town. The wealthy Schoener matriarch who had donated the land had modestly refused to have her name on it. She had declared it was not, after all, her name but had been acquired at marriage. So it had become known as the Mount Conover Cemetery. And ever since those days the rich and poor had lain down together on these hallowed grounds.

Hana had never before visited it at night. There was a different feel. Leaves turned white in the moonlight as they lay on the silvered grass. Angel arms reaching toward branches seemed to move in the uncertain gloom. Above all was the stillness. She passed the family plot where Grace Urich newly lay with generations of Schoeners who had buried their fears and prides. Women in childbirth. One suicide. Even a murderer who had been driven to desperation by a faithless wife in 1895. But mostly they had been sensible people who had lived good lives and died decent deaths —like her father and Aunt Sissy—and would, she felt sure, be horrified to find their descendant driving past their graves at 2:20 in the morning.

The path to the mausoleum was shorter than the winding road, but Hana had no intention of stopping and walking up the hill. It was only now that she realized she would have to park on the road and cross about thirty yards of grass and graves to the building.

What the hell was she doing out here by herself in the middle of the night?

But she drove on, knowing there was no answer to the question. She saw it as she came around a clump of boxwood beside the road. Remote and gray by day, by night it was starkly unreal. A house of the dead, designed with columns like some deserted southern mansion. Stained-glass windows looked dark, uncolored. The door was around the other side.

Hana pulled up as close as possible before turning off her motor. A few late crickets hummed a death song. She saw now why the grass appeared to be silver. Frost. Which meant her footprints would show. And the footprints of others. She squinted but saw none. Of course, there was the footpath beyond.

She sat still for a while, carefully looking in every direction. No sign of life or movement anywhere. But enough monuments, trees, and bushes to hide a very large cast. She gave most of her scrutiny to the mausoleum itself. For a good five minutes she stared at the window. There was no flicker of light that she could see.

She glanced at her watch.

Well . . .

No use postponing it any longer.

She opened the glove compartment, got out her flashlight and her can of Mace, and left the car.

Outside she was surprised how calm she felt. It was like the first TV commercial she had made. Once you make up your mind and go forward a kind of fatalism takes over.

Cold grass crackled beneath her feet, echoing,

almost as if she were being closely followed. She whirled. Nothing. Giving the building a wide berth, she came around to the front.

Of all the sights she had seen in her four decades of life, the one she saw now was the most awesome. The door of the mausoleum stood open. Before it, immobile as a statue, was the child, alone, her white dress limp, hair no longer confined in pigtails but fanning about her shoulders. A shawl hung on thin shoulders, inadequate protection against the chill. In her hands she held a doll. This time there was no suitcase. For one second Hana stared, unable to assimilate the sight. She did not know what might be beyond the girl in the dark mausoleum.

"Come here," Hana said.

Slowly the child turned her head. For moments she did not move, then, like a sleepwalker, she came toward Hana.

Hana ran forward, grabbed the girl's hand, and pulled her across the lawn toward the car. They had almost reached it when lights suddenly illuminated them. On another winding cemetery lane a car roared into life and started forward with a screech of tires.

Dragging the girl the last few feet, Hana jerked open the door of the car, shoved the child inside, fell in beside her, and locked the doors with her automatic switch. She fumbled, then found the key in her slacks pocket and managed to get the motor started. The other car was almost on them now, tearing out of the lane.

A number of shots were fired before Hana realized what was happening.

"Get down on the floor!" she cried as she

stepped on the accelerator. The Chrysler leaped forward.

As the other car careened in front of her, blocking the road, another shot was fired, this one penetrating the windshield on the passenger side. She could see the vehicle clearly now—a dark van with darker windows.

Hana spun her steering wheel, slid in a circle, and took off in the direction she had come. Frantically she tried to think; she knew this cemetery, and maybe they didn't. There was an area where she and Aunt Sissy used to walk on the way to the gazebo. Civil War soldiers—marked with granite squares low to the ground. If she had enough speed she could drive right across those graves toward the main entrance.

The child lay crumpled on the floor. Hana wondered if a bullet had gotten her. She could be dead, wounded, but there was no time to find out. Hana took curves as fast as she dared, skirting tombstones. The van was behind her again. She turned on her own headlights. No need for secrecy now. Near the top of another slope she plowed onto the Civil War graves, bumping over them toward the wider entrance road used by hearses.

To her horror, the van followed.

But now her mind was clicking as efficiently as when tackling carpet problems. Ahead, at the edge of the Civil War plot, loomed two ornate Victorian monuments, one an obelisk with stone drapery, the other a steeple carved with lilies and roses. Hana judged the space between the two was just wide enough for her car.

She put on a burst of speed. The van was gaining now. She took a breath and pulled in her stomach as if that would help, then plunged through the opening between the monuments. There was a slight crunch and shudder as the side mirror lopped off a stone lily. Then she was free, speeding toward the entrance.

Behind, she heard a crash, then yelling. Chancing a look in the rearview mirror, she saw stone drapery all over the front of the van. A tall figure sprang from the dark interior of it. Fire flashed as shots were fired after her. Breathing heavily, she concentrated on driving.

The iron gate.

Oh, God. What if they'd closed it? But they had not, and she sped through, tires screaming as she swung onto the main road. Through city and suburbs she drove, turning corners, going around blocks, always looking in the rearview mirror. Every car she saw she was afraid would be an enemy with guns.

"Are you all right?" she asked the child.

Without replying, the girl crawled onto the seat and leaned back wearily.

Hana knew how she felt. She herself wanted to crawl into a hole and sleep for a week. She wanted to go home. To Blue Spring Hill, where she was safe. Or would she be safe there? The alarm system was off. What a fool she'd been not to alert Mr. Fred. She wondered if she had been followed from there. She hadn't thought so, but today there were very sophisticated ways of tailing people; her own detectives used some of them. If these whoevers wanted the girl badly enough, they might be waiting at Blue Spring Hill.

To find a motel at this time of night would be almost impossible and also attention-getting. She could go to Elsie's place or to Mel Rosen—but they would want explanations.

In the end, she decided to go home. It seemed as sensible a course as any, and . . . damn it, it was where she wanted to go. She glanced at the girl, who was still, her head rolling with the movement of the car. Her doll lay sprawled on the floor where she had dropped it. An expensive Amish doll. Somebody had tried to reach this child with an expensive Amish doll.

Hana drove more slowly now, on a straight course for home, but she continued to monitor the rearview mirror. She nearly panicked when a car seemed to follow for a mile, but then it stopped in front of a house with the porch light still on and a man got out to stagger uncertainly toward the front door.

On this country road through farmland and woods there was nothing. Closer to Blue Spring Hill she looked for shadowy figures in parked cars, even though everything seemed peaceful, normal. Still wary, she turned into her own drive. Was it possible they had followed whoever brought the child to the cemetery? That they knew nothing about her? No, she decided, that wasn't possible.

Finally they were parked in her familiar space. She took the precaution to look carefully about as she had in the cemetery, although a precious lot of good it had done her there. When she was satisfied there was nothing more she could do, she lightly shook the girl's shoulder. The child grumbled, stirred, but didn't open her eyes.

Hana got out of the car and came around to the passenger's side. Nothing happened, but she still felt spooked. She lifted the girl, which proved more difficult than she had imagined. An eight-year-old was all arms and legs, she thought as she staggered to the house. It was awkward getting out her key, then stumbling through the door. The kid was slipping as Hana raced to a chair where she dropped her. She reset the alarm immediately. When she returned the girl was awake, looking about as though dazed. Hana realized then she had left the doll in the car. She hoped she wouldn't have to go back outside for it. Well, she certainly wasn't going to mention it unless the kid did.

"Come," Hana whispered.

The child got up by herself. Hana put an arm around the thin shoulders as they went upstairs. At the door to Hana's room Penelope Baskin and Kitty Fisher appeared, apparently on nighttime patrol.

Hana felt the child stiffen as she stared at the cats. She introduced them as family friends. The girl stood rigid. Penelope Baskin padded forward to sniff her shoes. The child whimpered.

Hana no longer wanted to think or deal with anything.

"You're tired . . . so come on inside. Kitty Fisher. Penelope Baskin. You go on patrolling."

She pulled the child into the room, shutting the door on the cats, who protested the violation of their personal rights.

"You can get acquainted with the house animals tomorrow. They're good cats. You'll like them when you get to know them."

Wide eyes surveyed her doubtfully.

"We'll also get you some new clothes and find a special room for you here," Hana went on. "For tonight you'll sleep with me."

She rummaged in a drawer until she located a T-shirt, which she tossed to the girl, then pointed her in the direction of the bathroom. The child went in and closed the door. Hana listened until she heard water running. At least she knew how to use a bathroom. Was she retarded, either emotionally or mentally? Or deprived? Certainly she had never been close to cats before, and Hana considered that definite deprivation.

Hana crawled out of her clothing, leaving the items where they fell. She put on her flannel pajamas and sat on the bed, wishing the kid would hurry. Kid. Girl. Child. Did she have a name?

Finally the door opened and her guest came out, looking incongruous in the oversized T-shirt that hung on her like a sack. Hana sighed.

"Listen to me—I've got to call you something. I know you're not much of a talker, but I can't say 'Hey, you' all the time, now can I? Will you please tell me your name?"

It was a whisper, low, almost lost in the silent, sleeping house.

"Grace. My name's Grace."

Chapter Twenty

HANA AWOKE EARLY. In fetal position, the girl—Grace—still slept. Moving slowly, Hana crawled out of bed. She felt stiff, as if she had done unaccustomed exercises. And there was a lot to do today.

Yawning, she put on a robe and slipped away to the kitchen, where Mr. Fred and Sal were having breakfast. The dogs had gone outside, but Penelope Baskin and Kitty Fisher lay on the hearth, indignantly ignoring Hana. Trouble sat on the table, waiting for a chance to grab Mr. Fred's scrambled eggs. Tersely, Hana explained about the child.

"That's worse than this cat you dragged home," Mr. Fred growled, lifting Trouble and dropping him to the floor.

Hana told them what she wanted done. There were two sunny rooms on the top floor, one of which had been used, generations ago, as a school. The other was a wide-windowed bedroom facing trees and the slope of the hill, unseen from the front of the estate. These rooms were part of the 1812 Annex and could only be reached by a private hall, easily secured.

Mr. Fred was sent to ready the rooms, with Trouble slinking after him. Sal was dispatched to the mall to buy clothing. She had been given a peek at the still-sleeping child to determine size.

"Do the best you can," Hana told her.

Sal sniffed. "Why, sure I can get stuff to fit her, all right. Haven't I been buying clothes for my sisters and brothers for years now?" She paused at the door. "I think I've seen her picture on milk boxes."

"The police checked all that and couldn't find anything," Hana assured her.

Sal sniffed again.

After breakfast Hana called the office, talked to Jimmy Klopp and Cindy Hefflefinger, and decided the business could survive her absence. Next she phoned Mel Rosen. This was much harder than the other call. Despite the fact that she didn't tell him how she had gotten the child, he hit the ceiling and advised her to contact the police immediately. It was some time before she could even get him to listen to her plan. When he heard it, he exploded again.

"Please, Mel," Hana begged. "People know I have this girl. She's in danger."

"You're probably right about that, but why should I put one of my girls in danger?"

"I wouldn't ask if I thought she'd get hurt. You'd be with her all the time. And I'll hire bodyguards to go with you. As many as you want. From what I've heard, that's one thing the detective agency is really good at—guarding people. It'll be broad daylight and—"

"Let the authorities handle it, Hana!"

"No! I'll tell them. I promise—but later. I don't want to lose her again. Give me a chance, Mel. I want to buy time, and this is the only way I can think of. Will you at least consider the matter and call me back?"

She hung up before he could reply. It was half an hour before he did call back. During that time Hana had the girl up and fed and sitting forlornly in the snuggery as if waiting for someone. The doll had been brought from the car, but, much to Hana's disappointment, even that failed to spark her interest.

"I made the mistake," Mel growled, "of mentioning this to Robin."

Hana held her breath. She had often met Mel's daughters, but she was not on intimate terms with them, which worried her when she considered further involvement with Mel Rosen. Robin, the oldest, had seemed to be particularly headstrong and spoiled.

"She wants to do it," he went on. "And I don't

suppose there's any real danger in it." He interrupted her grateful mutterings. "But I want four bodyguards. You got that, Hana? Four. At least one of them must be a woman."

"Agreed," Hana said meekly.

"I'll contact the agency myself," he snapped. "Since I'm better at dealing with them than you are."

Hana was only too glad to let him make all arrangements. He told her they'd be there at noon.

Sal returned with shopping bags full of uninspiring—what Aunt Sissy always referred to as "serviceable"—children's clothing. They unwrapped them in the upper rooms, which Mr. Fred had outfitted especially for the girl.

"It's a shame to use this antique school furniture," he fretted. "I do hope she's not a rough, energetic child."

They added a small table and a few oak chairs. The bed had been made; the new clothing was spread out on it. The doll was put in a place of honor. Stoically the girl watched the activity.

"What's the matter with her?" Sal asked in a low voice. "Doesn't she like what I got?"

"It's just her way," Hana whispered.

"Something's the matter with her, isn't it?"

"I don't know," Hana admitted. "I'm going to have the doctor check her out."

"Best do it pretty quick," Sal muttered.

Hana sent Sal and Mr. Fred below to wait for Mel Rosen. Then she sat on the bed to observe the child, who was seated on a small chair, her hands in her lap.

"I'm going to have difficulty calling you Grace," Hana told her. "I had a good friend named Grace. Did you know that? Did you know her?"

The girl stared at the floor.

"Isn't there anything else I can call you? A nickname, maybe? What did people call you where you lived before?"

Questions were definitely not the way to get through to this kid.

"Okay," Hana said briskly. "If you won't give me a name and I cannot call you Grace, I guess I'll have to make up something. How about . . . um, your hair is very light, so how about Sandy?"

The eyes looked at her with a shadow of resentment.

"You don't want to be called Sandy? Very well. But you have to tell me what you do want to be called, or Sandy it is going to be. Got that?"

The eyes dropped.

Hana said, "Sandy, do you know people were shooting at us last night? People in a van. Did you ever see that van before?"

"Honey!"

It was the loudest, most definite thing she had ever said.

". . . Honey? She called you Honey?"

Sullenly the girl nodded.

"All right, Honey. Do you realize we were in danger last night? There are bad people after you —us. We—you and I—could be hurt."

The girl nodded again, and this time she sighed. No, she was not retarded. Something else.

"Then you understand why we fixed these rooms for you. You're going to have to stay up here until it's safe and we have those people out of your way. Sometimes you'll be alone, but we just can't help that. We'll do the best we can. Do you understand what I'm saying?"

Another nod.

"The cats would be glad to keep you company. They like to prowl about the upper rooms here."

A violent shaking of her head.

"I have dogs, too. Would you rather have dogs for company?"

Again a shaking of the head.

"Honey, haven't you ever been around animals?"

That received no answer at all.

"The other places you lived. They had no pets?" Nothing. "Okay, let's talk about something else. Guns . . . shooting. Have you ever been shot at before?"

Body language. Cats had it. People, too. Honey did not respond verbally, but Hana was sure she saw signs of fear in the way the girl pulled back into her chair. Instead of probing further, Hana pointed out books and toys, crayons, papers, pencils. Then she went downstairs to spend the next twenty minutes thoroughly going over the clothing Honey had worn. She found nothing significant.

Mel Rosen drove up. With him were two men who looked like wrestlers and two equally competent-looking women. Mr. Fred and Sal hurried out to meet this unusual group and, under the cover of their bustle, Robin Rosen, who had been sitting on the floor of the car, was bundled into the house.

Mel was still complaining, but Robin, who was a progressive nine-year-old, insisted it was fun. The men remained outside the room, but the two women guards came inside while Robin was dressed in the limp white garment Honey had worn the night before. The shawl was draped over her head and shoulders.

"That's a woman's, not a child's," Mel said when he saw it.

Hana nodded. "I'm glad it's big so I can cover her hair. Robin's is too short and curly, and I have a feeling somebody's going to be watching even if we don't see them."

"You mean I've got to wear this dumb thing over my head all day?" Robin demanded.

"I'm afraid so," her father told her. "Unless you don't want to do this. You certainly don't have to, you know."

"I want to," Robin pouted. "It's like on TV. Kids always get to do stuff like this on TV."

Mel grumbled something about the influence of various forms of media upon impressionable youth, but he agreed when asked if he was ready. Sal and Mr. Fred waved good-bye. Hana, holding Robin's hand, led her to the car followed by the silent but alert quartet. Morosely Mel slid into the driver's seat.

"Don't look around," Hana cautioned Robin. "Just stare straight ahead, as if you're in a trance. Do you know what I mean?"

"Sure!"

Robin stifled a giggle, opened her eyes wide, and gave her impression of a zombie. The two women helped her into the backseat. Hana crowded in with them.

"Don't drive fast," she instructed Mel. "We want them to see us."

"Them? Them? What 'them'?" he demanded irritably.

The thems who acted on malls, then climbed into vans to shoot at people in graveyards in the dead of night. But she had not told Mel about the shooting.

They drove to the airport just in time for the group to catch the commuter flight to Philadelphia. The plan was simple. At Philadelphia International they were to lose themselves in the crowd. After this Mel would put on a different coat while Robin changed clothing completely in a rest room, stuffing Honey's things into a flight bag brought along for the purpose. They would then rent a car for the drive back to Conover. The bodyguards were professional enough, they hoped, to also vanish. Hana hoped the ruse would buy them time. Time to find out who the child was and what was to be done with her. Time to ensure her safety.

As she drove Mel's car back to Blue Spring Hill, Hana couldn't get the episode in the cemetery out of her mind. Why hadn't they grabbed the child before Hana arrived? Assuming, of course, that it was the child they wanted and they were not the ones who brought her.

She looked forward to the peace of Blue Spring Hill, but Sal was waiting to pounce when she got there.

"That girl is not normal. Maybe I never had kids of my own, but I've helped raise half my family and neighbors, too. And I never once saw anything like this."

"What's she done?"

Sal pursed her lips as she swiped at a perfectly clean hall table with her perfectly clean apron. "Done? She doesn't do anything. If I didn't see her move once in a while, I'd think she was dead."

Chapter Twenty-one

MEL AND HIS daughter returned home without incident. He had the kindness of heart not to dwell on the fact that he obviously considered the entire exercise a waste of his valuable time. But Hana was sure the time had not been wasted, because Blue Spring Hill remained outwardly calm, unmolested.

She knew the old house had a spirit of its own, composed of the compressed memories of the lives that had been lived within its walls. Now the feeling was intensified. She was sure even Mr. Fred and Sal felt it, because they were restless, out of humor. Like interference on a TV channel, the vibes in the house flickered and jumped.

In a strange way, everybody was aware of a presence overhead. Of empty rooms now occupied. Whenever Hana climbed the stairs, she did so with dread. She had a sense of waiting, and didn't know what she was waiting for. She, too, was irritable.

She returned to spend an entire day at Grace Urich's apartment. But no message came.

One day Sal, carrying Trouble, passed Hana in the hall and said, "She might have some awful disease. Heaven knows where she's been or what they've been doing to her. If *I* had my say, I'd make sure she saw a doctor right off. You did say you were going to do that, you know."

"All right, I will," Hana agreed with rather poor grace. "Where are you going with that cat?"

"To the kitchen, and I'm closing the door. He was kneading on the eighteenth-century carpet in the Lafayette room. If *I* had anything to say about him, he'd be declawed."

"I don't believe in declawing. It's not humane."

Sal stomped off.

Hana knew Sal was right about Honey. She'd been putting it off because she wasn't sure how Dr. Reifsnyder would react. When she called him in the afternoon that reaction was decidedly hostile. She was forced to remind him that her father had made it possible for him to attend medical school, that he was, after all, an old family friend. He obviously did not like to be reminded of these matters, but he arrived for a house call in his sleek Mercedes.

Harold Reifsnyder was a large man, well dressed, accustomed to authority and prosperity. He disliked having his comfortable routine upset by unorthodox happenings. Otherwise, he was fond of declaring, he would have specialized in obstetrics.

"I'm going to have to report this call to the police," he said pompously as he followed Hana up the stairs.

"Now, Uncle Harold," Hana said glibly, using his honorary title from her childhood. "I took the girl to the police when I first found her, and they have no record of her as a missing child."

"Then they know she's here and are still looking into the matter?"

"Uh-huh."

"Why is this mongrel following me?" he demanded. "I don't want it in the room while I'm examining the child."

Ghost, who had been padding after them, stopped indignantly.

"Go downstairs," Hana ordered.

The dog displayed his teeth in a silent snarl

aimed at the physician, then with a toss of his head obeyed.

"I have never understood your obsession with animals, Hannah Elizabeth Clara."

Fortunately the day was sunny, making the attic bright and cheerful. It didn't seem as bad to have a child locked inside rooms dazzling with light. Hana introduced the doctor. She had no idea what Honey's reaction would be.

It was as usual. Aloof, vague.

Hana left them alone at Dr. Reifsnyder's insistence and returned downstairs, where Ghost was moodily waiting for her.

"He doesn't understand that you're only human," Hana told him.

He yawned, then his sharp ears picked up a sound from the kitchen and he galloped off in that direction.

It was over half an hour before the doctor came down again. He sounded puzzled as he said, "Well, I cannot find anything wrong with her. Of course, I haven't taken a lot of tests, you understand. She'd have to go to the hospital for that."

"Is that what you're recommending?"

He hesitated. "I think not. Unless there are symptoms you haven't told me about." Hana shook her head. "I did a few simple things like testing her reflexes. Tried talking to her. Very withdrawn. I would recommend seeing a child therapist. Something's certainly wrong, although I doubt it's physical."

Hana was anxious to get rid of him, but he lingered, even had a glass of sherry. He insisted upon giving her names of therapists and asked to be kept informed. He knew about Grace Urich and allowed himself some curiosity. Hana satisfied as little of it as possible. When he finally did leave, his parting shot was "You know, of course, your father and your dear aunt would have been appalled at your bringing that unknown child into this house."

After Hana had firmly closed the door behind him, she went to the kitchen to report to Sal, who was busily scalloping potatoes. Sal was glad to hear no fatal disease had invaded Blue Spring Hill. She had built a small atmospheric fire in the walk-in fireplace. Ghost, disappointed in potatoes, had curled up on a rag rug for a nap. Trouble, bribed into virtue with catnip, rolled drunkenly.

Hana picked up a wagging Crumb and returned upstairs.

Because of the girl's reaction, all animals had been kept out of her rooms. Mr. Fred had been attempting to reach Honey by reading aloud. Sal had brought crafts, along with sewing and knitting, at which she was a master. Hana herself had furnished games, old and new. Aloud they had admired the Amish doll and questioned her about it. Nothing had met with response. Honey listened passively to Mr. Fred but apparently made no attempt to read herself. She wouldn't even try Sal's contributions, nor would she play games.

She seemed to spend most of her time staring through the window at the trees. The other thing she did was work in coloring books, some of which had been among the desperate purchases Hana had made. Given a blank sheet of paper, she would not draw, but she would spend hours with crayons. She worked neatly, precisely, and very carefully.

She was coloring a picture of a princess in a tower when Hana and Crumb came into the room. She dropped her crayon. Her mouth opened as she stared at the dog.

Hana had decided this small, considerably loving animal was the best creature to try on Honey. "This is Crumb," she said, smiling. "He's very gentle. I know you can hear what I'm saying, and I'm telling you he won't hurt you. Honey, look at me."

She stood holding the dog. She waited. So did Crumb, although not quite so patiently. Finally the girl looked into Hana's face.

"That's better. Do you believe me when I tell you that Crumb won't hurt you?" No reply. "I'm going to put him down. But I won't let him come near you."

Carefully, Hana lowered the dog to the floor. He wagged his tail, sniffing curiously toward Honey. Hana ordered him to go to the door and lie down. He obeyed. She picked up the crayon and handed it to Honey, who did not resume coloring. Hana sat beside her on one of the little chairs.

She told Honey Crumb's story. Of how he had been abandoned along the roadside as a puppy by people who didn't care about helpless creatures. She explained how he had been found and taken to an animal shelter. She told about seeing his large mournful eyes staring at her from a cage. How she had brought him home.

At first Honey had turned to stare out the window as Hana talked, but finally she began to look at Crumb.

"There are both animals and children who get lost and need help. And sometimes they've been hurt like my cat Trouble I told you about. Then they must learn all over again to be like other animals and other children who have homes. Trouble's trying. Are you?"

Honey looked into her face for a moment, then down at her own folded hands. Hana rose and slowly moved across the room to Crumb. She petted him; he wagged his tail.

"Don't move, Crumb," she whispered, then said to Honey, "Show me you're trying. Get up and come toward Crumb. Just a few steps. I won't ask you to touch him. Maybe some other day you'd like to touch him."

Hana continued to pet the dog. Minutes passed. Her legs became cramped from her crouching position, especially the right one. Wow. She'd soon have to get up. But she held on. Crumb sighed, rested his head on his paws.

Honey slipped from her chair and stood. For what seemed ages as her legs throbbed, Hana smiled at the girl. Then Honey took a step forward. And another. She was looking at Crumb. She stopped. Hana struggled to her feet.

"Do you want to touch him?"

Honey shook her head.

"I'll bring him up tomorrow. Maybe then. Or maybe not. It's your choice, Honey."

For a moment a flicker of expression crossed the child's passive face. What? . . . Surprise? Had she never been given a choice about anything?

Each day Hana went up with Crumb and talked about animals to Honey. On the third day the girl lightly touched the dog with one hesitant finger. A moment of triumph! It meant she could be reached. But ever so slowly. That thought sobered Hana, who had felt like celebrating. How long would it take to learn where she had come from and who had brought her?

At least it was a start. Perhaps if she could be taken out to the Fur and Feather Refuge . . .

Mel had called a number of times to inquire how things were going. He even offered to bring Robin over as a playmate, but Hana refused. She had enough to cope with, she didn't need his disturbing presence and all the questions it raised. Anyway, one couldn't trust kids to keep their mouths shut, although Robin apparently had kept their secret of the airport trip. Hana began to hope more than ever that the ruse had worked. She even began to hope that she could smuggle Honey out to the animal refuge for further stimulation.

Chapter Twenty-two

IN AN EFFORT to appear normal, Hana had resumed her custom of eating lunch in her favorite tavern.

As with many buildings in Conover, the tavern had been restored without resorting to paneling or plastic. The suburb had grown up around it, but it still sat on its parking lot, about a mile from Shaner Carpets, like an eighteenth-century anachronism. It had a porch, wide windowsills, large fireplaces, and wooden flooring. Hana had advised her lawyers that if the old building ever came on the market again, she wanted to buy it.

Most days she carried work with her and ate alone in "her" booth at the end of the barroom next to one of the fireplaces. The present owners were proud of her patronage and saw to it that she wasn't disturbed.

Which was why she was surprised when someone slid into the booth to sit opposite her.

Carl Reid. Obviously they were not aware that he no longer worked for her.

"I want to talk to you."

Crunch. Her stomach. But it wasn't the broccoli cheese soup. She had known that somewhere, sometime she would be hearing from the other side. But she had hoped it wouldn't be this soon. Not until she had decided what to do about the child.

"I can't imagine what we have to talk about."

He smiled. Furtively.

"I think you do."

She put down her spoon. "Would you like me to call the bartender and have you thrown out of here?"

"No, no! Please. I was hoping— See, I really liked working for Shaner Industries. It was just . . . well, I went crazy over that woman. Like I was hypnotized or something. My family is not very understanding." His tongue flicked about, moistening dry lips. "I was hoping maybe you'd give me another chance. Oh, not in your office—I wouldn't expect that. But . . . somewhere."

Hana watched him speculatively. "What do you really want?"

"Why do you think they asked me to check up on Grace?" he asked miserably.

The waitress brought her open-face grilled Swiss and tomato and looked uncertainly at Carl.

"He's leaving," Hana told her. "You are leaving, aren't you, Carl?"

The waitress moved away.

Carl said, "I guess Grace never told you that she and I had a thing going for a while after she started working for you."

For a moment Hana felt uncertain. It seemed so unlikely, but—

"She didn't want anybody in the office to know. She thought it would be awkward. Gossip and all that. She was ambitious."

"Why are you telling me this?"

"So you understand how much I liked her." He leaned across the table. "Everybody at the funeral acted like I had the plague or something. But I had to pay my respects. I wish we hadn't split up. Then maybe I wouldn't have gotten myself in so much trouble. Please. Won't you give me another chance?"

His voice had a tone she couldn't quite place. Perfunctory . . . Yes, that was it. As if he expected a refusal.

Watching him carefully, Hana said, "I'll think about it."

Quick dismay crossed his face before he masked it.

"Well," he said. "Well, thanks. Grace . . . would have wanted it that way."

It really was too much. Hana nearly choked on a bite of sandwich.

He seemed in no hurry to go. She ate quietly, waiting. He spoke about Grace. Surprising how much he knew. As he rambled, he appeared to gain confidence.

"We used to sit and talk a lot. She always said I was easy to talk to. I think she needed somebody to talk to." He took a deep breath. "It used to seem odd to me . . . how often she'd talk about kids."

Hana was glad she had chosen that moment to look down at her plate. Because now he was the one watching her closely. Her secret was a secret no longer. But why send Carl Reid . . . ?

"So?" she asked carelessly.

He shrugged. "She must have really liked kids. Especially little girls."

He talked around the subject, not coming out and saying anything. Hana finished the single glass of white wine she allowed herself at lunch and pushed away her plate. Without a word she threw money on the table, but as she stood she forced herself to smile.

"We'll talk again, Carl."

On her way out she looked at the booths along the wall and the people at the bar. Maybe *they* were watching, guns concealed beneath jackets or in shoulder bags. If so, she hoped it appeared that Carl's message had been well received. Maybe it would buy her time.

Nobody seemed interested in her. And although some people looked a little odd (not uncommon, especially in bars), nobody looked dangerous.

Hurrying back to her office, Hana did not even bother to check if she was being followed. She informed a surprised Mary Hafer that if Carl Reid called, he was to be treated gently—only, she would be "out."

Hana sat drumming her fingers on her desk. Just when it seemed she was making progress with Honey, the girl would have to be moved. But where? Since she didn't know what she was fighting, how could she make intelligent judgments? And until she decided the best course to follow, that can of Mace in her glove compartment wasn't enough.

This time she knew she could not call on Mel Rosen for help. After some hesitation she dialed Bill Longenecker and, without preliminaries, asked him to get her a gun. He laughed.

"I'm not kidding," she snapped.

"Oh, Hana, I didn't think you were. It's just that every time you call for a favor, your request throws me off base."

"A gun, Bill. I need a gun."

"Sure, sure," he snickered. "Anything you want. What're you going to do? Shoot Mr. Fred next time he digs up your lawn?"

He laughed again, as if he'd said something very clever and funny.

She waited until the levity subsided. "Make sure it's a nice little gun that's easy to shoot."

He was having himself a ball. "Nice little gun!" he chortled. "Right on. It'll be so easy to handle, it'll shoot itself."

She hung up while he was still laughing.

The man was an idiot.

Later in the afternoon, Pocky Reilly called. Did Hana realize that the latest commercial was causing a commotion all over the country? There was talk that Trouble was being considered as spokescat for a very popular brand of litter. Although the offer was tempting, Hana declined on the gray cat's behalf. Like the child alone on the top of Blue Spring Hill, Trouble was just settling in. But *he* didn't have to be moved.

Chapter Twenty-three

HANA EYED THE row of empty cans that had once held tomatoes, creamed corn, and unsweetened grapefruit juice and that now stood on top of a pile of soil from one of the digs on her front lawn. She raised the .22-caliber pistol with both hands as she had seen women police officers do on TV. She supposed she should have been more focused about it all and asked Bill the Great Comedian where he had obtained the gun. Mel Rosen would die if he knew she had gotten a secondhand weapon this way. Perhaps one day soon she'd have him take care of details, like a permit and all that.

Meanwhile, she intended to concentrate on learning to use the thing.

She pulled the trigger. The gun roared. Hana gasped, her ears ringing. She hadn't realized it would be so *loud.*

Mr. Fred came running from the house.

"What are you doing?" he cried.

"You can see what I'm doing," Hana told him peevishly as she squinted at the targets. Wherever the bullet had gone, it hadn't hit a can.

"You could kill one of the animals."

"I made sure they were all in the house."

"Wait here," he instructed, then went back inside.

She wished Bill had stopped laughing long enough to explain more of the intricacies of the weapon. She hated not to do things well, and now she suspected hitting empty cans was more complicated than it appeared. Her second shot also missed, but she knew where the bullet went by a small cloud of dust raised from a surprisingly distant pile of dirt. Unfortunately, it was just as loud as the first.

Maybe the sights of the gun were off. She'd vaguely heard of such things.

Mr. Fred returned wearing a holster complete with gun. He carried an official-looking target. She stared at him.

He said rather smugly, "After all, my position here carries a great deal of responsibility. I decided many years ago that if protection were ever needed I should be prepared to provide it. These days, one never knows."

"Whatever happened to 'kick them in the nuts'?"

He looked pained. "This is definitely preferred protection."

Deliberately he removed the pistol from the holster, raised it with both hands, and shot all the cans from the pile of dirt. The performance was not only loud, it was also most impressive. Hana congratulated him, then regretted her generosity as he became even more smug.

His was a Magnum. However, he conceded her .22 would do considerable damage, if she ever managed to hit anything. Galling as it was, Hana asked him for lessons.

It was agreed that the most convenient time was mornings before she went to the office.

Hana had only three days of practice before she needed the gun.

Chapter Twenty-four

IT WAS HALLOWEEN.

The day had always been special to Hana, a holiday low-key enough to enjoy with complete relaxation, unlike Christmas, which always came with so many demands, like forced marches home to the nest when one would rather spend the holidays at a ski resort with one's college friends. Halloweens had been enhanced by the flavor of autumn at Blue Spring Hill. Mr. Fred decorated with corn shocks, potted mums, and pumpkins. As a child, Hana always wore the costume of a European peasant. In it she roamed the grounds, pretending herself to be an ocean away, a princess masquerading as a pauper. It all culminated in Aunt Sissy's party for the children of the area, complete with Mr. Fred as a ghost.

Hana could not, she realized, create the Halloween of her own childhood for Honey. But she hoped to give the girl just a taste of it. No masks or costumes to cause fear, but certainly they could carve a pumpkin and share a bag of treats.

Hana asked Sal to bring the children of her own family who were young enough to enjoy it. But Sal refused. Halloween, she declared, was a pagan holiday.

After they had eaten, Hana brought Honey downstairs. Mr. Fred had a fire in the kitchen. The table had been cleared, with the pumpkin ready for carving. There were doughnuts, cider, and dishes of candy. As she pulled Honey into the kitchen, Hana explained what Halloween had meant to her in years past.

The animals, of course, had been invited. Trouble immediately knocked over a bowl of candy corn, sending them spinning across the floor. Looking bored, Kitty Fisher and Penelope Baskin sat before the fire. Crumb wagged pleasantly at Honey while Ghost helped Trouble pursue candy corn in a frenzy of delight.

Honey stared uncomprehendingly at the decorations. Hana drew her to the table as Mr. Fred prepared to work on the pumpkin. Honey blinked as he sliced off the top.

"Now it's ready to be cleaned out," Hana said cheerfully. "Come."

But Honey refused to participate. Hana, up to her elbows in slimy pumpkin guts and seeds, wondered why she had ever thought this such great fun. She let Mr. Fred continue as she lit candles on the ledges around the brick walls.

Soon Mr. Fred's pumpkin smiled in Honey's honor. It had ears, a triangle nose and rather eerie eyes. He placed a candle inside, then put the top back on. The eyes stared with fire. Fascinated, Honey stared back.

"Wonderful!" Hana cried. "Honey, isn't it wonderful?"

"It is good," Mr. Fred agreed as he contemplated his work of art.

"Ever have cider?" Hana asked as she poured it into pumpkin-decorated cups.

Honey still stared at the jack-o'-lantern.

"Maybe she's just not ready for it," Mr. Fred said, worried.

Hana was about to drink her cider when she realized the lights had gone out. Blue Spring Hill, house and grounds, was never left in darkness, but now, looking from the kitchen into the hall, it was dark. Very dark. The flickering candles had kept them from noticing.

"How long have the lights been off?" Hana asked with alarm.

Without waiting for a reply, she seized Honey's hand and pulled the child after her into the hall. She knew the house as well as her own body. Deftly she moved to the stairs. When the child stumbled, she picked her up. All she could think of was getting to her own room. To her gun.

Jesus, it was like the Old West. She should have kept the pistol in a holster on her belt instead of in her bedstand drawer.

She heard nothing. She wished for moonlight, any kind of light, but the night was as dark as the hall. If only she had thought to pick up a candle . . . But it was too late now. Stupid.

It seemed forever that she moved through blackness to her room. Once there, she set Honey down, then cautiously opened the door. One arm around the child, she groped forward. The bedstand was closer than she'd guessed. She bumped into it, swore, then fumbled with the drawer.

The gun was in her hand.

As soon as she felt safer she also felt a little ridiculous. It could be just a fuse. Suddenly the lights would come on and they would laugh. Mr. Fred was probably working on the fuse box this very minute.

But no lights came on.

Hana went to the window. Night hid even the trenches on the lawn. The alarm system was separate, but if they knew how to cut off the lights, might they not also know how to cut out the alarm?

Her eyes were becoming accustomed to the

gloom. She could make out Honey sitting docilely on the bed. Hana realized the girl had not protested. Running in the dark seemed natural to her.

Now what?

Well, she had the gun. But no flashlight. Okay. Was there really any point in prowling about looking for intruders? There were literally hundreds of places in this house to hide and from which they could pounce. Unpleasant thought—people who knew so much must know the location of her bedroom.

Still, it was the room with which she was most familiar. She didn't believe anybody could get in through the windows. That would take an acrobat. Therefore, all she had to do was face the door. Even if she couldn't hit a tin can, she could make a big fiery bang.

"Honey," she whispered, "we're going to stay here for a while. Get under the bed and stay there until I tell you to come out."

Wordlessly, the girl dropped to the floor and slithered beneath the dust ruffle. Hana sat on the bed, facing the door, both hands on her gun.

It seemed as though eons passed.

The house was utterly silent. Her fingers on the metal felt sweaty. She wiped one hand on her blouse, then the other. She wondered again where Mr. Fred was. Where the animals were. Her eyes began to ache from trying to stare into blackness.

When it happened, there was no conscious thought on her part. Only a gut-level reaction.

It came barreling through the window of the bedroom, smashing glass and frame. She didn't even realize it was human. It was only a dark blob at which she fired. Again and again. Then it was crashing into her and she was falling, slamming into the floor. On the way down something tore into her face, hitting her on the jaw.

Deeper silence and deeper darkness followed.

She might have been unconscious for a year or a minute. All she knew was that her mouth and jaw hurt and her head ached. She sat up, aware of cool air pouring at her through the broken window and on past to the open hall door. She seemed to be alone. She groped about but found no gun.

Lifting the dust ruffle of the bed, she whispered, "Honey?"

No reply. She reached beneath the bed. Nothing. What she needed was a flashlight. She couldn't find anything without light.

Hanging on to the bed, she pulled herself up. Happy Halloween, she thought groggily. Some party.

But once on her feet, she didn't feel as bad as she had imagined. A bit of nausea—not much. She went into the hall and paused, one hand on the wall to steady herself.

It was as if she was alone in a darkened world. No child. No assailant. No Mr. Fred. No animals. She moved forward to look down the wide stairs into the hall below.

She stifled a scream.

A fiery face looked up at her.

Shit. The jack-o'-lantern. It was no longer in the kitchen but on the hall table. Why would anybody do that? For light? Maybe. Holding cautiously on to the banister, Hana crept down the stairs.

At the bottom she took a chance and called out, "Mr. Fred! Where are you?"

A growl answered her.

Ghost stood beside the stairs with something dangling from his mouth. She reached down. "Let go!"

Obediently he released a bit of cloth. . . . Something from a pair of trousers? She patted him.

"Good boy."

The air was even cooler down here. She saw the candles in the kitchen flickering.

She and Ghost went in that direction. The back door stood wide open.

Flashlights.

Kitchen drawers. Yes, they were always kept in some kitchen drawer or other. Damn. She should pay more attention to her own kitchen. Except that it seemed to be Sal's and Mr. Fred's kitchen. If she had her gun she wouldn't feel so vulnerable.

Somebody had a gun. She could hear it being fired outside at some distance. Then she heard an automobile start up. She rummaged through drawers, upsetting Sal's order as she hunted. Outside Crumb barked. Ghost ran out through the still-open kitchen door.

Hana's hands closed over a small flashlight. It worked! A friendly circle of light guided her to the kitchen door. She shone it around hopefully. The dogs were out of sight. Trouble, hair on end making him seem enormous, came dashing across the parking lot and into the house.

Hana closed the door, locked it, then made her way back to the stairs. First she would search for Honey, then try to find Mr. Fred.

She paused at the foot of the stairs, shining her light upward.

At the top, Honey stood unblinking. Held in

both hands was a very real-looking gun pointed directly at Hana.

Carefully Hana lowered the light so that it did not shine into the child's eyes. Trying to keep her voice calm, she said, "Honey, it's me. Hana. The woman who brought you here. It's all right. Whoever else was here is gone now. Put down the gun. Lay it on the floor."

The girl appeared to have retreated into the trancelike state in which Hana had first found her. The pointed gun did not waver. Hana, speaking nonsense words she sometimes used for the cats, slowly came up a step. She tried five more, then paused.

The child's hands clutching the gun were taut and white-knuckled in the circle of light. She might pull that trigger any time. If she had the safety off . . . Hana felt sure it was her own gun. To be shot in the gut with one's own weapon . . .

"Put down the gun," she said more firmly.

Something moved in the darkened hall beyond the child. Hana was afraid to shine her light there, afraid to do anything that might cause the kid to fire. About her the orange glow from the jack-o'-lantern flickered across the hall. And upstairs God knows what was creeping toward them.

Then everything happened at once.

A figure behind Honey leaped forward to seize her arm. The pistol fired, a bullet biting into the ceiling above Hana. The flashlight revealed Mr. Fred holding the child. Hana ran up the stairs.

Honey, docile now, went limp in Mr. Fred's arms. Hana grabbed the gun, which had dropped to the floor. It *was* hers.

"Where'd you come from?" she gasped through her sore jaw.

"Back stairs," Mr. Fred panted. "I chased somebody. They'd been on the top floor. Must have known the kid was up there but didn't know we'd brought her down tonight. A man, I think. There was a car . . . he got away."

It had been bold, audacious. Like abducting Grace Urich in the middle of the pedestrian mall. People who wanted you to know they were present and would strike any time.

"He came through the window in my room . . . crashed through—"

"That's impossible—"

"He did it."

"Then he must have been an acrobat."

Which had already crossed her mind. A circus performer swinging on a rope from one of the many trees. The big trick was to get your attention to the middle ring.

"Let her go," she said wearily.

Mr. Fred released the child, who looked as if she might collapse.

"I'm going to take her into the corner guest room," she continued. "You go look around and see what you can find—a phone, a fuse box—"

"First I've got to get a flashlight . . ."

"They're in—"

"I know."

In the brown and lavender room, she gently pushed the girl into a chair, then groped until she found two blankets. Brown. Yes, she remembered. In this room the blankets were brown. Fingering them, she got an idea.

Mr. Fred returned from his expedition to report that wires had been cut, the phone disabled. The alarm system was jammed so completely he couldn't get it going again. He had checked one automobile to find the tires slashed, the car phone smashed. Unless a patrol car passed and investigated the absence of lights on the grounds—which was iffy—they were effectively cut off for the night. And it was only nine o'clock.

"They'll be back," Hana sighed. "It was a charade. Part of their strategy of fear."

"Well, we're armed. If we lock this door and barricade it with furniture—"

"Suppose they set fire to the house?"

Mr. Fred cried out in dismay. "Surely nobody would burn down Blue Spring Hill! What a monstrous idea!"

"Maybe they'll just use tear gas," Hana said soothingly. "One thing I know for sure. Sometime tonight people will come into this house. Dangerous people. There'll be enough of them to go over every foot of it, and they'll get us somehow."

"But—my God—why . . . ?"

Hana shrugged, then looked at the child, whose head drooped as if she were dozing. "I wonder if she can keep quiet? I mean, really quiet."

Mr. Fred grunted. "Her? She never talks. Why should tonight be any different?"

"She was frightened enough to grab that gun, wasn't she? She could be frightened enough to talk."

"Maybe we can find another gun for her and she can help us fend them off."

"Don't be ridiculous. I have an idea." Hana knelt before Honey. "Listen, we have to hide. We're afraid those people might come after us again. Do you understand what I'm trying to tell you?"

The girl raised her head a little, looking at Hana through half-lidded eyes. She nodded almost imperceptibly.

"You must not talk. Nor cry out. You must come with us, do what we tell you and keep very still. Can you do that?"

Honey sighed with world-weariness.

"She's done this before," Mr. Fred said wonderingly.

"I'm sure," Hana agreed, rising. "Come. We're going outside."

"Are you insane? At least here we've got a chance to hold them off until morning."

"Mr. Fred. I've found a use for the trenches you've been digging all over my front lawn."

Hana gave him the brown blankets and, over his whispered protests, they went downstairs. She could feel her heart beating, her body acknowledging fear. Pausing at the foot of the staircase, they listened. Nothing. Hana blew out the candle in the jack-o'-lantern. Dragging Honey, she crept toward the conservatory with Mr. Fred following. Coming up the drive, one could not even see this conservatory, for it was grossly Victorian in architecture, an eccentricity of the flamboyant Maude Evans Schoener, who loved flowers, glass walls, gingerbread, and domes. This had been her sanctuary, and after her death tolerated although carefully screened by a wild growth of rhododendron bushes to protect the architectural purity of the house. It was full of towering ferns, banana trees, bird of paradise plants, all crowding around a fake waterfall that incongruously ran over a granite, tombstonelike cliff.

Her father, Aunt Sissy, and even Mr. Fred had been unable to confine Hana to the house, because as a child she had discovered the secret of the odd conservatory, a secret that made her wonder about Great-Grandmother Maude. A door to the outside had been sealed shut generations ago. But in one glass wall—if you knew the trick—a panel opened outward, giving enough room for even an adult to creep through.

Without using the flashlight, Hana maneuvered the wrought-iron studs and opened the secret door.

"So that was how you did it," Mr. Fred said, sounding annoyed.

"Easy, once you know how."

He put a hand on her arm. "You're forgetting something."

"What?"

"The dogs."

They could find Hana anywhere.

"How are we going to hide?" he demanded. "They'll send the dogs after us."

"The dogs won't cooperate with them. Ghost had a piece of somebody's pants in his teeth."

"They won't mean to, but you can bet they'll sniff us out and let these people know where we are."

Even though he was probably right, she snapped, "It's the only chance we've got. Don't come with us if you'd rather not."

But he did. They slipped through the opening, which Hana carefully closed after them. The night air felt cold, as if previewing November. Getting through the rhododendron thicket proved to be a problem. Hana considered remaining there, but it was too obvious. When they weren't found in the house, the woods and the high rhododendron would be the logical places to search.

She hoped they were not leaving too much of a trail. Honey moved through the twisting branches as if she had spent her life hiding in thickets. Hana led the way, going slowly, trying to disturb the plants as little as possible. Mr. Fred swore a couple of times under his breath as sharp, dry twigs tore at the blankets in his arms. They finally reached the other side, where they paused again.

She had remembered correctly.

For weeks she had watched the trenches increasing in length along with their mounds of soil. She had noticed them spider out toward the boxwood and azaleas. She had also noted their steady crawl toward the rhododendron. A pile of soil and rocks was little more than ten feet from where they stood in the shadow of the thicket.

Hana dropped to her stomach and crawled toward the trench.

The child, never seeming to question anything, wriggled along. Mr. Fred swore again before he joined them. At the protecting mound of dirt they could go on hands and knees. Crawling along with her rear end nearly in Mr. Fred's face, Hana hoped he would never tell Sal. Or a reporter. What a tabloid would make of this trek, she could well imagine.

The trenches were darker than the night. Gravelike. The crawlers had nearly reached the center of the maze when Hana found one that suited her purpose. Wider than most, it was quite shallow. She slithered into it, then reached up and pulled Honey after her. There was some resistance this time. The child was shaking her head.

"It's okay," she whispered.

Mr. Fred slid down. Hana helped him spread a blanket on the bottom of their trench. They lay down together, Honey in the middle. The other blanket they pulled over themselves. Then Hana began to claw at loose dirt. Mr. Fred got the idea and worked from the other side. Honey whimpered.

"Shh," Hana cautioned.

She had two broken fingernails before she was finished.

Mr. Fred murmured, "Your father would turn over in his grave."

Funny he should think of graves.

They were now covered with a thin layer of soil. They had part of the top blanket to pull over their faces if necessary.

Waiting began.

Irreverently the words of a song came to Hana's mind: "This is a lovely way to spend an evening . . ." An old tune, one Aunt Sissy had loved. Suddenly she wanted to laugh hysterically. Whether or not anybody came looking for them, she would have to do something with this kid. One night in a trench covered with dirt was only bearable, two unthinkable. Especially with Mr. Fred. She wondered if he would demand overtime.

Now that the activity was over, her jaw began to hurt. Also her back. Something was poking her.

Felt like a bone.

Oh, God.

They were probably right on top of another corpse. She fought an urge to dig it out and hit Mr. Fred over the head with it. But then, if it weren't for his ridiculous hobby, what would they have done? Probably gone to bed and spent a comfortable night. Because most likely nobody else would come, nothing would happen.

She stirred, trying to ease her back.

After a long time she was aware that Honey had fallen asleep.

Thinking about it now, Hana felt sure the child had held a gun before. Honey knew what a gun was, knew that she had to hold it in both hands. Even knew enough to remove the safety.

Had this child killed? It was an awful thought, but today children did. In Northern Ireland. In the Arab countries. They killed and were killed. They were prostituted and abused. It had become an insane world. An insane decade.

The key to Grace's disappearance—and death—lay with this child. She had to be made to talk. If they were alive in the morning. If they were not, she wondered what Dr. Reifsnyder would say when they were found murdered here together.

Dr. Reifsnyder.

His brother was her dentist. When Mary Hafer at the office had been afraid to have a root canal, Hana had recommended Dentist Reifsnyder because he used hypnosis therapy. Maybe lying in a trench for hours covered with dirt was good for mental stimulation.

They would hypnotize Honey!

Wonderful idea. Why hadn't she thought of it before?

She couldn't wait until morning.

Actually she couldn't wait until morning for other reasons, too. It was a most uncomfortable bone she was lying on.

At one point Mr. Fred muttered, "If I ever get out of here, I'm going to quit. Do you realize all they'd have to do is push that heap of dirt over us and we'd smother to death?"

"Shh!"

She had seen a flash of light inside the house. Unless Penelope Baskin and Kitty Fisher were hunting her with flashlights—and despite their intelligence she rather doubted that—somebody was in there. She hoped the animals were all right. At least the cats would be. They were good at games of hide-and-seek.

Mr. Fred must have seen it, too. She sensed his tenseness.

They pulled up the blanket, covering their faces. When Hana peeped out, as she couldn't resist doing occasionally, she saw more lights inside. They were certainly in there, hunting. Later the lights were everywhere on the grounds, accompanied by muffled voices. Beams swung among the trenches, once passing right over them.

A clear voice sounded only yards away. "They could be hiding in those fucking bushes. They've got to be somewhere."

Hana started, gulping to quiet her breathing. She heard Mr. Fred wheeze a little.

Moments later, crackling and cursing came from the direction of the rhododendrons.

She wondered what would happen if these people hung around until dawn. Until Sal arrived alone to begin her daily chores.

But after what seemed ages the voices ceased. No more lights swung about. Hana thought she heard cars start up somewhere beyond the estate, but it could have been her imagination. She felt the bone on which she was lying must surely have penetrated her rib cage by now. Warily she moved, then sat up. She wanted to look at her watch, but to turn on the flashlight might be suicide. They might have left a guard. It could be the same ruse they had used before.

Mr. Fred, too, was probably on artifacts, because he stirred stiffly, turning on his side. As far as Hana could tell, Honey still slept. Thank fate for small favors even at the worst of times. She rooted about beneath the blanket. It was a bone—big sucker from the feel of it. Seemed to be attached to something. Why had they buried their bloody soldiers here?

At least the pain in her jaw had dwindled to a dull ache.

She slid down again, turning onto her side, facing Honey. They would have to remain for at least another hour. Maybe longer.

She thought of Grace in her trench in town. But she soon drifted from that awful picture. Actually this bed was quite comfortable now that she had moved off the bone.

Hana awoke when Mr. Fred shook her. She nearly screamed. It was a grave. She was in a grave!

He was standing up, as was Honey, whom he was brushing off. Hana sputtered as dirt got into her mouth. The sun shone, the estate looked deserted.

"I think we should clean up a bit before Sal arrives," Mr. Fred said formally.

Hana decided she felt lousy. She needed coffee, food. Yes, and a bath. Groaning aloud, she struggled to her feet. They helped each other out of the trench.

Walking back to the house, Hana noted the child's continued passivity even now and impatiently felt like shaking her. She was the most frustrating kid Hana had ever met. No bounce to her. No childish glee that the sun was up and they had survived the hunters of the night.

But then, maybe she felt lousy too.

Hana never asked Mr. Fred how he did it, although she guessed he had probably walked to a public phone booth. However, by the time she had bathed herself and the girl the police were already there. They radioed for the company that had installed the alarm. The electric people were also on the way, as was the phone company, a carpenter, and two garages.

Sal, who arrived soon after the police, was uncompromisingly disapproving of the entire business and retired to the kitchen to make breakfast. Kitty Fisher, Penelope Baskin, and a subdued Trouble came out from wherever they had been hiding for plates of raw ground round as a treat. A policeman located Ghost and Crumb penned inside a gardener's shed. Either the enemy was not infallible or was afraid of dogs.

"Ghost must have been giving them a hard time," Hana told Sergeant Kochen as she patted the animal's head. "We were worried they might lead them to us."

Pushing his glasses into place, Kochen looked morosely at the wagging tail. "He's going to make one hell of a witness."

To Hana's horror, Mr. Fred had also located his archaeology students, who were already busy in the trench where Hana, Mr. Fred, and Honey had spent the night. Her bone was being excavated. Honey was restored to her rooms on the top floor with the assurance that a police guard would be there.

As soon as they were finished with her, Hana

gladly left for the office. From there she called Dr. Reifsnyder at his home. She knew he didn't like it, but Hana never let that stop her.

"Hannah Elizabeth Clara," he said, "I've been thinking about you ever since I examined that child."

Sounded bad. Her formal name usually meant he was about to pull rank.

"I just have a favor to ask," she said quickly.

"Oh, I do, too. I wish you wouldn't call me at home. I am not a private physician retained exclusively by the Shaner family. My office has a secretary as well as an answering service. In the future call me there."

"Of course I will," she lied.

"And if you're looking for another house call, let me tell you—"

"No, no. What I want is for your brother to hypnotize Honey. And I'd like you to be present when he does it. She seems so fragile—"

"No." He said it loudly.

"Okay, then we'll do it without you."

"I think not. I'm dialing my brother immediately, and when I get through talking to him, he too will refuse to participate in this."

"I must get into that girl's head—"

"Not this way. I want her to see a therapist who specializes in children's problems. If you recall, I gave you names of people in Philadelphia whom I can highly recommend."

"Will they hypnotize her?"

"Certainly not immediately. She's suffering from trauma, and we must get at the root of that. This may take time."

"Like how much?"

"Months. Conceivably years."

"Well, couldn't we hypnotize her first? If I promise I'll cooperate in every other way, will you reconsider?"

"I really cannot take the responsibility."

"Oh, come on, Uncle Harold! I've even been getting through to her by using my animals—"

"Animals!" he cried. "Just what I might expect from a meddling amateur. I insist you stop whatever you are doing immediately and get in touch with—"

Their conversation terminated abruptly as Hana hung up. She dialed his brother immediately, but the good doctor had the advantage of not having to look up the number. By the time she reached her dentist, the doctors Reifsnyder were in complete agreement. There would be no hypnosis.

Hana, accustomed all her life to getting her own way, was angry. Of course she could find a hypnotist—Hannah Elizabeth Clara Shaner and/or Shaner Industries could find anything they wanted. But she hesitated. To go ahead without a doctor's approval might be unwise. Obviously the girl *did* need help. Still, what good would a therapist be if she was kidnapped? Maybe the best thing would be to get her out of town.

Unfortunately, Hana had no confidence in Philadelphia.

She felt tired. She needed the weekend to sleep. She'd have to hire private muscle to guard them. If the alarm wasn't fixed, maybe Sergeant Kochen would let them spend the night in jail.

When Hana found herself seriously considering this alternative, she decided it was time to put the entire matter out of her mind and get on with business.

That evening she returned home to find another Revolutionary War skeleton had been unearthed. God, they had spent the night in his grave.

Whenever Hana was upset, she always went to her kitchen. It had been her refuge as a child. As an adult, she still found it a source of comfort, warmth, and good smells. Sal was baking potatoes.

"Never saw such a skinny kid," she muttered. "Well, I'm going to fatten her up some while I'm cooking for her."

"Is she still upstairs?"

"With a policeman in front of the door," Sal said disapprovingly.

Hana perched on the brick ledge in front of the old fireplace and stared into the flames. November already, she thought. A time for fires and baking apples.

She realized Sal was hovering. Which was odd, because Sal rarely ever hovered.

"Is something wrong?" Hana asked.

"Oh, no. No. Just—I was thinking some. . . . Why don't you bring that little girl out to the farm tomorrow?"

Hana stared up at her. "Why, thank you. I never thought of that. I'm not sure—"

"It'd maybe do her some good to be around other kids. Our Annie's even her right age, I'd say."

"But something might happen—"

"On the farm!?" Sal asked, scandalized.

Chapter Twenty-five

SAL PAUSED IN her sweeping, leaning on her broom, looking about. Hana sat on a porch rocker, idly surveying the hazy landscape. Even in early November some trees remained colored, and piles of golden leaves littered the lawn where the children played. A cidery odor of windfall apples drifted from the orchard, although the trees had long been harvested.

Maybe this was what gave Sal her energy, Hana thought. Even on her day off she wasn't resting but was sweeping, baking, and tending to inexplicable farm matters.

There were five Nunemachers young enough to play with Honey. They had apparently been given time off from farm chores, which they appreciated, and had been instructed to include this strange girl in their games. The three girls had braids, and dresses longer than fashionable. The boys, in shirts and trousers, were less noticeably of a sect apart. Honey, wearing a dress of Sal's choosing, looked surprisingly like one of the group.

At first Honey had remained on the porch with Hana, watching them play. At Hana's urging she then sat on the steps. Finally the ten-year-old called Annie took Honey by the hand and wordlessly drew her into their circle. It was incredible, Hana thought, how sensitive these children were. Perhaps in their young lives other children had made fun of them.

They played hopscotch, a child's game Hana barely recalled. They used a stick to draw a series of numbered blocks in the dirt of their lane, and a worn rubber heel served as the "potsy" to toss into the various squares. With Annie still holding her hand, Honey stood watching. Sal tapped her broom on the edge of the porch, then went inside.

With the sun warm on her back, Hana felt the tension she had been under easing a little. She thought sadly that for her there could be no real rest until she had solved the mystery of Grace Urich. On a day like this, she wished she could sweep it away as Sal had swept the porch.

Young Nunemachers suddenly began to cheer. Hana saw Honey hopping on one foot through the numbered blocks. And smiling!

Sal's mother had made the meal to which they were invited. This supper, eaten at the long kitchen table, was plain but plentiful. Hana had not tasted *schnitz und knepp* in years. It was served in a large iron pot placed in the center of the table, and was full of tender ham with an appetizing broth, to which dried apples and potatoes had been added and cooked soft. On top floated large, fluffy dumplings. Honey doubtfully surveyed this assortment on her plate, then shyly peeped at the other children, who were hungrily eating. At first she tasted it slowly, but soon was eating as rapidly as any of them. Sal and her mother beamed.

After supper it was too cool to sit on the porch, so they moved to the parlor. The children played a spelling game in which Honey refused to join despite coaxing. Sal cut short the entertainment, sending the five siblings off to do homework. The older woman tactfully located her mending.

"I'm glad you came to visit my family," Sal told Honey. "Annie especially likes having you here. Will you come again?"

"Oh, yes."

It was the first enthusiastic thing the girl had ever said in their presence.

"Good." Sal smiled, placidly smoothing her apron as she leaned back in her rocking chair. "Annie'll be glad to hear it. Next time you can help with the chores. Annie's the one who gathers eggs. Maybe you can do that with her. You ever do chores?"

The question was completely relaxed and casual the way Sal asked it, but for a moment it seemed Honey would not answer. Then she nodded.

"Um, good," Sal murmured. "I wouldn't want Annie to think there are children who never work. I really wouldn't want her playing with children like that."

The woman in the corner continued sewing. A clock ticked somewhere. From upstairs came the softness of children's voices.

"I dried dishes," Honey blurted. "I never did before that, but I dried dishes. She said I should. She said . . ."

The sentences were disjointed, awkward. Hana held her breath.

". . . said I should call her Grandmother . . ."

"I'm glad she had you dry dishes," Sal said calmly. "I did when I was your age. Still do sometimes. Did she ever have you dust?"

They discussed dusting. Hana bit her lip to keep from butting in. *Get the woman's name. Sal, while you've got her talking, get the woman's name!* She tried to catch Sal's eye but was ignored.

"She sounds like somebody I'd like," Sal said. "I

think it was nice she asked you to call her Grandmother."

Honey sighed. Hana knew she was slipping away.

"What was her name?" she asked.

Sal glared.

"Don't know."

"Annie never lies," Hana said. "It's against her religion to lie."

"That's right," Sal agreed. "In this house we are not allowed to lie. The Bible says, 'Thou shalt not bear false witness.' "

Did she understand? Or was it instinct that here was a safe haven? Hana never knew.

But Honey was talking.

"Her name was Doris. I saw it on a letter. Doris. And the rest of it was real funny. H-Y-L-A. The letters looked funny together like that."

"Oh, I know that name," Sal smiled. "Hyla. It *is* a funny name. Mother, didn't we know a family by that name on Duke Street?"

"No," the sewer replied firmly. "We never knew anybody by that name."

"Her house was on King Street," Honey whispered before she lapsed back into her usual silence.

Chapter Twenty-six

THE AMAZING THING, Hana thought as she parked the car, got out, and put money in the meter, was that a Doris Hyla actually lived on King Street. She was listed not only in the phone book, but also in the courthouse records. She had been a resident there for twenty years. Not exactly a transient citizen.

The house had been restored to the original brick, was well kept, obviously loved. She rang the bell. The door was opened by the woman she had seen in the rest room at city hall the day Honey had vanished. Hana stared in surprise. The woman started to close the door. Recovering in time, Hana stuck her foot in it.

"I'll call the police!" the woman threatened.

"I'm here to talk about a missing child named Honey," Hana said, talking fast. "Girl about eight. And I know she stayed with you. Will you let me inside, just in case somebody is watching the house?"

Apparently frightened, the woman abruptly stepped back. Hana entered, looking about as Hyla peered out suspiciously, then closed the door and slipped a sturdy chain into place.

The inside matched the exterior: white plaster walls, woodwork painted Colonial colors. Antique furniture. It had all cost money.

Doris Hyla led the way into a small, tidy living room.

"Is anybody else in the house?" Hana asked.

The woman shook her head. Apparently something had robbed these people of their ability to communicate with words.

"So you live here alone?"

The woman stared at her without answering.

Hana took out her checkbook, an activity she had found often eased awkward situations and contributed to the conversation.

"My name is Hana Shaner. I saw you at city hall, and I know you recognize me from there. As I said, I also know the girl called Honey lived with you in this house. Now, you have your choice. Speak to me privately. Then I will write a check, the amount of which will depend on what I think your information is worth. Or, if you prefer, I can call Sergeant Kochen at police headquarters. It won't take him long to get here."

"No! . . . Please."

The woman started to talk. She had received a phone call from a man—it was definitely a man—whom she did not know. He offered her a great deal of money to keep a child. He seemed to know she was a widow who needed money. She was instructed to tell neighbors the girl was a granddaughter.

"I was told there was nothing illegal. Just that the girl's mother couldn't take care of her for a time. The way she seemed, she'd been in one foster home after another, if you asked me. Not that I was paid to think, mind. I just did what I was told. Don't have many friends since my husband passed on. Told neighbors who saw her she was my granddaughter, just like he said. I'm a bit of a loner, so it wasn't hard. Even so, I'd never have done it if I thought harm would come to the child."

"Who delivered her to you?"

"Why, nobody," Doris Hyla said. "At least nobody I saw. A car pulled up. The kid got out alone.

It was a big car and had those kinds of shiny dark windows you can't see through. It stayed right there at the curb until I got the kid inside, then took off and I never saw it again. She walked right up to the door like a grown-up person. Had her little suitcase. She wasn't any trouble. Never said much. Did what I told her to."

She had been there six months. Doris Hyla had never made any attempt to question her. She was well paid, and that was enough for her. That, plus an undercurrent of fear, because somebody knew so much about her. Nobody called to check what was happening. Nobody was watching the house —at least so far as she knew. Money had been regularly deposited in her account.

She admitted she was sorry when it was over.

It happened very suddenly. The girl liked to color. Liked to watch TV, too. Her favorite programs were old reruns of "I Dream of Jeannie." She was really into that. So she'd been watching it one day while Doris was preparing dinner. When she came to call the child, she wasn't there. The TV still played, but the girl had gone.

"You didn't call the police? Anyone might have taken her."

"And what would I tell the police? Huh? What *could* I tell them? Anyways, I knew it was them. They came and got her is all."

"What about her clothing?"

"Gone. Everything. They must have been upstairs. It was frightening, let me tell you. I had all my locks changed after that."

She heard nothing more for nearly a year, then received a call to go to city hall. The voice was more muffled this time. Could have been the same man, or even a woman. She was to go into the lavatory, bustle about, creating a diversion. Later, outside, she was told she would be given the girl to keep for an unspecified amount of time. She hesitated to get involved again, but, after all, nothing bad had happened the other time and she always needed money. So she went to the bus stop exactly as directed, except something obviously went wrong. The child had not been delivered. After waiting for about an hour, the woman had gone home. No one had contacted her since.

"But why you?" Hana wondered. "Out of the thousands of widows in this area, why you? Who did you know? Who knew you?"

Doris Hyla shrugged helplessly. "I've asked myself that. I've wondered if maybe it was somebody who knew Hem, my husband. We always called him that. Short for Hemingway, because he used to think he was a writer. He did sell a couple of short stories. Had a few plays done."

Hana felt a sudden hope. "Plays? Where?"

The woman sighed. "I don't remember. No place big or important. At least, it never seemed important to me."

"Maybe you have his theater contracts among your papers."

"Oh, he never had a contract. It was just little stuff, I tell you. Hole-in-the-wall kind of places."

"Here?"

"Out of town."

"New York?"

"Maybe. Yes. I think there was one in New York, though beats me why anybody'd want to go to a place like that when they could go to Broadway."

"There must have been programs. Even small theaters have—"

"Oh, yes. He had some of them, all right. Used to show them around like they were something."

Excited, Hana envisioned names and places that could lead to the end of her quest. "I'd like to see them."

"I just bet you would, but I got rid of all that junk when he died."

Disappointment turned dreams back into windmills in her mind. "How did you get rid of them? Did you sell them to a dealer or—"

"Who'd pay anything for that trash? I burned them."

"Everything?"

"Sure. Programs, stories, plays, poems. I like things neat and easy to clean."

Defeated, thinking of poor Hem's impossible dreams, Hana mentioned names of everybody she knew connected with Grace Urich. Nothing registered. Then, even though she could hardly look at Doris Hyla's stupidly placid face, she wrote a check for a thousand dollars and noted in her checkbook that it was for charity.

"If I were you, I'd use it to take a little trip."

"But I don't like to travel," the woman said forlornly. "Not alone. Not since Hem died. He was the one liked to go places. Had a good job, you know, so we traveled. I don't understand any of this. Do you have the girl? Is she all right?"

"I think so," Hana said vaguely. "But I haven't got her. I'm looking for her."

"You the mother?"

"I'm a friend of the mother."

"Well, all I can say is you'd best tell your friend she should do something about her girl. Send her to a special school maybe. The kid never talked.

Didn't know anything. I thought there was something wrong with her. I'd worry if she was mine."

Driving home, Hana went over the interview in her mind. She had wanted to assure the woman that Honey was safe, but it seemed wiser to be noncommittal. Despite her shortcomings, Hyla had apparently been reasonably good to the girl. Maybe Honey had been able to relax there. Maybe that was why they'd managed to reach her even in a limited way.

She pulled into her parking lot at home, turned off the motor, and sat thinking about Hem Hyla and his plays. Maybe she should turn her team of computer-wise PIs on to Hem. Not that she expected much from that direction. But perhaps in some obscure directory of failed playwrights . . .

Hana went into her home, then paused to listen. She always did now, afraid intruders might be there.

Fear.

Bloody awful. Ghost and Crumb came to greet her. She patted them absently, then went to the kitchen.

Sal was still there, but getting ready to leave.

"It's meatloaf," she said as if delivering bad news. "In the oven. Mr. Fred knows what to do."

Hana told Sal about Doris Hyla.

"I don't know what's going on," she finished. "But one thing I'm certain of is that I've got to hide that girl. I have to put her somewhere she won't be found."

Sal's eyes were on her face. "Think you can?"

"I don't know. Apparently Grace didn't manage it. She tried, but she didn't manage it."

"Grace Urich is dead," Sal said sharply.

"Well . . . Yes, of course she is. But this has

something to do with Grace, and whoever—for whatever reason—killed her knows that girl is here. I have to get her to a safe place."

"I'll take her."

It was said so matter-of-factly that for a moment Hana thought she had misunderstood. Then she shook her head.

"Just because we had one successful visit, and Honey calmed down and told us something, doesn't mean it would work on a . . . well, not exactly permanent, but let's say . . . on a regular basis. She could be there for a year, maybe more. And we didn't exactly sneak out there. They probably know about that visit."

"Now, you listen to me," Sal said, adopting one of Mr. Fred's less attractive tones. "You can't put a child in one of your safe-deposit boxes in a bank. Children aren't that easy to hide. They need things. They need schooling."

"I know that."

"What they don't need is to be penned up alone in a couple of rooms in an attic."

"You know it's not like that," Hana said angrily. "They're nice rooms. And it is not even an attic!"

"Don't you raise your voice to me, Miss Hannah Elizabeth Clara Schoener. You'd have some trouble getting somebody else to put up with you and your animals and Mr. Fred."

"I'm sorry—"

"You should be."

"Sal, have you thought out this offer? Really thought about it? It could be dangerous."

"That never stopped the Lord Jesus Christ."

Hana took a deep breath. She never felt equal to Sal's heartfelt religion. Indeed, she wanted to stay away from it. Sal knew she had the advantage, and she took it.

"The best place to hide some straw is in a haystack. We have lots of kids out there on the farm. If she was to look like us, dress like us, who'd be the wiser? I talked to my mother about it after you left. She's sorry for the girl, wants to help."

"Suppose they find out? Suppose they come to the farm?"

"Suppose the Day of Judgment comes tomorrow?"

"Could you handle it, Sal?"

"The Lord gives us the courage to handle what we must."

Sal's offer was, of course, the answer to the problem. Maybe the only sensible one, because obviously she couldn't keep Honey here much longer. But to think of involving other children . . . the bright and pretty Annie, with her long pigtails. Annie would obviously be the one closest to Honey. Suppose they found out, and suppose Annie was there when they came to get Honey . . . ?

"I just don't know what to do," Hana admitted.

"Of course you do. You must agree. You have to. It's the only practical thing to do."

Their eyes met.

Hana finally nodded. "All right. But on one condition."

"Ja?"

"You use hired men from time to time on the farm?"

"Well, sure we do, but not as often as we need. The boys do most of it, but—"

"Right. I am going to hire a strong, strapping bodyguard to work as a hired hand. He'll be paid a bonus to be there all the time. To live in with your family."

"I don't know if Mom would like that—"

"It's the only way I'll agree to this. I mean it, Sal."

"He'll do chores? Farm work?"

"Absolutely."

Sal grinned. "Then I think I can get Mom to say yes."

By the following day it had all been arranged. The beloved computer at the detective agency had located a free-lance security man who had done bodyguard work and as a teenager had lived on a farm. His Germanic background plus a gift of blarney from his mother's side won over Sal's mother immediately.

The computer, however, could not locate Hem Hyla's playwriting career. Theater, evanescent at best, had failed to be impressed even for one brief spot of fame, which had flickered out.

Mrs. Nunemacher altered three of Annie's outgrown dresses to Honey's measurements. A suitable story had been delivered to the children. Honey would not go to school immediately. She was recovering from an illness (only a white lie; there are all sorts of ills) and was a relative (the human race is all related though Adam and Eve) and needed peace and quiet. The Mennonite Church to which they belonged was alerted that a needy child would be among them. They closed ranks without asking questions.

A chilling rain was falling one evening as Sal drove back to her farm at her usual quitting time, apparently alone. A short time before, Mr. Fred had conducted a circus on the front lawn, running about, loudly herding startled cats and dogs in out of the rain. Under the cover of that diverting activity, Hana and Honey had crawled from the house and the girl had been tucked into the back of Sal's old station wagon, where she lay curled on the floor, covered with blankets. At Blue Spring Hill Mr. Fred turned on lights on the top floor. He carried up a tray of food, which he also ate up there.

"She didn't even say good-bye to the animals," he fretted when he brought down the empty tray.

"She didn't say good-bye to anyone."

Mr. Fred was always grumpy when it rained. "I don't see why I have to eat the food. Couldn't I just carry up an empty tray?"

Hana shook her head. "You never know who's watching. Or where."

That night she couldn't sleep. Wedged uncomfortably between purring bodies, with Ghost and Crumb sprawled across the bottom of the bed, she knew they couldn't keep up the charade for long. Whoever watched—and that they were watching she had no doubt—would soon discover that the girl was gone. Maybe even now they were padding through the house. She kept the gun under her pillow, the door bolted.

At breakfast she snapped at Mr. Fred. "When are you going to fill in those terrible trenches on my lawn?"

"It's raining," he said stiffly.

"Today, yes. But it's been a dry, beautiful autumn."

Trouble leaped onto the table to lick catsup from Hana's scrambled eggs. She pushed him to the table's edge, where he jumped indignantly to the floor.

"Why don't you train this cat?" she demanded. "What am I paying you for?"

He pulled himself erect, his dark eyes looking blackly at her. "To keep Blue Spring Hill in good condition and to recover historical artifacts. I am not an animal trainer."

Trouble hissed at both of them, then stalked from the room.

Before he stalked too, Mr. Fred said, "One more week should do it. Then we'll cover the trenches. Before it freezes. You," he continued accusingly, "haven't even inspected the treasures in the annex. We have cups, bullets, half a water canteen, the remains of four soldiers, plus an assortment of body bones from incomplete corpses. And a lot of other surprises."

Contemplating the enormity of this collection, Hana added more catsup to her eggs, tasted them, shoved the dish from her, and ate a slice of toast. It had to be, of course, the morning Elsie arrived for a cup of coffee.

"I haven't seen much of you lately," she complained, helping herself.

"I've been busy, getting back into the office routine, you know."

"Hey, this is me—Elsie. Your best friend."

Debatable.

Elsie's large eyes blinked accusingly over the rim of her cup. "Office routine is like meat and potatoes to you. Second nature. No, Hana. You've been avoiding me."

Hana sighed. It was going to be one of those days.

"Don't be ridiculous. Why should I be avoiding you?"

"Because you're mad at me."

It was just awful when Elsie got like this.

Hana endeavored to keep some dignity in the scene with a crisp "I assure you I am not angry. Just busy."

Elsie shook her head with all the vigor of a temperamental five-year-old. "You're mad, all right. I know it. Bill knows it. And we know why. You have such an unrealistic—even puerile—attitude toward tourists. You just cannot bear it that we're working out this crime tour against your will. You're like a spoiled, willful child, Hana."

Hana was about to say "You take that back!" but stopped herself in time. Wow. Maybe Elsie had a point.

Elsie continued. "Well, we can't let this come between us, so I'll tell you what I'm going to do."

Hana stiffened. Oh, no. Not *that.*

But it was just *that.*

Oozing guidelike cheer, Elsie said, "I will personally escort you on our tour. The entire tour, so that you can see we are not violating the privacy of any living persons. You will be taken to see all the crime scenes in Conover County!"

"Elsie, no! I mean, thank you. I'm really touched, but I'm just too busy . . ."

Elsie stretched out her long neck just as Kitty Fisher did when she needed a sympathetic pet. "It won't take that long, for goodness' sake. After all, you won't be climbing on and off a bus with thirty-five other people. Please, Hana. Give a little for a change, all right?"

It was really hitting below the belt, and Hana was aware that Elsie knew it. Even so, if Elsie Hardinger were not such a devoted animal person—if she hadn't been absolutely invaluable when they were starting the Fur and Feather Refuge—if she weren't, damn it, such a good friend . . .

But she was. Hana refused, however, to let her get away with it too easily. It was those stinging references to her being spoiled that made her insist on returning the favor by conducting Elsie on a tour of the 1812 wing and a full description by Mr. Fred of the artifacts recently dug up. She knew Elsie cared nothing for either Revolutionary War bones or old halves of water canteens, so she considered it suitable penance. She herself stood it as long as she could, not able to pull her eyes from the skulls, one of which had hair still attached, then stopped Mr. Fred midsentence.

Later, she decided even the skulls were preferable to the tale Elsie spun about a grisly murder that had happened on a farm only two miles beyond Blue Spring Hill. Hana had never heard of the tragedy, but then, it had occurred in 1927. Lovingly Elsie lingered over the details of the jealous husband and the hacked bodies of his wife and her lover.

"We have permission to tour the barn, where it happened," Elsie gloated.

The next one was easier to take, because it involved a trip into the wooded slopes of the Scotch Mountains, where a group of brothers in the last century had stolen horses and chickens from area farmers. Back in the city, Elsie kept her tales to herself for a while but looked as if she might be silently purring over a particularly choice item.

Déjà vu. Hana had driven these streets recently.

Suddenly she knew where they were going. To King Street. Where Doris Hyla had lived with Honey.

She did not like the creepy sensation along her

neck and back. Nobody knew about Doris Hyla. Except herself. Sal.

They were within a block of the place. She could see the house now. Police cars and an ambulance were parked in front.

"Well, well," Elsie murmured, slowing.

She pulled in to the curb, eyes bulging as she watched.

"How did you know about this place?" Hana asked tightly.

Elsie looked a little scared. "Bill told me. He said this woman kept that girl here for a while. We were planning to do a drive-by. You see, we don't want to disturb anybody, but we do want to tour the places connected with Grace Urich. You know—make as much of a mystery of it as we can."

Hana swore.

Sergeant Kochen was coming out of the house, a bright green turtleneck visible beneath his trench coat. Men followed with a stretcher. The face of the victim was covered.

"She's dead," Hana said. "She's dead."

"Maybe it was an accident of some sort. I'll try to find out."

Hana seized her arm. "Drive me to your office so I can talk to Bill Longenecker. Then I want you to take me back to Blue Spring Hill to get my car. Move!"

"But the tour—"

"Damn the tour!"

If Kochen saw them, he gave no sign. But then, he apparently had his mind on the business at hand. She wondered if he knew about Doris Hyla's connection with Honey.

Craning her neck, Elsie drove slowly past the

activity, after which she speeded up in angry silence. She pulled into her parking space in the lot behind Bill's office and slammed on the brakes. Without a word, Hana got out of the car.

She didn't even look at the secretary as she hurried into Bill's private office. He was involved with his computer, looking up with a frown that changed to a smile.

"Hana! Did you like the tour? Great, isn't it? Elsie's done a terrific job of discovering—"

"How did you find out about Doris Hyla?"

"Who?"

"The woman who was hiding Honey."

"Oh . . . that kid?"

"How?"

Elsie entered. "We never finished the tour, Bill. Got to Doris Hyla's house and I guess she's dead. Which will be great for the tour—"

"This office will be on the tour in just about two minutes, because I am going to kill both of you," Hana snapped. "I can see the headlines—Double Murder in Tourist Office."

Elsie sighed sadly. "She just won't understand what we're trying to do."

Bill cleared his throat. "Elsie, maybe you'd better go."

She was willing. Hana suspected she was itching to get back to the scene of the crime.

"Go on," Hana agreed. "I'm sure Bill will be glad to drive me home."

"Oh, certainly, certainly!" Elsie zipped out of the office.

"She does get a little carried away," he said uneasily.

"Take me home. We can talk on the way."

Without waiting for his reply, Hana hurried

from the building. Elsie was already pulling from the parking lot. Breathing deeply of the cool November air, Hana tried to calm herself. Maybe it was time to terminate her friendship with Elsie. There were others who ran the refuge now. Good people. And even though she hated to use friends and then discard them, Elsie was driving her crazy.

Bill came out almost immediately. As he unlocked his car door, he glanced guiltily at her. They left the lot more slowly than Elsie had done.

He said quietly, "I'm sorry."

"Who told you about Doris Hyla?"

"Carl Reid."

"Carl—? When did you see him?"

"He came here. Two days ago. I was surprised too. Hana, he needed money. Claimed he had to get out of town."

"Did you call the police?"

"What for? It's no crime to need money."

"Give him any?"

"Well . . . naturally I refused. At first. Hardly know the fellow. Except I've seen him occasionally. Knew he worked for you."

"So you did give him some."

"He knew about our new tour. The crime tour. He said he could give me useful information."

"My God, Bill—"

"What's so terrible? How'd I know the stuff was about Grace? Could have been about any one of a hundred crimes. Even when he started talking about her I didn't think it was all that important. . . . Hey, you advertised for that kid in the paper. So what's the big secret?"

"Doris Hyla was a secret."

"Not to Carl. He knew all about her—how long she had the kid. How the kid got there and left."

"What else did he tell you?"

"Well, we talked about Grace. He said she was different from what any of us knew. Did you know she was a karate expert? It's a fact. If you can believe Carl Reid, that is. She kept a gun and knew how to use it. He said he'd been told her apartment was a fortress."

"Did he say how he knew these things?"

"Some woman told him."

"Name?"

"Search me. He was frightened, Hana. He admitted it. Said he had learned more than they wanted him to know."

"They?"

"Whoever. He wasn't about to tell me that, for Christ's sake."

"How much did you give him?"

They were on the bypass now, headed for the country. "Eight hundred."

That wouldn't take him far. Still, it was a large amount for the information Bill said he had received.

"Do you have any idea where the girl is now?" Hana asked.

He looked uncomfortable again. "With you. That's what Carl said."

Hana let it drop.

They rode in silence for a while, then Bill said, "I guess you're wondering why I gave him that much."

"Uh-huh. That's exactly what I was wondering."

"I felt sorry for him. The guy was really scared, Hana. And Grace Urich was murdered, so that means there are pretty mean people running around loose. I thought just maybe the money might save his life."

Possible. Carl did have a forlorn way about him when he chose to. He'd certainly been forlorn enough when she'd dug him out of the coal dirt. Their conversation faltered, then died. If Bill had gotten more information from Carl, he didn't intend to share it. She insisted that he drop her at the gate to Blue Spring Hill.

"Maybe we could have dinner soon," he said wistfully.

"I'll call you," Hana told him, then walked rapidly away.

The mists had melted with the morning and the day was becoming warmer. There were still colored, if tattered, leaves on some trees in her woods. Doris Hyla, who hadn't wanted to travel, was taking a journey now. Hana hoped it had been quick and painless. Carl was probably on the run for his life, but would eight hundred dollars take him far enough? These people seemed able to find out everything. She wondered if Honey was safe.

Ahead she could hear Mr. Fred's voice and the sound of digging. Damn the Revolutionary War.

Chapter Twenty-seven

It was late when Hana left her office. Only Mary Hafer had remained as long as she. Elsie had called in the middle of the afternoon. Hana had refused the call but after reading the message given to her had called back.

Ingratiatingly Elsie told about her return to King Street. Doris Hyla had been stabbed. Sergeant Kochen apparently did connect it with Grace Urich's death. However, he hadn't known about Hyla's keeping the child until Elsie herself helpfully informed him. She wanted Hana to remember how helpful she was being.

After leaving the office, Hana intended to drive home.

She hadn't thought much about Grace Urich lately as the emphasis shifted from the dead woman to the living child. She wanted to see Honey, assure herself that the girl was all right.

But she realized undue visits to Sal's farm would draw attention in that direction. She'd have to rely on Sal's verbal reports and even then be very careful.

Mists from meandering streams that wandered through farms and meadows were oozing across the land. Hana liked the grays and blues of November. Here and there the somber colors were slashed with unexpectedly vivid memories of autumn. Getting dark early now that daylight saving time was over . . .

What was it Grace had said . . . ? Last year. Yes, an evening much like this. She'd been depressed, and they'd gone for a drink together. She'd said, "I feel like a bird . . . you know. I'm always being polite and staying for dinner when I'm the dinner." It had seemed like an odd statement at the time. In retrospect, even odder. Was Grace afraid? Like Carl, did she really want to take money and run? But she hadn't taken her money. Had she stayed for dinner instead?

Okay. Suppose—just suppose—Grace were alive tonight. Suppose she was seeing this day, hearing the cry of those migratory geese. . . . Well, suppose she was, where would she go?

It was almost automatic. Hana drove to the CarPark.

That damn apartment. Well, okay. Grace would go there. But should Hana herself go again? Why not? It was still early. Check it out just once more and then close the damn thing forever. Rent it out again or let that weird Robie Holmes use it for storage. Maybe Robie could live there. Somebody that strange should be able to inhabit the place. Hana just couldn't understand this crazy punk thing the kids had. The Flower Children of the sixties had been so much more . . . normal.

Walking along the quiet mall, she was conscious of a weariness within herself. Always before she had been successful, whether it was in her carpet commercials or the business itself. College, too. Well, except for Mel Rosen. What was she going to do about Mel? Maybe she should ask what they were going to do about each other. . . . She'd been so preoccupied with Honey and with murder she hadn't felt capable of coping with the idea of a new relationship. They had to talk. If this was ever over, they had to talk.

She turned in at the alley. Robie's shop was already closed. She unlocked the downstairs door, then paused to look around. Damn the place. It always gave her the creeps, yet she couldn't stay away. Quickly she went inside and up the stairs. As she put the second key into the lock she felt a strong urge to turn and run. But weariness had produced a kind of lethargy, an ennui.

She turned the key and pushed open the door while she still stood in the hall.

Big, fat climax.

Empty.

The letdown left her even more tired. She closed and bolted the door. She turned on lights. Then she realized she was hungry. Should have bought something at a take-out. Better, she should not have come. It was almost dark.

God, she was getting as flaky as Elsie. *Come, take a tour through the haunted spaces of my mind.* She went into the kitchen. Maybe there were crackers. Or tea. She opened the refrigerator. Oh, good. Yogurt. Not fattening and . . .

Half a dozen cups of yogurt?

She stood, stupidly staring at them for some seconds. Slowly she took a cup, checked the date on it, got a spoon, opened the cup, then took it into the living room and ate it.

Somebody had been here. Some living person who ate yogurt. There would probably be other signs of their occupancy, but she felt in no mood to look for them. She should call Mr. Fred or Mel Rosen—certainly not Bill—to come and get her.

Galling.

"Hi. It's me again, back at the apartment. I'm tired of it all. I quit. Take me out of here."

No, she was too proud to do that.

She sat still for a few minutes after she had finished her yogurt and began to feel better. Finally she rose, threw away the plastic cup, and looked into the bedroom. The bed had been slept in.

There had been a number of times in her life when Hana felt she was operating on automatic pilot. Doing what had to be done without thought or plan. This was one of those times, as she went about the apartment turning off lights. She looked out the window. She wasn't even surprised to see the figure lurking below.

She took the gun from her shoulder bag. She would no more go without it now than she would leave the house without her shoes. The person below must know she was there, because he/she had seen the lights. Had she been followed? Stupid to let a brief ennui make her careless. She realized she hadn't even checked the rearview mirror.

It would be so out of character—ludicrous even —for her to come bursting through the door and say, "Freeze!" But she couldn't very well sneak up on the person, now could she? They'd surely see or hear her come out of the front door. If only she could sneak through a window and across the roofs and— But they were barred.

Anyway, it was even more outlandish than the "freeze" business.

She unbolted the apartment door, listening, then carefully opened it. The automatic light in the hall was on. Great. She'd be backlit when she opened the lower door. And if the person did not "freeze," what would she do then? Shoot? She wasn't even sure she could see to do that, coming into the dark of the alleyway from the bright hall. Besides, she might accidentally kill somebody if she fired.

At the bottom of the stairs she straightened her

shoulders, put herself on automatic, then jerked open the door, galloped onto the wooden stoop, blinked with authority into the darkness, gun gripped in both hands, and shouted, "Freeze!"

An amazing thing happened. It worked.

He wailed, "Don't shoot!" and came forward with hands raised high. Light from behind her fell on him.

Carl Reid.

"What the hell are you doing here?" she demanded.

"Followed you. From the office. I was hanging around out there."

She really was a lousy detective.

"I wanted to talk to you. Hey, could you put that thing down?"

Watching him carefully, she lowered the gun to a more comfortable position. She couldn't recall whether or not she had taken off the safety, but it would look uncool to check it out now.

"What do you want?"

"Money."

It was amazing how he had changed since the days he had worked for her. He whined. He even looked different. Seedier, unkempt.

"Your family has money."

"They won't give me anything. They say I've been mixing in affairs I shouldn't. I can't even talk to them anymore. And I've got to get out of town!"

"Sell your car."

"I did. To the guy who pulled me out of that shit up there in the mountains. There was damage, so I didn't get—"

"Bill Longenecker told me you got eight hundred dollars from him."

He seemed to forget the gun as he came forward. "Hey, what's that? I need enough to get out of the country, tide myself over while I stay out of sight. I won't even be able to work for a while."

"That's rather melodramatic, isn't it, Carl?"

"What the shit are you talking about?" he cried. "They're going to kill me if I don't!"

"If they're that dangerous, why did you tell Bill Longenecker about Doris Hyla?"

"I had to tell him something so he'd give me money."

"She might not have been killed if you'd kept your mouth shut."

He moaned, covering his face with his hands.

"Did you know she'd been stabbed?"

He shook his head, looked over his shoulder, then moved closer. "Can't we go inside?"

"No. I won't go anywhere with you."

"But it's not my fault. That bitch got me into this. That beautiful bitch," he said bitterly. "I was crazy. And I even fell for it twice. But she was so—"

"We've been through that, Carl. What did she have you doing this time?"

"Hanging out. Around people I know. You. The others. Reporting back."

"To her?"

The little snake. How much had he seen of Honey?

"Sure, to her! Who the fuck else?"

"And who did she report to?"

"The actors, I guess."

The casual answer was such a shock that she almost killed him. The safety had been off. A bullet snapped into the bricks of the pavement.

He was crying again as he dropped to the stoop,

his hands around his middle. For an awful moment Hana was afraid she really had shot him.

"I'll tell you what I know," he sobbed. "It's not much. She was talking to them. Actors who were doing something on the mall."

"Actors don't kill people or kidnap them. They put on plays and they're out of work a lot, but they don't kill. They may bore an audience to death occasionally, but they don't do these things."

"These actors do."

"Do they have a name? Like Mutilation Workshop or Theater Kill or something?"

"I never heard one. Look, all I know is I heard her talking one time on the phone about acting on the mall."

"Are they real actors, Carl?"

"I don't know! I didn't even want to know this much. . . . See what it's got me into? I wish I'd never met that bitch!"

He was a disgusting sight, cowering there on the steps. She wished she didn't feel sorry for him. She had to face the practical problem of what she must do now. She had fired a shot, yet nobody seemed to have heard. Unless these mysterious actors were lurking about offstage somewhere. But she didn't trust Carl enough to take him into the apartment. Nor was she about to go out into the mall right now, either alone or with Carl.

"All right, I'll help you," she decided. "Come to my office tomorrow morning prepared to make a statement of everything you know. We'll put it on tape. Then I'll match the sum Bill Longenecker gave you. As a goodwill gesture. Or severance pay, if you like."

He was wiping his nose as he looked up at her. "But what'll I do right now?"

"Go home."

"They won't let me in."

"Then slip away into the dark. There are plenty of alleys in the city—all sorts of places to hide. I'm sorry, Carl. I really am, but it's the best I feel I can do."

She went inside while he was still pleading with her. Bloody awful.

Upstairs once more, she looked down on the alleyway. He rang the bell for about five minutes. Then something apparently frightened him and he moved rapidly down the alley and away into the night. She hoped he'd be all right. There had been enough death.

She had not bolted the apartment door; nor did she turn on a light.

She sat on a chair in the far corner of the room, her .22 in her lap with the safety definitely off.

She waited.

Chapter Twenty-eight

SHE DIDN'T REALIZE exactly when it was she fell asleep. The dream came so easily it seemed like just another distorted reality. She thought she was sitting in the 1812 Annex at Blue Spring Hill. Mr. Fred was with her, busily and happily stacking skulls of dead soldiers along one of the walls.

Students kept opening the door and entering with buckets of skulls. The door opened again. . . .

Hana jerked awake.

The door of Grace Urich's apartment was opening. Against the light of the hall she could see a slim silhouette for a moment. Then the door closed, the bolt was shot across, and the person was inside the apartment with her.

Breathing quietly through her mouth, Hana's fingers tightened around her pistol. She expected the light to be turned on, but it was not.

She wanted to softly say, "Grace?"

But she had this ugly vision of Grace, dead and rotting, walking through these rooms. She could again discern a dark outline as the person moved toward the bedroom.

And bath. No light, but soon the toilet flushed. It flushed away the vision of the dead walking. She knew she had to make a move now. If she turned on the light, it might blind the other person, but it would also blind her. Suppose the person ran? It was the same problem she'd faced below. Would she actually shoot? Or if they didn't run, how could she hold a gun and dial the police?

While her mind pondered these questions, her body took action almost as if it were an independent agent. She was walking into the bedroom. No, running. Dashing. Switching on the light, her gun pointed at the blurred image. The light was behind her, on the wall. Shining on the girl and into the girl's eyes.

She looked like Grace. A young Grace. And for a moment Hana thought it was Grace before her eyes adjusted to the light and her mind clicked into the memory of the teenager she had chased through the alleys. That older version of Honey. The girl sat on the bed and had been taking off her shoes.

"Don't move," Hana ordered.

"Shit!"

She threw the shoe in her hand, hitting Hana in the stomach. Then the girl was on her feet, charging toward the door. A thrill of excitement swept through Hana. Gripping the gun but not firing, she grabbed as the girl passed her. Flesh. A thin arm. She dug in, knowing she hurt. As the teenager yelped, Hana dug harder, now with her nails. She swung the girl in a circle, bringing her around in front, pushing the gun into her ribs.

She could feel the tenseness in the other body. She herself felt great. My God. It was a rush. No wonder people got into this. Maybe she could become addicted.

But that lasted for only one isolated, fantastic moment. The second after, she still had the problem of what to do next. Trying not to show her indecision by slowing the momentum, she pushed the girl before her, moving into the living room. Deftly she swung the girl around again and shoved her into a chair.

"Stay there!"

The girl moved as if to rise.

"I'll shoot!"

"You fucking won't!"

"I fucking will! Want me to prove it?"

Rubbing her arm, the girl suddenly looked uncertain. So far so good, Hana thought. But she knew she needed help. And considering what she was doing might be illegal, probably her lawyer would be most helpful.

Keeping between her captive and the door,

Hana backed to the phone and dialed Mel's number with some difficulty while still pointing her .22.

The housekeeper answered. Mel wasn't home. He wasn't at the office, either. She left a message on his machine, then dialed Mr. Fred. She was beginning to sweat.

The girl had stopped rubbing her arm and was smiling, as if she guessed Hana's discomfort. If Mr. Fred didn't answer, maybe she'd have to resort to calling the police. And what would she tell them?

Mr. Fred answered. She invited him to come immediately.

Later, at Blue Spring Hill, nobody was happy. Mr. Fred declared he would never do such a thing again. He said it was kidnapping, plain and simple. And now they were holding this young, unknown person on the top floor of a historic shrine. Hana announced that it was her home, not a historic shrine, but even she had qualms about locking a defiant, obviously mean-spirited individual in Honey's old rooms. With Honey, she could believe she was rescuing a child. This teenager left no doubt she was being imprisoned, not rescued. She cursed them, using a creative, fluent vocabulary.

"We'll wait until I can get ahold of Mel Rosen and have him question her. After that we'll either call the police or—"

"Or what?" Mr. Fred demanded, his big head bobbing in a hostile fashion.

"Whatever Mr. Rosen suggests. After all, he is my lawyer."

"No lawyer will want to get mixed up in this."

"Mel will!"

But she wasn't sure. She felt glad Sal had gone home for the day. She hated to think how her Mennonite sensitivities would have reacted to this sort of . . . rescue. She tried to distract Mr. Fred by talking about his bones. Even that didn't work.

The animals, too, were upset, because the girl was pounding on the door when she wasn't viciously kicking at it. Frequently this was followed by the sound of breakage in the schoolroom. Ghost growled. Crumb howled.

"In a historic shrine!" Mr. Fred repeated, then stalked off to the kitchen, followed by a parade of indignant animals. Only Trouble exempted himself, sitting in front of the locked door, switching his tail as if ready for a fight.

"This premises is guarded by an attack cat," Hana shouted to the door. "Now stop! We'll let you out as soon as my lawyer gets here."

"Tell him to bring along one for me, because I'm going to sue!" the girl screamed, adding a variety of inventive obscenities.

The word *sue* always made Hana nervous. There was a lull in the banging, however, probably due to bruised knuckles. Hana tapped lightly.

"Do you want something to eat or drink?"

She was told where to put the food and drink. For one so young, their guest certainly did have a disgusting mouth. A person ought to be civilized even if being held captive.

Temporarily.

It wasn't as if she had *actually* been kidnapped.

Hana dialed Mel's home again. This time there was no answer at all. It was two hours later when he finally called and said he'd be right over. A very uncomfortable two hours they had been, the last filled with ominous silence. A dozen times Hana had been tempted to open the door. But a dozen times she decided she did not dare. She no longer felt herself a physical match for the wiry creature penned in the rooms, and she doubted she could count on Mr. Fred now. Trouble continued his vigil. At times he rose on his hind legs to scratch the woodwork.

The first thing Mel said was, "I cannot believe a woman in your position would do such a thing! My God, Hana, what's gotten into you?"

She explained. He waved aside the explanations as if they made no difference. She suspected the police would have the same reaction.

They hurried upstairs. He ordered her to unlock the door immediately.

Uneasily she did so.

Trouble leaped into the room. They followed.

Looking young and vulnerable, the girl sat on a too-small chair. It was amazing that language such as she had been using could come from those rosebud lips. Hana put her hand into her pocket, on her gun. If Mel realized she still carried it, he chose to ignore the fact.

"I'm Mel Rosen, Ms. Shaner's attorney." He smiled.

"I'm the one needs a lawyer."

"Now, now. I'm sure we can clear up this little misunderstanding without hard feelings on anyone's part," he continued soothingly. "You are . . ."

"Grace."

He looked at her now as if noting the resemblance for the first time. Trouble sniffed at her.

"Grace what?" Hana asked tensely.

Insolently. "You know."

Mel looked annoyed. "You are not Grace Urich. Grace Urich is dead."

She leaned forward, chin on hands, eyes dropping to the area of his crotch. As she continued to stare, he stirred uncomfortably, attempted a few questions, then checked his zipper.

She kept on staring. Mel sat down and crossed his legs.

"Ms. Shaner meant you no harm, young lady. In fact, she wants to help you. We all do. Believe that. We wanted to find and help Grace Urich, but all we succeeded in doing was locating her body. Did you know that Ms. Shaner handled all the funeral expenses and buried Grace in her family plot? We would now like to discover who killed Grace and why. Will you help us?"

She slouched down in the chair, still peering at his fly. Awkwardly, he uncrossed his legs.

"What's the matter? You getting a hard-on?"

Mel cleared his throat. "As a matter of fact, you're rather a turnoff."

"Yeah? Well, don't get the idea that I think you got such a great crotch. It's just that I don't want to look at your fucking face."

Mel rose. "Hana, may I see you in the hall for a moment?"

Hana called the cat, who was seated on a chair beside the girl. He refused to come.

She hesitated. "Do you mind if he stays?"

The girl looked at the cat. He looked at her. She shrugged.

"Come, Hana," Mel said impatiently.

She joined him, and he quickly closed the door behind them.

"You either turn her over to the police or let her go. Immediately."

"She was just trying to get your goat, Mel."

"She's dangerous. She may holler rape—anything. I wouldn't trust that one any further than last week."

"But she was living in Grace's apartment. She looks like Grace. And Honey. I know she can help us."

"I am officially recommending that you notify the authorities! I don't know what's going on here, and neither do you. If you are hiding that child, turn her and this one over to the police and get out of it while you can."

"Oh, I don't know what to do—"

"Do what I'm telling you, damn it! I'm your attorney. Listen to me. I'm telling you to take the only course possible."

"I'll think about it."

"Hana—"

"I said I'd think about it!"

He swore, then strode down the hall and on to the stairs. Hana watched him go for a sad moment, before she returned to the room.

The girl had risen and was staring out the window, as if contemplating escape in that direction. Trouble, too, stared at the scene, competently considering this interesting possibility.

"You'll kill yourself if you try to get out that way," Hana told her.

"Maybe it wouldn't matter."

"It must matter to somebody."

She gave a bitter laugh, one far too old for her years.

"My lawyer tells me in no uncertain terms to either turn you over to the police or simply let you walk out of here. But I think there's another solution."

"Grace" turned warily, as if poised to sprint for the door.

"You were hiding out in Grace Urich's apartment," Hana said quickly. "Which means somebody's after you. Somebody besides me, because I'm not really a threat to you and I think you know that. My suggestion is that if you must hide, why not hide here? Maybe not in these particular rooms, but downstairs the 1812 Annex is full of junk and would be a great place to hide if you don't mind sharing space with old bones. Think about it. Stop running for a second and think. Maybe you could rest. Maybe it would help you solve some of your problems."

The girl's body language told Hana she had struck home. There was a relaxation of tension, a moment of giving in to . . . what? Her world-weariness maybe, or perhaps physical fatigue. Slowly she came and sat on the chair again.

Trouble gave a look of regret at the window escape route, then followed her. Hana waited.

Finally the girl said, "My name's Abby."

"Abby what?"

"Don't push! Don't ask questions, damn it. If I decide to tell you anything, I'll tell it, but don't think you're going to hear no big fat fucking confessions. Maybe I'll stay, and then again maybe I'll just decide to walk the fuck out."

Even a bad deal is better than no deal at all.

"You want to sleep here, or do you want me to make up a bed downstairs—?"

"Here. I'll sleep here. Tonight. I have to think."

"Do you need anything?"

"Uh-uh. Not from you or anybody else. I take care of myself."

"I thought a spare toothbrush—"

"Go stick your toothbrush up that shyster's ass!"

"So don't take a toothbrush. It's no big deal if you want to go around with fuzzy teeth," Hana snapped, turning to the door.

"Hey! You. This is where you kept Honey, right?"

Hana hesitated. "Yes. It is."

"Where is she?"

"Someplace safe."

Abby laughed again. It was a horrible laugh, more in keeping with the mausoleum in the cemetery than these cheerful rooms on top of Blue Spring Hill.

Chapter Twenty-nine

THE NEXT MORNING Hana overslept. No wonder, she thought as she groggily made her way to the bathroom. She could hear the rain, could sense the gray of earth and sky. It would take the last of the leaves.

While showering, she planned her day. Get money for Carl Reid. Cash. She didn't want him running about with her check in his wallet.

She wondered if the girl, Abby, was still upstairs or if she had run away during the night. Mel Rosen would be happy if she had. Poor Mel. She really was a trial to him.

Kitty Fisher and Penelope Baskin were waiting for her when she got out of the shower. As usual, Kitty F. complained about the weather. She had faith that Hana had complete control of such matters.

Hana chose a maroon sweater and skirt, which she wore with a very special scarf she had bought last spring. It had an intricate design of maroon, beige, and white, but it was the material that had attracted her so much. Whichever way it was tied, this material slipped into the most compact knots she had ever seen, then, when untied, resumed its original shape. She brushed her hair, realizing it needed a trim. Damn. She'd missed her last hair appointment. Grace would never have allowed it to happen. Cindy Hefflefinger tried to keep up with her schedule, but she just wasn't . . .

She went downstairs to find Mr. Fred working by himself and in a foul mood.

"Sal's not usually this late," Hana said, glancing at the clock.

"She didn't used to be," he growled darkly. "But lately she seems to be very busy at home."

Ghost rubbed against her, wetting her nylons. Both he and Crumb were soggy and somewhat muddy. Sal would never have permitted that.

"We're putting up a canopy so we can work on the last trench. We've got to finish."

"I hope you have everything you're ever going to dig out of my lawn," Hana snapped as she helped herself to coffee.

"We think so. Unless, of course, new information turns up."

"And just when do you intend to start filling in?" She could be as testy as Mr. Fred any day.

"Over the weekend."

The rain had ended by the time Hana finished breakfast. Still no Sal. She had Mr. Fred make up a tray, which she carried to the top floor of the house.

She hadn't really expected Abby to be there, but she was. Sleeping as if totally exhausted, with Trouble curled beside her. Trouble stretched, yawned, and dismissed Hana with a flick of his tail. Hana called Abby softly, then carried the tray downstairs again. The girl could have breakfast later.

Mr. Fred and the muddy dogs had gone out.

By the time she reached the hall closet to get her all-weather coat, he was back inside.

"It's the cops!" he cried. "One of the students saw the car. That girl—we've got to get her out of here!"

"How could they possibly know she's here?"

He was actually wringing his hands. "I don't know. Maybe she called them to come and rescue her."

"Now, just calm down. I'll talk to them. If they do know about her, I'll take full responsibility—"

"I'm the one held her down on the way over here." His big head bobbed dismally. "And she'll tell. God knows *what* she'll tell."

Hana realized he was right.

"Keep them down here as long as you can," she told him, then ran up the wide stairs and kept going until she reached the rooms on the top floor. Abby still slept. Hana shook her. Trouble hissed. The girl moaned, then opened her eyes.

"The police are here," Hana said urgently. "They may know about you. If they do, they'll search the house. Not much we can do about it. Maybe you can get out the back door. That is, if you don't want to see the police."

Without looking at Abby again, Hana left the

room and went downstairs. Her warning had been virtually useless, she realized, when she saw that Sergeant Kochen was already inside and showing Mr. Fred a search warrant.

"What's the meaning of this?" she demanded haughtily.

"These 'gentlemen' insist we have a young woman here who has information about Grace Urich's murder," Mr. Fred said, matching her tones.

But the sergeant and the three officers with him were affable and cool. Kochen politely handed her the search warrant.

"All entrances to the house are guarded," he informed her conversationally. "So if you were upstairs warning somebody to leave, I'm afraid it was wasted effort."

The man was a swine.

She mentally apologized to swine as she stalled for time by frowning over the search warrant. He patiently explained it to her and pointed out the official signatures.

"I'm afraid I must insist on having my lawyer present during this search," she finally said, doing rapid calculations on the amount of time it would take Mel Rosen to reach Blue Spring Hill.

Kochen looked as if he was enjoying this. "Certainly, certainly," he agreed, beckoning his assistant.

That cheerful officer popped open Hana's front door to reveal Mel on the porch. Staring at his unhappy face, Hana knew how the police had found out about Abby.

Mel cleared his throat as he came into the hall. "The search warrant is in order, Hana."

"She just wouldn't take my word for it," Sergeant Kochen beamed. "Now we can get started."

With much the same attitude as Mr. Fred's lawn diggers, they went charging up the stairs.

"Go with them. Keep an eye on things," Hana ordered Mr. Fred.

He looked unhappy as he complied.

Hana followed Mel Rosen into the living room, where one of her placid ancestors in white lace cap and gray satin gown smiled benignly down. The room, subdued as a November day, seemed unaffected by the invasion of police.

"Were you afraid to come in and face me?" she demanded.

"Certainly not."

"Then what were you doing hanging around outside?"

"I was on my way in. The police drive faster than I do." He licked his lips. "I wonder if I might have a sherry?"

She went silently to the table with the decanters and poured drinks for both of them into the delicate antique crystal. As she took a sip, she realized the house was amazingly quiet, considering that a search was going on. Perhaps they had already found her.

She had not asked Mel to sit down.

Finally, after more sherry, she asked, *"Why?"*

"Damn it, Hana," he said, then stopped and drew a deep breath. "I told the police about that young woman because I care about you."

"You have cops running all over Blue Spring Hill because you care about me?" she asked furiously. "I'm going to fire you. You've violated client confidentiality."

"I didn't do this as your lawyer—I did it as your friend!"

Hana put her glass on the table. "Leave my house."

He sat on the sofa.

She started for the door. "I'll have you thrown out."

"Hana."

She paused.

"Sit down," he said. "Please."

"I don't want to sit down. I want to get you out of here."

He sighed. "Listen to me for just a minute. You've been on awfully thin ice. With that child . . . and now this girl. My God, you heard her yesterday. All that sex talk. She's capable of accusing anybody of anything. And she might even be a murderer. But you barge right ahead—taking the law into your own hands, putting yourself in the position of facing criminal charges. I decided I had to get that kid into police custody before you got into real trouble. Now, if you want, I'll leave. But at least I know I've done what I could for you."

He had risen and was facing her. She was still angry. She *wanted* to be angry. She really did want him out of there, but she heard herself asking him to sit down. He did. She poured more sherry for both of them.

"Damn you anyway," she said quietly. "You had no right . . . but maybe you have a point—about Abby. I'll admit she could be a problem."

"She could be lethal." He held his amber drink up to the wan light coming through the window. "This is beautiful."

"My God, Mel!" Hana cried. "We're having a

fight and you're admiring the color of your sherry."

He grinned sheepishly. "Maybe I am weird, but you're no prize yourself, lady."

"Was your wife a prize, Mel?"

She didn't even know why she asked it except it was something she'd been wanting to ask for a long time and she was just mad enough to do it.

There was silence broken only by the ticking of the old clock. He still held his glass before him as if frozen in time. As if in the amber liquid he was seeing a face he no longer wanted to see. Then, in a strange kind of slow motion, he finally set down the glass.

"No. She wasn't." He seemed to shake himself out of a daze and force himself to look at her. His voice was flat. "I suppose people do wonder why I don't ever say anything, but . . . It was bad. She beat Robin. She was abusive. She needed help. But she wouldn't accept help. I was afraid for the girls' lives. About a year after the divorce she killed herself."

Hana felt ashamed of herself. It was a personal tragedy that he would have told her about someday—some quiet day if their relationship ever resumed. But she had meanly forced it out of him.

Helplessly she said, "Mel . . . I'm sorry . . ."

He shook his head. "I should have told you long ago. I should talk about it sometimes. I know that. It's just—"

Sergeant Kochen stomped into the room.

"She's gone," he announced.

Hana blinked at him, for a moment not realizing who he was talking about. Mel rose, staring at Kochen.

"I'm damned if I know how she got away," Kochen said bitterly. "We'll keep looking, but I'm sure we're not going to find anyone. But since it's a large house with lots of hiding places, we'll keep at it." He moved in to Hana. She stood her ground. "What I want from you right now is your story of how that girl came to be in this house."

Hana glanced at Mel, who nodded briefly. After a moment's hesitation, she gave an expurgated version of encountering Abby in Grace Urich's apartment, omitting mention of guns and coercion. She said she was only trying to help the poor soul, who certainly had nothing to do with the crimes, and she really had no idea where or why the girl had gone. Kochen was obviously dissatisfied, but there wasn't much he could do about it.

Long before the police were finished, Mel had returned to his office. As soon as the official search was completed, Hana returned to the top floor, but except for traces of fingerprint powder, it appeared undisturbed. Penelope Baskin and Kitty Fisher came out of hiding, but Trouble, too, had disappeared.

Sal still had not come.

Hana felt unnerved, anxious. She called the farm, but there was no answer. She got in touch with the detective agency. The security guard she'd hired for the Nunemachers had reported the day before. There'd been no trouble. A soothing operator she spoke to was sure they'd know if there was any untoward disturbance. He was even starting to talk like a computer. She called her office. Nothing other than ordinary business was happening there. Carl Reid had not shown up asking for money. She wondered about that.

She was just hanging up the phone when Trouble came purring around her legs.

"Where have you been?" she asked.

Mr. Fred came down the main staircase and replied for the cat. "He was up on the roof. With her."

"The roof?"

"Apparently she crawled out to escape the police. That cat followed. Two of a kind, if you ask me."

"It's a wonder they weren't killed. That roof's terribly steep."

"Well, they weren't. She's back now. In the room. Thank God your father and your aunt aren't here to see such goings-on at Blue Spring Hill."

Leaving Mr. Fred to ruminate about the bad times into which the historic mansion had fallen, Hana ran to the top of the Annex. Trouble followed, obviously hoping for another expedition.

She opened the door. Abby sat on the bed as though the last few hours hadn't happened.

"Mr. Fred says you were on the roof. With the cat."

Abby nodded.

Hana went to the window, opened it, and leaned out. This alone was enough to make her queasy. But then, she never was good with heights. Keeping her eyes on the roof rather than the ground, she could see that if one had the guts, it would be possible to crawl along the coping, onto a narrow ledge, then up to the main roof where the large chimneys were. Anyone behind the chimneys would never be seen. Still, it was amazing that a cat would go along with a crazy human attempting it. Cats were, after all, the most intelligent of creatures.

"It was raining," Hana said with some awe. "Those tiles must have been wet and slippery."

Abby shrugged.

Trouble leaped happily to the windowsill and placed a tentative paw outside. Hana picked him up, dropped him back into the room, then closed the window.

She turned to Abby. "I've been accused of a lot of things lately, and I suppose some of them are true. I've been told to let the police handle this. Maybe I'll decide to do that. I want some answers about what's going on, or I'll hold you right here and have the police come and get you. And this time you won't be out on the roof!"

"You go to bloody fucking hell," Abby said easily.

Hana grabbed the front of the girl's blouse, yanking her off the bed. "Grace Urich is dead! The woman who babysat Honey is dead! And now I can't find my friend Sal Nunemacher! Talk to me!"

She slammed the girl back down.

Abby looked scared. "Grace'd kill me."

"Grace is dead."

Abby said nothing.

Hana went on. "We checked the fingerprints. Fingerprints don't lie."

Abby's voice was heavy. "Everything lies. In my world, everything lies."

"But if Grace Urich is alive . . . who did we bury in her grave?"

Abby stared sullenly at her.

"All right," Hana said. "I'll ask Grace. *You take me to Grace.*"

Abby spit in her face.

Hana struck her.

For a moment they were still, eyeing each other.

Hana said calmly, "I won't take no for an answer, Abby. I want Grace Urich. I've been looking for her for a long time. You might as well cooperate, because you aren't getting away from me."

"You won't do anything to me."

"There's more than one way of doing things to people," Hana said, slowly taking the gun from her pocket and trying to talk tough. "I have a lot of money and a lot of influence. I can have you locked up in a padded cell so legally secure you'll never get out."

Eyeing the gun, Abby sat up. "Yeah . . . Okay, why not? So I'll take you to Grace. But no gun. Not when we get there. You got to leave it in the car. Grace'd kill me if I brought anybody who had a gun."

Hana hesitated. Grace was her friend. So, despite everything, it had to be all right. Reluctantly she agreed.

But for now she slipped it into her pocket. They went downstairs, Abby in front, followed by Trouble, who had been watching with excitement.

Mr. Fred came into the hall from the direction of the kitchen.

"I'm really worried about Sal," he said. "There's still no answer out there."

"We're going to her farm right now," Hana told him. "I may not be back for a while, because there are a few other things I have to do after that."

Like finally finding Grace Urich.

She got their coats out of the hall closet. In the

parking lot Abby said, "Can you borrow a car someplace?"

"What?"

"Even before you go check on this woman Sal, we better get another car."

Impatiently Hana unlocked the doors. "Why?"

Abby flopped into the seat. "Bugs."

Her car bugged? Hana'd never thought of that, which confirmed her amateur status, she decided. She wondered if she was up to the next few hours. But as Mel had said, she had barged into this, and the only thing to do now seemed to be to keep on barging.

"We'll get another car," she agreed.

Hana drove rapidly to Shaner Industries. Inside, she kept a firm grip on Abby. Siamese twins. A few people looked at them in surprise. Mary Hafer most of all, when Hana asked to borrow her car. They exchanged keys with Mary Hafer, who was still looking doubtfully after them as they left.

Hana drove rapidly, taking a few precautions to throw off any tails. Probably amateurish attempts, she thought bitterly.

"Which direction are we heading when we leave Sal's farm?" she asked.

Abby was leaning back, eyes closed. "I don't even know where this fucking farm is, so why don't we wait and see?"

Deciding the time for battle was when she was not behind a steering wheel, Hana let it pass. The sun came out, making the world look brighter. Sending mud splattering, she spun Mary's two-year-old Ford onto a lane through apple orchards.

Now that she had time to think, a panic was rising within her. It would be too much—Sal and

Honey, the whole family maybe. She glanced at Abby, who was passive, seemingly uninvolved. Damn her. Damn them all. As she skidded to a stop on the graveled area beside the barn, Hana had an awful feeling of what she might find.

Sal must have heard the car, because she came from the house immediately. Hana got out of her car fast, eyes on Sal. Thank God she was all right.

But something was wrong, and it could only be Honey. The child was either dead or had been taken away. For a moment she stood staring at Sal. She was aware that Abby, too, had come out of the car and stood idly looking about.

Finding her voice, Hana called, "Where's the kid? . . . The bodyguard? What's the matter here?"

"I should have called," Sal said dully. "But I didn't know what to say or what to do. I was praying for an answer."

"It's Honey, isn't it?"

Sal shook her head. She was looking at Abby. "She's all right, but I don't think we should talk about it."

"Then what's wrong?" Hana cried. "Where's . . . what's-his-name? The guy I hired to watch over you?"

Sal wore a gray woolen shawl, which she wrapped more tightly about herself as if it were protection from a world crowding in on her.

"Working in the dairy barn."

"Get him."

"We don't need him. Not for this."

"I want to talk to him—"

"No. You come along once," Sal insisted.

After her tiff with Mel and the traumas of the morning, Hana felt the last thing she needed was a trip around the farm. But Sal had gone on ahead, grimly, rapidly, with authority.

"Come with us," Hana ordered.

Abby shrugged and trotted down the lane by her side.

The land had not lost all the colors of harvest. A few pumpkins remained in the fields. There were also remnants of yellow-grained corn where birds were feeding. Sal marched doggedly on ahead, not turning to see if they were keeping up, not talking. Hana tried speaking to her, but Sal continued walking as if she had not heard.

Yet Hana knew Sal too well to doubt that they were going to meet with something very unpleasant on some remote corner of the farm. Sal never lost a day's work without good reason. Nor was she taking this walk for her health.

It was a meadow with a stream meandering through. A place of grazing cows and the daisies of summer. A few large sycamore trees for shade. A calendar scene, even this late in the year. Watercress rippled green in the brook. The uncut hedgerows were bright with the red and orange of ripe bittersweet and full of birds feeding on seeds.

Sal entered the meadow on a little-used footpath.

"How much farther?" Hana asked.

Sal kept moving.

It was in the far corner of the field. They could see it now. Soil. Freshly dug.

Finally Sal spoke. "My brother checks over the farm this time of year—sees what needs mending in the way of fences. We don't get out this way much in summer. Too much work with the crops. Mostly we let the dairy cows in here. Annie's pet goats, too. Anyways, when he was here last week he saw some dirt that looked like it had been dug up some time ago. He's the one goes down the road to see television shows on Buddy Kawoski's set a couple times a week. It gives him funny ideas. So he got a shovel and started digging, thinking maybe he'd find buried treasure. He found buried treasure, all right."

Sal pointed.

It was a shallow grave, and he had been there for some months. Hana forced herself to look. She didn't think she knew the man, although it was almost impossible to tell.

"Does the bodyguard know about this?"

Sal shook her head. "Buddy had the good sense to keep his mouth shut for a change. He's scared."

"I'm glad it was nothing worse. I was worried about Honey . . . all of you—"

"Worse! How could it be worse?" Sal demanded with unaccustomed vehemence. "I don't want police around this farm. Especially now. I've been tempted to cover him right up again, even though I'm not sure that's not a sin."

Abby had been standing a little apart, humming a slow sad tune that was barely audible. She turned to Sal.

"It's okay. You can cover him up and forget about it."

They looked at her. She moved forward to stare dispassionately into the shallow grave.

"Nobody's going to miss him. Nobody's going to ask questions, either. Hey, I know you got Honey here. So just cover him up again and forget it."

"Who is he?" Hana asked faintly.

"I don't know his name. Don't matter."

Hana wanted to open her mouth and scream. She wanted to fill the air of the pasture with shrieks until the wild birds flew in startled circles. And maybe throw herself onto the grass and wail.

Instead she asked quietly, "Who killed him?"

"Why, Grace, of course," Abby said, sounding somewhat surprised. "Who did you think?"

"I didn't know," Hana murmured. "Why did she do it?"

"Because he tried to kill her, why else? He got into the hall . . . you know, through the front door, into where the steps are. So she got him instead. Broke his windpipe, I think. She's great at karate. What I mean, he was dead, man. Real dead. So I helped her bury him. She'd been out here to visit Sal one time, walked around the farm and spotted this pasture. You know. In case she ever needed to bury somebody. That's only common sense, right? We thought the shit would grow over it and you'd never notice."

Sal's eyes were closed, her face turned heavenward.

"He's a human soul," she whispered, but Hana wasn't sure whether she was speaking to God or to them.

"Not anymore," Abby said nonchalantly. "I don't think he had a soul any more than he had a name. Hired gun. Killer. Hit man. Know what I'm talking about? If he had a soul, it's rotting in hell right now. Go on, cover him up. No big deal. It's what usually happens to them."

Sal's eyes popped open.

"Are you related to Honey?" she demanded.

"If you say so."

"How? How are you related?"

Abby shrugged. Hana moved closer.

Abby looked at her, then said, "Oh, what the

hell. What does it matter? I'm Abby, Grace's sister."

"And Honey's her daughter, isn't she?" Hana asked.

"Yeah."

"She could grow up to be like you," Sal said with sad wonder. "Have you ever been to church, young woman? Have you ever thought about your own soul and where you'll spend eternity?"

Abby groaned to Hana, "Let's get out of here."

"In a minute. Sal, maybe Abby's right. Maybe it would be best if you just covered him up."

The woman looked stricken. "That's not a Christian burial."

"I bet you're real good at saying prayers," Abby snickered. "So say a couple before you shovel the dirt over him."

Sal flinched. "Don't say things like that."

Hana patted Sal's shoulder, trying to comfort her.

Abby said impatiently, "Hey, you want to talk to Grace or what? We haven't got all year, you know. This guy'll keep."

"Can we help you?" Hana asked Sal.

Sal shook her head. "I think it would help most if you take this Abby away now."

"Great. Let's split," Abby said enthusiastically.

Hana felt glad she had slugged this kid. Obnoxious person. Not at all like Grace. Then she looked down at the mangled body again. But Grace had done this thing. Her Grace. Her friend. . . .

"I'll call you," she told Sal lamely. "Come, Abby."

They retraced their steps down the lane. Hana

looked back only once to see Sal still standing with her shawl clutched tightly about herself. Alone in the pasture. Hana hoped she was praying. She even hoped the prayers would be heard somewhere.

Chapter Thirty

GRACE URICH STEPPED from behind an outcropping of rock.

Hana exhaled a deep breath, partly because of the climb through seemingly pathless forest and partly because she had reached the end of a long search.

A momentary triumph washed away, leaving loss and sadness. The woman standing before her was not the Grace Urich she had known. She had only been playing the part of her Grace as she was now playing a . . . what? Survivalist? She was dressed rough, armed, and vaguely reminded Hana of Israeli women soldiers she had once met. The woman gestured with comedic theatricality.

"Want me to hum a bit of my theme song? It's called 'Amazing Grace.' "

Hana could find nothing to say.

Grace waited a moment, then continued. "Nice of you to drop by while you were in the neighborhood. I'm alone too much. Of course, yesterday I wasn't alone. The piano tuner was here."

"After . . . all this . . . I'm in no mood for jokes!"

"I always said you were a marginally inspiring person, Hana. Come. Walk into my parlor."

Grace slipped back into the forest, as camouflaged as a wild animal. Hana hesitated, even though she knew there was no turning back. It seemed ages ago that they had crossed the Appalachian Trail, and they were now so deep in the Pennsylvanian woodland she had no idea where she was.

"She said for you to come," Abby said impatiently. "I mean, this is what you wanted, right?"

"Right. . . ."

Actually, wrong. She had never wanted this kind of hike through the wilderness. Another mile of it and she'd be flat on her face in the dead leaves. But thankfully, after a few hundred yards they came to a sheltered area amid boulders. Although Spartan, it was a camp. Abby threw herself onto a sleeping bag beneath a camouflaged tarp as if she, too, had been exhausted by the climb.

Hana, neither dressed nor conditioned for mountaineering, dropped breathlessly onto a log. There were a million questions she wanted to ask, but for the moment just breathing seemed more important.

Grace laughed. "Poor Hana. I sure jogged you out of your rich, complacent world, didn't I?"

Hana, who hated to be made to feel ridiculous, felt ridiculous.

After a false start she managed to gasp, "I guess I rode out on a white charger to rescue you while all the time you were very competently taking care of yourself."

"I got dangerous just after I learned to read," Grace grinned. "How's Honey?"

"All right. I think."

As the woman dropped to sit cross-legged on the ground, Hana realized she looked thinner. But there was hardness in her lean limbs. The nearly bare woods around lay silent, as if waiting. It was almost as weird as the dream Grace had told them about at the summer picnic.

Grace . . .

"What am I to call you?"

The smile was faint now. "You've always called me Grace."

"But that's not your real name."

"It'll do."

Even now, even here, Grace whoever seemed in no hurry to talk. Abby had apparently lapsed into total lethargy.

"I want to know what's going on," Hana said firmly. "I want to know now. You owe me that much."

Grace seemed to be considering this during moments of more silence. Hana stirred uncomfortably on her damp log.

"You're really dredging for answers, aren't you?" the woman asked softly. "I'm still dredging for questions. But I don't expect you to understand that. Still . . . I suppose you've a right to know. But you're not going to like it."

"I didn't like the trail of bodies I was following to get to you, either. Who did we bury in my family plot?"

"My sister."

"Abby's your sister."

She was droll now. "A person can have more than one sister."

"How did this sister get your fingerprints?"

"Really, Hana. Couldn't you guess? All we did

was substitute a set of her prints for mine in your company files. To prove to official wisdom that she was indeed Grace Urich. After all, I still had my keys to the office."

"Why?"

"I was safer dead."

"Safer . . . from whom?"

"Rolf Bedlow."

"Who's he?"

"There's no easy answer to that one." She frowned thoughtfully. "Description? Okay. An attractive man—six foot three inches—a genius in his own way. He's done a little of everything in his time—in the sixties theater, later government work—has a brilliant scientific mind, too. He actually invented a new kind of telescope about ten years ago."

"But what's he doing now?"

"Making an atom bomb. Just a small device, of course."

The air around Hana felt colder, the log damper. "For the government, I hope . . . for the government?"

Grace's voice had turned colder too. "Rolf is an anarchist. A terrorist if you like."

Hana felt sick. "And you?"

She looked surprised. "Me? I was just looking for a chance to melt some icebergs with my hair dryer. Eleanor—that's my sister—and I were thumbing around Europe one summer when we met these fantastic people. It's so great to get out where you meet real people. Like Rolf's group. We'd never known anybody like that. It was all so emotionally freeing. Didn't you ever feel an urge to violence?"

"No," Hana said vehemently to cover a slight twinge of guilt.

"No, I don't suppose *you* would. At first they didn't trust us. It's not easy to be accepted in these circles, but Rolf . . . he liked me. So he let us play along for a while. Nothing serious—practicing karate, target shooting, making simple bombs. It was rather like charades."

"But you knew it was real. Surely you guessed where it would lead. Why didn't you get out?"

"Because she's crazy," Abby said, coming to life. "Because our whole family was always crazy. Like she and Ellie went off to Europe with only a couple hundred dollars besides plane fare. And Mom and Dad let them go. They didn't care—they were always at the community theater anyhow. Everybody in our house was always acting and pretending. Like she pretended Old Rolf was in love with her."

"He was in love with me," Grace snapped. "Abby's never understood any of us. You can't either, Hana. These people were like a family. So close, so dedicated to ideals. It was wonderful."

"If it was so great and you enjoyed it so much, what happened?"

"Well, once we became part of the real action it was frightening as well as exciting. And Rolf—he was so charismatic, but after a while . . . I realized he was a little . . . What? Strange, you might say."

"I'm sure I would," Hana agreed dryly.

"I loved France, and so did the others. But he insisted on returning to this country. To this area. The nuclear power plant here in Pennsylvania—the one that had the 'accident' some years ago. That's why he's here. He considers this the best place to collect the material he needs. And to work in quiet. He can't very well get to Chernobyl, you know."

The horror of it took Hana's breath. "Is he— How close is he?"

"I'm not sure."

"You've been helping him—that's why you got a job here."

"No, I'm not helping him. Not in this."

"Then why are you still here?"

"There's nowhere to run," she said simply. "Once you enter the terrorists' underworld, you're trapped in that world forever."

Hana wanted out. Right then. Get to a phone, call the FBI, Sergeant Kochen—anybody. Questions, answers meant nothing now. She struggled off the low log.

Apparently Grace read her thoughts, because she put her hand on her ready revolver. "Don't even try it. We're not finished talking."

Helplessly, Hana looked at Abby. "How do you fit into all this?"

The girl groaned.

Grace said, "When we came back, Eleanor and I looked up our family. Mother and Dad were both dead, but we found Abby."

"My lucky day," Abby sneered.

"How can you trust her if she feels so negative about what you're doing?"

"Abby's cooperative when she must be."

"Sure," Abby agreed. "You got a gun to your head, you cooperate. Hey, man, I was old enough to understand. Which is more than I can say for Honey."

"That's where things began to split wide open for me," Grace admitted. "When Honey was born.

Kids don't belong. I began to want a seven-day-a-week life. Know what I mean? But you have to understand—I loved him. I love him."

"This Rolf—? He's Honey's father?"

She nodded. "Everything got more complicated. Children talk, and talking cannot be tolerated, because it jeopardized the safety of the entire group. So the child must be kept confined. Away from other children. Away from life. One of the other women . . . she found a home for her baby, but I kept thinking we could work it out. We couldn't. Honey just wasn't developing properly. She saw things she shouldn't have seen at that age. Rolf—he wasn't sensible about it."

"What did he do to her?" Hana demanded. "What did *you* do to her?"

Grace slid to her feet. "Damn you, Hana Shaner! Nothing. What I did was the best I could. When I realized that things were wrong with her, I wanted to get help. I thought she might be . . . you know, autistic. And she kept getting worse. I had the problem of Abby, too. She never did fit in."

"It sucked," Abby moaned. "You never could have any fun. Couldn't meet other kids. Rolf's so weird. I hate him. I'm scared of him, too—everybody is."

"Did she force you to go with them when they took you away?"

Abby sighed. "Oh, shit. I wanted to go. They were my sisters, and everybody else was dead. Only, I didn't know how rotten it was going to be. At first it seemed pretty exciting."

Hana looked at Grace. "Couldn't you have sent Abby and Honey away?"

"It wasn't safe to let anybody go," Grace said dully.

"You went."

"Rolf—he agreed to let Honey and me go. I was supposed to take off first, set up a fake ID—we'd gotten good at all that—and settle in around here where he could keep an eye on me. So I did just what he said—except after I got a job and an apartment, he refused to give her to me. He'd taken her to some woman to look after instead. A small gray box of a woman. I didn't like her. Everyone has her face. I was half crazy. Tried to reason with him, and finally he did let me have her. By that time I had the apartment I'd rented from you and had pretty well fortified it. But I was afraid to keep her with me. Rolf could change his mind any time—he seemed to be getting more erratic. So I hid her and told him she was in Philly getting treatment. I got away with it for a long time. But it was all coming apart. . . . Eleanor was unhappy. She was scared stiff about this nuclear bomb business. She wanted out too, so she'd been keeping a notebook with names and places and things that had gone down. Enough to put everybody away for centuries. I couldn't believe she'd done that—it was so dangerous. One night she came to the apartment with it. Abby was with her."

"Did Rolf know about the notebook?"

"Of course not. He'd have killed her immediately if he had. She was in terrible danger just for splitting. I had to help. So I went out for breakfast as usual next morning and looked around. Everything seemed normal, and I hoped Rolf was busy enough with his toys to give us a little time. I didn't know he was right there on the mall. I sure didn't see him. They must have been watching and set up their show after I got back to the apartment. They'd used shows as distractions before. There are all kinds of people in the group—a few actors, an acrobat. One guy was a carpenter and is really good with his hands."

"Eleanor went out and walked right into them?"

"She looks—looked a lot like me, so we dressed her in my clothes and she was supposed to take my car and get out of town. I needed more time because of Honey. If worse came to worst I was to take the notebook to the FBI and ask for protection. We thought if they were around, they'd just follow her, thinking it was me—"

"It was stupid," Abby cried. "I told you it wouldn't work—Rolf would know it wasn't you. If I'd gone along like you wanted, I'd be dead too. I wouldn't go. I stayed right there in the apartment."

"And pretending to be a theater troupe, they waylaid Eleanor on the mall in front of an audience. . . ." Hana said in wonder.

Grace nodded. "I'm sure they injected her and loaded her up with props. I just hope she was still unconscious when they killed her. As soon as I realized they'd got her, I knew we had to get out of there."

"Why didn't you go to the FBI at that point? They'd have protected you."

"Would they? After Rolf got Eleanor, I wasn't even sure he didn't have somebody planted there. You don't know how he is. I decided Honey and I would go underground."

Abby said, "I told her that's what she should have done—taken Ellie's old book to the FBI. But she was too scared. I said I'd do it, only she wouldn't give it to me. So I just ran and hid. Got in with some punkers. Wow. That is out of nowhere. They were just as weird as Rolf."

Hana found herself clinging to a rock as if she couldn't stand alone. "This book—did you destroy it?"

Grace squinted upward at the gray sky. "No."

"Where—"

"Oh, you'd never find it, Hana. It's a miracle you located the clues I left for you to follow."

"You wanted your sister found and given a proper burial—"

"I wanted people to think I was dead. I wanted you to take Honey."

"Then why didn't you just contact me? And ask me . . . without all this—"

"She thought it was funny," Abby said. "She's got a real creepy sense of humor. That's why she went for Rolf."

"Not funny," Grace amended, "but certainly interesting and intriguing to use a mausoleum and a tape recorder. As for the receipt . . . Well, I needed clothes. There was this big sale, so I thought I could slip in and nobody would notice me. But the kid who waited on me—I'm sure she figured it out. She was the one who pointed out the restorations—and when I saw them, I knew that's where Rolf had put Eleanor. Too convenient, too like him. He always tried to do things with a flair."

"You took the receipt for the blouse to the apartment?"

"I wanted to give you a trail to follow. I couldn't believe how incredibly slow you were, my friend."

Hana felt a tightness in her throat. "Were you my friend, Grace? Were you really?"

The eyes were wide, wonderful, as Grace's eyes had always been. "Your soul, Hana, has a very comfortable quality."

"Oh, really—!"

"And remember, I kept the picture of the company picnic."

"Why? Because you felt comfortable with my soul?"

"Because it was a memory of a happy day."

But there was something mocking in the way she said it.

Hana turned away. "Rolf was awfully close that night I came to get Honey in the cemetery."

"I know."

"You were there?"

"You didn't think I'd let Honey alone in that place, did you? I was just inside the mausoleum."

"Why didn't he grab her before I got there?"

"He—they didn't know we were there. They must have followed you."

"A bug on my car, or somebody told them. Grace, are Sal or Mr. Fred—"

She shook her head. "No, but Rolf has an archaeology student on the payroll."

"And a cop at city hall?"

"Oh, that guy was one of Rolf's actors. They were watching you all the time. I sent that fool woman Rolf had boarded Honey with for distraction and succeeded in getting my girl away from there. Your cop thought Rolf was the one had grabbed her, and since it was risky hanging out there, he split. Rolf must have been furious. But you see, I couldn't let you turn Honey over to the police. He would have gotten her right away."

"I never saw you—"

"Oh, but you did. I was the policewoman who passed."

"You were right there under my nose?"

"There's a whole lot that's right under your nose. I signaled to Honey. She is obedient—came to me, right out through the front door. You were too busy giving autographs, and Rolf's ham was too busy acting. But he saw Mrs. Hyla, knew she'd had Honey in the past, so I guess he thought she'd gotten the kid."

"What else is under my nose, Grace?"

"Sure you want this?"

Hana nodded.

Grace shrugged. "Rolf has someone he always sends ahead when he's about to make a major change—like a move to another country. That person scouts around, makes arrangements for places to live, maps underground sewers—all that."

"Who?"

Grace was obviously enjoying this. "Elsie Hardinger."

"No! I don't—"

She laughed joyously. "Believe it. She's one of Rolf's early converts. She's always the one who goes in before the rest of us arrive. Stays until he's ready to make another move."

"As a tour guide—"

"Makes a great cover."

"But she's been here for years!"

"Not that many. Think about it. She's infiltrated well is all. And remember, it takes years for a group like Rolf's to build an atom bomb. It's a lot more complicated than one might think." Again, the bedeviling amusement in her eyes. "And one can direct operations from here as well as from anywhere in the world."

"But Elsie's so—"

"—smart. It takes a lot of brains to play the fool. She doesn't have too high an opinion of you, Hana. She thinks you're very gullible."

"She identified the body as you, not your sister."

"Must have suited Rolf's purposes. After all, I had an identity in the world, and Eleanor didn't. A number of fake passports, of course, but not an established ID like mine. I think they hoped to stop all inquiries, including yours. At least we were in agreement about that."

"Do you know why she took me to Doris Hyla's home?"

"She must have had some idea of you and her discovering the body together. Or was curious to see if it had been discovered."

"Did she kill Mrs. Hyla?"

"Oh, I doubt that. There are others better suited for those assignments, including Rolf himself." Grace continued dispassionately, "I suppose it's my fault the poor woman bought it. When I got her to go to city hall for me, Rolf must have considered her a turncoat—thought she was knowingly helping me. Really, she had nothing to do with anything. Just that Rolf used one of her husband's stupid plays long ago when he was working with a little theater group as cover. He did that sometimes."

"It's horrible . . ."

"Lots of that going down today."

"But to kill for so little reason—"

"Hey, it was no little reason to Rolf. To stand in Rolf's way is to invite violence." Grace was studying her. "I'm sorry you had to get caught up in the middle of this. I don't care about people like Carl Reid. He's just a fool, but when I found out they'd drugged you—"

"How can I believe anything you say? I don't even know you."

Even as she said it, Hana shivered a little. The damp was getting to her.

"Believe what you want but I felt like shit when I found out about it," Grace sighed. "Sometimes I think they do things like that just to cut the rich and powerful down to size. And to do it in public is a real challenge."

"I thought it was a warning—and to get the receipt."

"They didn't know about the receipt. At least I don't think they did. But naturally they wanted to search your bag. And you're right about the warning. They wanted to scare you. They weren't anxious to have you in that apartment and getting on my trail, so they set Debby on you."

"The waitress from The Feathered Duck . . . ? I had her in my hands and I let her get away."

"Isn't she good? Really went after Carl."

"She was the woman who got Carl Reid in such a state?"

"I'm telling you, she's good."

"Isn't anything the way it seems anymore?" Hana asked sorrowfully.

"Not much. It's part of the fun of living in the eighties."

"I'll take the sixties any day."

"I know you would. Revolutionary games can be fun, and it was all games back then, wasn't it? You wore rags, but they were designer rags."

"We had ideals," Hana said angrily. "Nobody

ever had to barricade themselves in an apartment to get away from us the way you barricaded yourself behind bars and locks to get away from these terrorists!"

"Ever find my trapdoor?" Grace asked, sliding into a lazy voice.

"Trapdoor—?"

"You and your slaves overlooked it? Hey, I must have done a good job."

"Where was it?"

"Living-room closet, above the drop ceiling. I could get in and out without anybody knowing. Went over roofs and down a fire escape into one of those cobblestone alleys."

"So that's how you got Honey in there. . . . Grace, were you in that apartment the first night I stayed?"

"Wouldn't you like to know?"

"Not really, because I don't think I care anymore," Hana said slowly. "Not about you. All I care about now is Honey. I'm going to keep her away from you and the rest of them." She stood erect, forcing a confidence she did not feel. "Now I'm going back down this mountain to my money and the rest of my creature comforts, and I intend to forget I ever knew anybody named Grace Urich."

"You're not going anywhere."

Damn. If only she'd hidden her gun on her person. Or at least her can of mace.

"Like hell," she said, then turned and began walking rapidly away. A shot echoed. A bullet pinged against a rock. Birds in a green laurel thicket squawked and flew in an exodus of fear.

Hana stopped.

Smoking weapon in hand, Grace came to her. For a moment Hana had visions of a shootout.

"What do you think you're going to do about all this?" Grace asked.

"Go to the police."

"Oh, Hana, use your head. They won't listen to you unless you have some kind of proof. Like . . . maybe Eleanor's notebook."

Grace returned the gun to her hip holster, then walked slowly back to the camp. After a moment, Hana followed.

"Even if I had it, they'd need you to testify."

Grace shook her head, hair rumpling forward onto her face, making her look strangely like Honey, young and vulnerable.

"Believe me, the book would be enough. There are so many names and places, they could get anything they'd ever need if they just dug a little."

"But are you," Hana asked, "going to give me the book?"

"That depends."

"On what?"

"If you're willing to follow instructions."

"Whose?"

"Mine."

Abby stirred, yawning loudly. "Better do it, woman, or we'll all be dead meat."

Hana loathed that phrase. Even more, she loathed the idea that she would have to follow some nebulous plan of this woman's or she might be . . . Just that. Dead meat.

"What do you want me to do?"

The sleepiness, the shifts of friendliness were gone now as Grace said crisply, "You have to get the police to cooperate with you and do just as you say. Hold the book over their heads—blackmail them with it. With your business background, you ought to be good at that. You *must* get Rolf and his entire group together, or they'll scatter, go underground, and continue collecting nuclear material. If not here, then somewhere else. The only way you have any chance to stop them is to get them all together. Unsuspecting. And the FBI and the police must be made to realize this. That it's the only way."

Helplessly Hana shook her head. "But how could we get them—this Rolf and . . . everybody. Why would they do it?"

"Use bait."

"Bait . . . ?"

"A person, Hana. A person as bait to bring them out."

"Not Honey!"

"Of course not Honey! I'm the traitor. The only person who has ever eluded Rolf even for a little while. If they've got me they figure they can pick up Honey anytime. Me. Hana, I'm your bait."

There was something very nearly like exultation in the way she said it. Almost . . . crazy. But then, maybe Grace Urich was. Maybe they all were.

"It's dangerous," Hana ventured.

"Oh, very dangerous. And there's no guarantee they'll even fall for it. They've got eyes everywhere. Up to you, Hana. You'd be doing the old world a favor, you know. An even greater favor than the invention of Dutch Blue."

Now Grace was laughing at her. But when Hana thought about the other Grace, it had been one of her charms. She always seemed, even then, to be standing just off center laughing at everything, even the most awful carpet crisis when a vat of Dawn Red had accidentally been mixed into a vat of Noon Yellow and a whole advertising campaign for something called Round Orange had been born. Grace had actually thought that was *amusing.*

"I'm not sure," Hana said, "that I'm quite good enough to take on an entire terrorist organization."

"I'm not sure about that either," Grace admitted. "But I don't see anybody else around, do you?"

Hana swallowed. Grace was right. There was nobody else.

The woman waited for a moment, then went on. "Contact dear Elsie. Tell her you found me. But that you don't know what to do with me. Say something's wrong—that I won't tell you where I've been or what I've been doing. You've hidden me at the Fur and Feather Refuge."

"Our animal shelter?"

"It's logical, isn't it? Arrange to make another animal commercial. The last one was so good they want another at the same place, right? And you want everything to appear normal until you can make plans to get me out of the country. Tell Elsie all this. You need extras for your scenario. I know Rolf—he'll figure it's good cover for them. Sometimes I think he's still an actor at heart, because he loves to do stuff like this if it furthers his plans. Elsie will contact them, don't worry about that."

Elsie. Funny, comfortable, infuriating Elsie who had read to her when she was ill. The enormity of the betrayal suddenly settled on Hana as bleakly as the gray clouds were settling over this ancient, worn-down mountain.

"It's time to go," she said hoarsely, wondering if she could take any more. "Past time. Give me the notebook and I'll try. I can't promise more than that. I'll try to do everything the way you've planned."

"You really think I'd carry the book around with me?" Grace asked. "Too dangerous, my friend. I wanted to give that notebook the best chance to get to the authorities, whether I was dead or alive."

"Then where is it?"

"In your safe-deposit box."

"My safe-deposit box? How on earth did you—"

"Oh, I'm very good too, Hana. Even better than Debby. And almost as good as Rolf. Almost . . . You see, he was an excellent teacher." Grace brought out a hip flask. "One for the road? It's a long hike back."

Numbly, Hana shook her head.

Grace took a long swallow. "Why, Hana," she said, wiping her mouth. "Remember that we have nothing to drink but drink itself."

And she laughed.

As Hana and Abby turned homeward, Hana was glad it was all downhill. The thought came to her when she stumbled over a protruding tree root that this same thing had been said of life after forty.

Suddenly she was no longer tired. She was angry. Deftly she stepped over the next root in her path.

Chapter Thirty-one

THE FIRST THING Hana did the next day was visit her safe-deposit box. She would not have been surprised to find it undisturbed, with no notebook anywhere to be found. But there it was, right beneath a pile of bonds. She sat in the small booth, staring at it for some minutes. A cheap spiral notebook of a kind usually reserved for student doodling during dull classes. Warily she opened it and began to read.

The words set her teeth on edge like the sound of a dentist's drill.

It was all that Grace had said. And more. Hana flipped through the opening pages, glancing, skimming paragraphs. She didn't want to know all this. One could be kidnapped and executed for knowing far less. If Rolf Bedlow had had any idea Grace's sister was recording these things, no wonder Eleanor was dead. Grace had said he didn't, but maybe Grace didn't know everything. Without reading further, Hana snapped shut the book, hesitated, but since she couldn't think of anything better, slipped it beneath the bonds again.

Nervously she returned to her office, feeling as if she wore a sign on her back: I HAVE SURVIVED THE NOTEBOOK. I KNOW AN UNHEALTHY AMOUNT ABOUT INTERNATIONAL TERRORISM. But no, she hadn't read it—just glanced at it, which was a far different thing. Focusing on how much she didn't know, Hana dialed Elsie Hardinger. To simulate spontaneity, she had planned to stutter over a few words. The stutter came very easily now as she explained that what she needed for her new commercial were not actors, but real people. Um . . .

larger-than-life real people, if Elsie knew what she meant. Elsie did. Hana suggested that since her friend had so many contacts in her line of work, surely she could select some very interesting faces and bodies. Elsie agreed that she could.

Hana plunged on, dropping mysterious hints about Grace Urich—just enough so that Elsie could figure out that Hana had found her. A laugh —which sounded near hysteria in her own ears— as she said, "I was right and you were wrong." She managed to whisper innuendos about the Fur and Feather Refuge, then hung up fast.

God, she hoped the woman known as Grace had their reactions figured out right.

Cindy Hefflefinger seemed wired and kept explaining away her relationship with Carl Reid, even though Hana had not asked. Cindy had seen Carl recently. He had asked for money.

"But I don't know where he is now," she complained.

"It hardly matters," Hana sighed, rubbing her forehead.

She instructed Cindy to make a call to Mel Rosen about the commercial. With so many people involved, she wanted him there.

She herself called the police to set things up with them. That turned out to be a lot worse than the call to Elsie.

"Are you insane?" Kochen demanded. "You want me to contact the FBI and say—*what?*"

Hana explained as best she could, then explained all over again to a superior with whom Kochen connected her. She realized she was sweating as she told about the notebook. No, she would *not* bring it in. She resorted to the famous Shaner Dignity. They Knew Who She Was, after all. They would just have to take her word that it contained volatile information. The superior was suitably impressed.

The FBI, too, may have known who she was, but was not at all impressed by the fact. The agent who arrived at the office only half an hour after Hana had dialed Kochen was a middle-aged stout woman who looked as if she should be making pasta commercials on TV.

She carefully identified herself as Emily Fanelli, listened while Hana explained that she had no intention of turning the notebook over to anybody until Rolf and crew were in custody, then casually suggested they go to the safe-deposit box for the book. Hana, still refusing, found herself on the way to the bank, accompanied not only by motherly Fanelli but by two other agents and a driver.

Later, as they took away the notebook, she dourly noted that they certainly had a way about them. Logic was on their side, too. Naturally the United States government had a right to such material and was the best possible protector of it.

Back at her office with the notebook safely in federal hands, Hana realized a great sense of relief. At least she didn't have the information on her conscience. Surprisingly, however, the government—in the person of Emily Fanelli—agreed with Grace Urich about Rolf Bedlow. Fanelli had actually beamed when she heard the plan for his capture. She and the others eased themselves out of the picture, leaving Hana to go forward on her own.

She sat at her desk, feeling like a zombie. No, a robot. She wondered why she had fought so hard for answers when those she found were all so unpleasant. Well, after it was over, she would immerse herself in carpets and Dutch Blue clothing. She'd had enough excitement this fall to last her a lifetime. Her career as an investigator would definitely end with this case.

Hana helped herself to an afternoon brandy from a bottle kept for visiting VIPs of the carpet world and drank to peace and quiet and a safe world in which to enjoy one's carpets.

She awakened that morning, almost wishing it were raining. But it was Indian summer all over again. Or perhaps this was the real Indian summer. Sal always maintained that true Indian summer came just before winter set in, after the leaves had fallen.

Hana dressed in a rich warm rust outfit that had been carefully hand-knit for her by Sal's mother. Sal was back on the job. Nothing more had been said either about Honey or the body in the field. In fact, everything appeared to be normal.

Pocky Reilly herself had been ecstatic over the prospect of another commercial at the Fur and Feather.

Mr. Fred had not shared her joy.

"Maybe you'll even find another cat out there," he had muttered sarcastically.

Hana had smiled.

She kept smiling all the way to the refuge. She had allowed Abby to return to Grace. If they melted into Shakespeare's thin air, it didn't matter now. Rolf and the others would be caught.

Mel arrived, looking legal. Elsie came, along with Bill Longenecker, who said he wanted to observe with the idea of using the refuge in a TV spot for his travel agency—dogs dressed as people barking about a trip. Plenty of time to tell him later that she didn't approve of dressing dogs like people. Hana busied herself with Pocky.

"Where's my crowd?" Pocky cried.

Hana found herself wishing she had not eaten Sal's corn fritters that morning. Suppose Rolf and company didn't come? Maybe they had watched during the night and had seen the enemy sneaking into place. Or suppose they did come, but in true terrorist fashion with guns and bombs? The thought froze her. People . . . the helpless animals in the shelter— What had she done?

But it turned out that Grace was right. Rolf couldn't resist swallowing the bait. He had come for Grace, and through her, the notebook.

They arrived in nondescript cars—fourteen people, if she counted correctly, led by a tall, princely man with goatee and hair as white as her own. They were indeed larger than life. One young woman with marvelous red hair looked suspiciously like Debby the waitress, but Hana couldn't be sure.

Hana had more disquieting moments as they walked forward, mingling with the employees of the shelter and the TV crew. They shook hands. They were friendly, personable. It was hard to believe. . . .

Pocky Reilly surveyed them ecstatically.

Again the area was covered with Shaner carpets. Shaner Tonebrown to match November subtlety.

The scenario they were working with called for Hana to act the role of the director of the refuge. She would be surrounded by dogs in the opening scene—their own mixed with a goodly sprinkling of police dogs, trained to attack on command and delivered to the shelter the day before. Hana the director is afraid the carpet will be ruined, the patron who donated it offended. Then many people arrive, all anxious to adopt dogs. The animals are taken away by the people who troop merrily down the lane to the woods. The commercial ends with Hana discovering the carpet is still in perfect condition and her worry was needless.

Pocky was addressing them through a bullhorn. "We'll try to make it in one take. It'll be too crazy to get it together twice. I mean, all these dogs . . . Wow. Anyhow, we want spontaneity. Everybody know what they're to do?"

A dog nibbled at Hana's shoes. Another, obviously a police dog, sniffed her suspiciously, either on the trail of drugs or Hana's own natural English lavender cologne.

Nervously she wondered when these people would make their move. If Grace was correct, it would be after the taping.

"Punch and cookies afterward!" Pocky shouted cheerfully. "Hana Shaner herself will show you over the facilities here if you like, people. So please stay."

Please stay. Check all bombs at the door. Hana was smiling at them. She couldn't seem to stop smiling.

Her face felt frozen.

Taping began. More dogs were let out. Hana was surrounded by a cluster of them. There was barking, snuffling, whining. She felt faintly dizzy. Forcing down the corners of her mouth, she expressed concern for her carpet. She was trying to watch the crowd that was milling beyond the TV crew. Rolf was smiling too. The woman with the fuzzy red hair moved toward a shed in which the riding mower and other implements were stored.

And suddenly Hana knew—as surely as she knew she was surrounded by dogs—that Grace and Abby were inside that shed. She tripped over a small but eager terrier and went down amid yapping and howling. Dogs licked her face. The suspicious police dog tried to stand on her shoulders. Pocky kept the tape rolling.

Hana struggled to her hands and knees. A dog rooted her behind; she leaped to her feet. Pocky was yelling for the Surge Forward.

They surged.

Hana lost sight of everything but dogs and people. Faces, flying hair, tails, tangles of bodies. Barking. Growls. Hollering. Then the mass retreated, dogs and people, back toward the lane. Instant cams following. Hana found herself staggering about on Tonebrown, alone.

She saw Grace Urich.

In the midst of the dogs and people, she saw Grace, arm held by the woman with red hair, and right behind her was Mel Rosen. It was only an instant flash, but it was enough.

Hana screamed.

She bellowed for Mel to help, for police, for the FBI. She shrieked about Grace Urich. There was a lot more screaming. Barking became hysterical. Police poured from the woods with more dogs. There were commands to attack. Confused canines moved in circles. People tripped over them. Emily Fanelli was glimpsed climbing into the lower branches of a pine tree pursued by a snarling German shepherd. Shelter dogs dashed off into the forest. The woman with red hair was flat on her face, then crawling away pursued by two delighted collies.

Grace had vanished.

Pocky Reilly shrieked above the commotion to "Keep taping! Keep taping!"

Shots were fired.

Hana pulled her own gun but stood irresolute. The scene down the lane was so incredibly confused.

Then she saw Rolf sneaking along the side of the cat house. His pistol was in his hand. The look on his face reminded her of the summer-theater stage manager left to command untrained extras filling in as citizens of *Inherit the Wind* town. A calico female inside the screen enclosure jumped up and purred at him hopefully.

For just a second, Rolf was distracted by the cat. Hana leaped forward, both hands on her .22.

"Drop it, Rolf! Drop the gun!"

The next few minutes ran together in Hana's mind like a tape being fast-forwarded. She saw Rolf's gun dropping at her command, saw relief on his face as he looked toward his left.

Mel Rosen moved into her vision from behind the cat house. He held a Magnum pointed at her.

Rolf's director was there. She knew it. Horribly she knew it.

She never really heard the shots she fired. With surprise she saw Mel fall, his Magnum falling with him from a bloody hand.

Chapter Thirty-two

IT WAS HOURS before the shelter, the police, the FBI, and even the entire countryside around the Fur and Feather Refuge were back to normal. Mel Rosen was taken to the hospital in an ambulance. Elsie was arrested, as were the others, including Rolf. Before he hastily left, Bill Longenecker was heard to say he had changed his mind about a dog commercial for his agency.

The FBI called in the CIA.

Some police dogs were inadvertently kept at the shelter for two days. One shelter dog joined the police force after proving she had the right stuff. For a week after, country people were bringing in strays that had wandered off during the chaos. Three dogs found receptive rescuers who just "kept them overnight" and in the end notified the shelter that they were adopting. The calico cat, whose picture was in the paper beneath a caption that called her "Feline Heroine," received half a dozen offers of homes. She selected a country estate, complete with a stocked goldfish pond on the terrace.

Pocky vowed the commercial was the best ever done and planned to enter it in competition for an award. Portions of the tape were also used on national news broadcasts. Everybody spent long hours talking to the police and the FBI. Emily Fanelli was not among the interrogaters, having broken her ankle falling out of a pine tree. Rolf had not achieved his position in the international terrorist community without being known to federal agencies, but it was Sergeant Kochen who broke him and got him talking. He did it by bringing the shelter dog that had joined the force into the interrogation room.

One look at the dog and Rolf went berserk. At first he babbled incoherently that the animals of the world had risen up against him for betraying his first commitment in life, which had been to do environmental plays to save the natural world. Then he went on to specific information, including the location of his nuclear stash and also where to find the sharply honed antique fencing sword that had been the murder weapon. It was a souvenir from his theatrical career.

When Rolf began to bark and howl, Sergeant Kochen left him to a police psychologist.

Hana was aware of these things as they swirled past her. She herself talked to Kochen, then was escorted to a small interrogation room where an FBI agent named John was waiting. The room was clean, polished, and smelled faintly of spray wax. Sitting in an old oak chair across the table from him, she felt almost drowsy, as if her body were rejecting these things that were happening. In all the confusion of the past few hours she felt she had lost something—her businesslike grip on reality.

She realized Agent John had repeated a question.

"No," she said dully, "I had no idea Mel Rosen was involved in anything like this. Not before today."

"How long were you in possession of that notebook?"

"I don't know. She—the woman, Grace Urich—put it in my safe-deposit box, but I didn't know it was there until just a couple of days ago."

"And you didn't read it?"

"Only a little—the beginning. I didn't want to know any more."

"Then you didn't read the material relating to Mel Rosen?"

"No. He really was the director of this thing, wasn't he? Rolf Bedlow was just a front?" She heard herself talking. She wanted to say these things, because maybe she could believe them if she heard them out loud. "He must have been sitting safely in the background raising money and financing their operations. He must have been the one obsessed with constructing an atom bomb. Maybe that's why he came back here—to get next to local people he could use. Maybe . . . blackmail. I guess it had to be that. He told me he returned because of his divorce. He told me . . ."

Oh, God, she wanted to cry out. Things were clicking into place, becoming real again, and it hurt like hell.

The young man looked sympathetically at her. "I'm sorry to have to tell you this, but there are strong indications Mr. Rosen killed his wife. Possibly she hadn't known of his involvement in these things, or perhaps she had gone along with him until it got too heavy."

It was like having her face slapped. Hard. Repeatedly. She put up her hands to ward off his words.

There were more questions. Somehow she stumbled through the interview, all the time some thread in her mind repeating, "Was it all an act? Or did he really want me?" But that no longer mattered, because he was a killer—and worse . . . much worse.

At one point she asked, "Why did he send the police to my house to get Abby?"

"He told us he hoped to frighten her into running to Grace. He was desperate to find Grace Urich and the notebook. That's how we caught him. He was too desperate. He felt that unless he got that book, everything was over for him."

"He told you this at the hospital after—"

Agent John shook his head. "No, he's here now. He's taped up and his arm is in a sling, but otherwise he's all right."

Hana stared at him for moments before she managed to ask, "May I see him?"

He looked startled. "Are you sure you want to?"

She nodded.

"Well," he said, "I think it might be arranged. At least for a few minutes."

They weren't alone when she saw Mel. Two FBI agents stayed with them. He was sitting in another room, much like hers. He looked pale, worried. Even now, it was hard not to respond to that look of pain in his eyes. To believe that the bright young man of twenty years before had become so twisted. Had some of it been there all the time? Was that really why they had never made it together? She asked the question she had come to ask.

"For God's sake, Mel—*why?*"

He turned his face away from her. Late-autumn sunlight coming through the arched windows reminded Hana of a college room a long time ago. A meeting. Students for a Democratic Society—SDS. On almost every campus, a uniform of blue jeans, protesting the Vietnam War, sometimes with violence. Even Hana herself . . . and Mel. Definitely Mel. He'd been very involved, meeting people, loving it. After their last summer, had he gone into it more deeply, perhaps wanting to prove something to himself? Or to her.

"I'd like to leave now," Hana said, her voice breaking.

Mel did not talk. It was Rolf Bedlow who recovered enough to give them details in exchange for a lesser charge. He reinforced everything in Eleanor's notebook. When Hana read the reports later, she felt no anger, only sorrow. Mel had chosen not to stand up and be counted, to be in the front lines with the bombs. He had complacently taken his place in a small community, surrounded by family and friends, while enjoying a rich secret life of intrigue in which he indulged his fantasies of a world ruled by those who controlled the armies of anarchists and terrorists. He was really a great director.

Finally it was over, and Hana returned to Blue Spring Hill. All sorts of messages had come for her, but she decided to wait to answer them until she was more calm and the memories of Mel and their times together were put away in somber black-and-white photographs of youth and not the living-color slides she had been mentally experiencing this autumn.

Sal, Mr. Fred, and the animals were waiting.

The trenches on the lawn had been filled in as if they had never been there. Straw and grass seed covered them in hopes of a mild winter, or at least a prolonged fall.

"Everything here has been taken care of. We will, of course, be cataloging the remains we have found during our excavations—" Mr. Fred began.

"Now, you just stop that kind of talk for once!" Sal told him with unusual anger. "Miss Hana, have they been arrested? All of them?"

Without answering, Hana helped herself to a sherry. Trouble and the other two cats sat on the carpet contemplating her. Together they made a picture of feline perfection. To a chorus of purring, she dropped into a chair beside them. She didn't want to look at Ghost and Crumb. She had seen enough dogs to last for a while.

"Two people escaped into the woods and haven't been found," she told them wearily. "A woman who once called herself Grace Urich and her young sister Abby."

"Do the police know about that?" Sal asked.

"It's the biggest case that ever happened around here," Hana said. "There's the local angle with Elsie and . . . Mel. There are all those odd people who belonged to Rolf Bedlow's group. But they aren't really very communicative, I understand. I don't think anybody is too anxious to search all the mountains in the state for two rumored people who may not even exist."

"We know they exist," Mr. Fred objected.

"No, we don't. Grace Urich is listed as dead and buried. Fingerprints are on file to prove it. Abby . . . Well, hardly anyone has even seen a girl named Abby. We'll let it go at that."

"But what about . . ." Sal stopped.

Hana had been thinking about that, during the times she wasn't thinking of Mel.

She said carefully, "There are a lot of children in your family. If you and your mother are willing, Honey would fit in without much notice. She must have medical help. I'll pay for that and donate to your family and to your church if you'll—"

"I wouldn't do it for money," Sal snapped. "But I'll do it. We'll give her a Christian name and see how it goes. For a while anyway. Mom and I think she'll be better if she can just settle down once and belong someplace."

Sal and Mr. Fred returned to their tasks. Ghost and Crumb, wondering what they had done to be so ignored, went outside for a romp.

Hana and the cats sat looking at the Shaner carpet beneath their feet. It was worth looking at, too.

Dutch Blue.

About the Author

Award-winning Roma Greth began writing mysteries after having been active in the theater for many years. Readers will find her characters fascinating as well as unconventional in this, her first mystery novel. Roma makes her home in the Pennsylvania Dutch country.